Intruders in Paradise

UNIVERSITY OF ILLINOIS PRESS

Urbana and Chicago

Intruders in Paradise

JOHN SANFORD

San

Manufactured in the United States of America

C 5 4 3 2 1

This book is printed on acid-free paper.

Six of the pieces in this book have appeared before:
"The Mighty Fallen," "A Land to Love," and "A
Gringo: Do You Speak English?" in *A More Goodly
Country;* "The First Knee on Canada," in *The People
from Heaven;* "The Poor Get Screwed, He Said,"
in *The Season, It Was Winter;* and "The Gastonia
Strike," in *A Walk in the Fire.*

Library of Congress Cataloging-in-Publication Data

Sanford, John B., 1904–
Intruders in paradise / John Sanford.
p.   cm.
ISBN 0-252-02343-9 (alk. paper)
I. Title.
PS3537.A694155   1997
814'.54 — dc21
96-52685
CIP

◆ *Dance us back the tribal morn!*

—Hart Crane, *The Bridge*

This region is inhabited by men and women who go about either quite naked or clad in feathers of various hues. They live in common, with no religion and no king. There is the greatest abundance of gold and pearls. . . .

—legend on an ancient map

To Maggie
1905–89

"Why am I in this book?" she said.
"Why would you not be? You've been
in all the others, even the two I wrote before
I knew you."
"That pleases me; it means you always
knew I was somewhere in the world. But
I'm not in the world now, Johnny. I'm eight
years dead."
"You're still here. Where else could you be?"
"Don't you believe in another world?"
"I believe in you."

Contents

Intruders in Paradise

Scenes of the National Life, 1

The Birds of Farewell Street

Here lyeth ye body of Mary ye daughter of
John & Sarah Green hew was born in 1715
and dyed in 1716.

Her slate, in the Burying Ground at Newport, has worn but little.
The letters and numerals are hard at the edges still, their serifs still are
plain. The lines that once guided the carver guide now as they did then,
and the eye drifts across the monumental story of a one-year life—a
few words above a pair of doves and a bowl piled with fruit. The fruit
remains uneaten, the birds have never flown, the one at their feet and
the two on the stone.

Pictographs of a Celestial Display *

All the Dakota bands saw that storm of stars in the November
sky. Of the Ogallalas, American Horse and Cloud Shield saw it, and
Swan the Minneconjou, and the Brule named Battiste Good. It rained
stars that night, and they drew them falling, a squall of four-point stars
pouring down the sky. *Plenty-Stars Winter*, it was called in the Dakota

*The Leonids, a star-shower of 1833.

I

pictures, *The Winter the Stars Moved Around*, and on buffalo-hide, the year is still here—all along the Missouri, that meteor rushes yet.

Print from a Wet-Plate Negative*

From her pedestal of skirts, she stares past the camera, at a man, perhaps, or another woman. The light seems to be going, as if time were still running in the picture and the hour growing late. A private place, that collodion world, and yet at any moment, the man outside may enter it—or the other woman.

Seven Frames of Film†

In the seven stills on the strip of celluloid, the same man stands with his hands upraised. In each, there's a slight but progressive change of position, suggesting seven stages of a single motion, a series begun before the first and ending beyond the last. It's the hands that seem to move, to catch a ball, it may be, or to wave at someone passing by—or, in view of the gun you hold, to be reaching for the sky.

5¢ Ride to Harlem‡

Snow lies on window lintels, and down at the street stare snow-browed eyes. There, hitched to a car, four horses steam: in the vaporous air, they seem to have reached a boil. On the tracks they stand between, they make one roundtrip a day—five miles north to Harlem and five miles south to here. And on the morrow, they'll do the same—being beasts, they'll do the same. And when their hearts begin to fail, they'll do the same one day and die.

*Unidentified photograph, 1859.
†Kinetoscope of Thomas A. Edison, 1890.
‡Photograph by Alfred Stieglitz, 1893.

Two Hundred Girls in a Caramel Factory

The little girls sit at long tables, wrapping and packing
the caramels.
    —Jane Addams*

They have foreign names,
those little girls,
tie-tongue combinations
in Polack, Spic, and Czech,
and for three cents an hour,
they sit beneath the boilers
and sort your caramels.
They work an eighty-hour week,
those little girls
with bohunk names,
with Slav and Serb and Galitz,
and side by side they sit six days a week
and wrap your caramels,
your plastic cubes,
your cubic candy,
and for their labors on your sweets,
they're paid in coppers
and other benefits
such as curvature of the spine,
anemia and scrofula,
enlarged glands in the neck and axilla,
mitral insufficiency,
deafness and defective sight,
syphilis (though rarely),
and TB.

Off-Season at Saratoga†

The overdressed hotels are closed, and their shuttered windows
peer at barren trees. Vacant now the verandas, and there's none to sup
up *Empire* spring (for eruptions of the skin), nor *Patterson* (for the
purge), and at *Columbian* (salts of iron), no hands are cupped save those

*Hull-House Papers, 1910.
†Photograph by Silvia Saunders, 1931.

of fallen leaves. Plush, this place, clinquant, flash, and somehow lewd, but in the autumn sun, the elms write themselves on the walls, and the whorehouse aura somehow goes.

Okie Madonna*

Her gown is made of a pair of sacks, raveled at the edges now and coming unsewn at the seams, and from a throne of torn ticking, she stares through the camera as if the camera weren't there. Held in her lap, a child sucks at a tit shown by a slit in the burlap, and he too stares, not at nothing far away, but at an enemy world that begins with you.

Writing from Afar

tele (distant) + *graphicus* (to write)

Along all roads and rights-of-way, wire—and wire too through the wheat, uptown and down dale, and streeted in the woods—the very air is wire, wire the very earth. *One volt resisted by one ohm allows one unit of current to flow, an ampere of dots and dashes.* A rhapsody of trash is streaming by, offers and acceptances, numbers, names, and times of arrival, sums, quantities, terms, covenants, assurances of love, cold fact and the coinage of the mind—base metal in the main, but now and again a grain of gold.

For Broken Things

The Indians could not bear to part with their dead. They built scaffolds of skin and poles and there displayed them with the mane of a highly-thought-of horse, with a hackamore made of braided hair. And so they stayed, those shades of men and parts of ponies, till their bones were picked by the birds and air.

We do as they did: we too put our dead on view. Having many, we cord them, rear them ever higher on the lone prair-ee. We stack them wrung and riven, stove in, sprung, and blind; we raise them aghast to the sky, an offering to the Okie of Things That Roll No More. But the

*Photograph by Dorothea Lange, 1937.

4

Great Manitou will not take them. He lets the robbers make off with their organs, their weapons, their secrets.

Inscription for Passing Sinners

Behold, it cries in lithic tones, God is great and greatly wrathful, and beware lest He brush thee away. Take care to turn from other idols, remember the Book of Remembrance and the day of darkness, remember how short the time. Behold, it warns from the boulder's round and the canyon wall.

For the Sequoia Sempervirens

It is told that a traveler, having come from far to gaze upon and marvel at the redwoods, found a pair of woodsmen engaged in felling one of the great trees. He asked why they were thus killing a plant seeded in the time of Charlemagne, and they replied that they were making room for cabins. "Cabins?" the traveler inquired. "Cabins for whom?" And they said, "Cabins for people like you, who come to see the trees."

Shawondasee and Other Winds

They bring these days no incense from the cedar trees, no perfumes of weed and herb; they bear no ozone freed by lightning, nor are they seasoned with the salt of the sea. Instead, they come laden with minute quantities of death, and breath by breath we die of Mudjekeewis, Wabun, Kabibonokka . . .

Judas in Peru

> The Sun, parent of mankind, sent two of his children to
> gather the natives into communities and teach them the
> arts of civilized life.
>   —Prescott, *Conquest of Peru*

Valverde, chaplain to Pizarro, was a Dominican friar. Born in Spain,
devil knows where or when, he was slain on the Isle of Puna in the Gulf
of Guayaquil. If eaten by the Indians who slew him, he'd've made them
a lean meal, for, as a man of God, he was sworn by a solemn vow to the
austere disciplines of his order—to poverty, to silence, to fastings long
prolonged, aye, to a life of beggary void of comforts and possessions.
But, alas, Fray Vicente was far, far from the way of Christ and farther
still from the Lord's.

Pizarro, whom he served, was a Spaniardo captain and a natural
child, which is to say he was a bastard born and a bastard by trade.
Abandoned in infancy on the steps of a church at Truxillo in Estrema-
dura, he was suckled, some say, on the paps of a sow. A thin beginning,
thinning still more with time until at last he seems to cast no shadow at
all . . . but stay! There's the fellow on Hispaniola, forty years old now
and owing more than he's able to repay.

From Darien came word, and he heard it, of a place in the mountains to the south, a place rich in gold, which to its benighted people
was merely the tears wept by the Sun—whereupon he sought and ob-
tained a *capitulación* giving him the right to explore and conquer the
domain. Blood, much blood, would he shed to attain his heart's desire:
he'd stain the very snows of the Andes red. But when all's told against
him, what was he but a bloodletter by vocation? His lifework was death.

How, though, of Fray Valverde, *el hombre de Dios* and soon to be
bishop of Cuzco? What plea can be made for the Dominican, clad not
in casque and corselet but in habit and mantle, armor more impervious
than steel? What will absolve him who was sworn to silence, to self-
denial, to mortifications of the flesh in the name of the Savior? What
can soften the sin of one learned in the Word whose own was spoken
falsely?

Aware? How could he *not* have been aware of the ambush Pizarro
had in store for the Incas in the square of Caxamarca—how, when he
had helped to prepare it? Pizarro's plan called for murder, and Valverde

6

knew it when he celebrated a mass blessing the enterprise—thereby making it a mass murder in very truth. Disposing his men of the foot and his cavalry so that they were hidden from view, and concealing as well his twain of cannon, the captain left the vast plaza empty for the arrival of Atahuallpa and his retinue, all of them unarmed as agreed—and trusting Pizarro, the simples in their thousands came. They came, the nobler among them appareled in fine-woven stuffs of striking dye and adorned with jewels and the plumage of vivid birds. They came, those gullible children, bearing the Son of the Sun on a litter of gold.

It is told that, finding none in the great square to greet him, he inquired after the *strangers*, as he called them, at which appeared Fray Vicente, a crucifix in one hand and a breviary (a Bible, some say) in the other. At once he began a harangue on the mysteries of the Trinity, on man's fall from grace, and on his redemption through the Christ. From such mouthings, incomprehensible to the Inca, he proceeded to exhortation: *Believe as we believe, renounce your inferior god, or burn in eternal fire!* But deep in ignorance, Atahuallpa laid hold of the Bible (or breviary) and cast it to the ground, whereat, outraged by the profanation, the friar hied himself to Pizarro, crying, as some heard it, *Fall upon this prideful dog! I grant you absolution!**

Pizarro fell instead on lesser dogs. At a signal, a gun was fired, whereupon out from their hiding-places poured the Spaniardos, the strangers, and shouting the name of their patron, James of the Sword, they hacked their way into the stampeding Incas—and the slaughter began. And slaughter it verily was, for, as said, the children of the Sun, babes and sucklings all, had brought no weapons along, nor even had they done so would slingshot and arrow have availed against armor, the musket, and the overmastering power of the charger. In all directions they fled.

It was a flight to nowhere. Pent within the walls of the plaza, driven by their attackers and self-propelled by fear, they merely milled about in a frenzy, and they trampled each other to death even as they were being shredded by blade and ball. More than ten thousand lay dead when the work ended (*mas de diez mil*), more than ten thousand dogs sprawled on the stones of the square. Atahuallpa, though, was taken alive, ostensibly out of respect for his exalted rank, but actually for his value. Ransom for his person was fixed at a quantity of gold sufficient to fill the chamber he was held in—a space measuring 17-by-22-feet—

---

* *Este perro lleno de soberbia, salid á el, que yo os absuelvo!*

to a height as high as Pizarro could reach, a ransom that would come to 2,500 cubic feet of gold.

The metal in such profusion had never yet been dreamt of, but from far and wide in the empire, it came to redeem the descendant of the Sun. Never having taught themselves the uses of money, the Incas had none, and they brought instead treasure in the form of works of art and veneration, and with it they filled the measure demanded. Then and then only was the true face of the conqueror revealed.

Accused of trying to incite insurrection against the Spanish crown, Atahuallpa was given a trial that consumed the better part of an hour, and being found guilty of the charge, he was sentenced to be burned at the stake. He deserves to die,* said Fray Vicente, but he sought all the same to save his savage soul. With the promise of a milder death—by strangulation—he induced the Son of the Sun to accept baptism, bestowing on him his new designation: Juan de Atahuallpa. They could've thrown away the garrote: the name alone would've killed him.

In his epistle to Titus, Paul declared that a bishop must be blameless, and in his epistle to Timothy, he added this, that a bishop must be apt to teach. How, then, did Valverde become bishop of Cuzco? Blameless he was not, for it is established in more than one *relación* that he encouraged Pizarro to commit murder with his promise of absolution. Nor did that example establish him as the kind apt to teach—that is, to teach aught but greed, brawling and striking, and a taste for wine.

Teach! What could he have taught those whose lives were civilized before he was born—yea, even before Dominic, who founded his order in the thirteenth century? What did the forsworn friar know that the Incas had not known long? He thought them barbarous, but already they were astonishingly skilled in the cultivation of crops, in the construction of canals and systems of irrigation, and in the making of roads, these last finer than any yet seen by the Europeans. But there was more, and it was most remarkable—their ability to build houses out of blocks of stone so truly hewn (with what? with *what?*) that a knife-blade could not be made to fit between them. Teach! Could that false priest have taught the Incas social ways? There were neither rich nor poor among them, all had land, none was idle, and famine was unknown, as were

El Inga fuese condenado a muerte.

8

theft and prostitution. Was Valverde the man to offer them better? Far more likely, he'd've taught them the uses of money.

The friar was eight years away from death on the Isle of Puna. If his slayers ate him, they must've broken their teeth on his heart.

THE JESUITS, 1632

The First Knee on Canada

We caught fireflies in the darkening meadows,
and threading them into on-and-off festoons,
we hung them up before the altar and the Host,
and they made light for God, Ghost, and Jesus
while we, adoring, put the first knee on Canada.

> *Who's that nailed to the cross, Black-robes?*
> *If he's an enemy, let your chief eat his heart,*
> *but if he's an Okie, you've killed yourselves*
> *unless you burn tobacco and invite him down.*
> *Take our advice about such things, Black-robes;*
> *listen to us, for we know the ways of the land,*
> *and you, on your knees like women making food,*
> *have already offended us with your ignorance:*
> *fireflies must not bow down to graven images!*

We said, "Unhappy infidels (meaning Dogges),
you that live in smoke only to die in flames,
repent you and choose between Heaven and hell!"

> *We said, "The sky is the palace of thunder,"*
> *but it was clear that they did not understand.*
> *"The sky," we said, "the blue wigwam overhead,*
> *the sky is the home of thunder, understand?*
> *and thunder is a turkey cock, a cock but a man,*
> *yet in one thing he is neither man nor bird,*
> *in one thing strange to all that walk or fly:*
> *he comes forth only when the wigwam is gray.*
> *He comes forth like a man, though, grumbling,*
> *and he flies down to Earth to gather snakes,*

snakes and other objects that we call Okies,
and if you see flashes of fire as he descends,
that fire attends the beating of his wings,
and if the grumbling now and then is violent,
be sure his children have been brought along.
Indian babies know all this. Why do you stare?"

"Which do you choose?" we said. "Heaven or hell?"

We said, "Heaven is a good place for Frenchmen."

"Which do you choose?" we said. "Heaven or hell?"

We said, "The French will not feed us in Heaven."

"Which do you choose?" we said. "Heaven or hell?"

We said, "Do they hunt in Heaven? Do they dance?
Do they make war or hold festivals in Heaven?
If not, we will not go, for idleness is evil."

"Which do you choose?" we said. "Heaven or hell?"

We said, "If our dead are in hell, as you say,
if for want of a few sprinkled drops of water
our babies live in hell, we would go there too."

We wrote, "We find that pictures are invaluable
in bringing about conversions among the Hurons;
we have learned that these holy representations
are half the battle to be fought against them.
We desire some more showing souls in perdition,
and if you sent a few drawn on paper or canvas,
with three, four, or even five tormenting devils
visiting different punishments on the damned,
one with pincers, another applying fire, etc.,
they would have a lasting effect on the savages,
especially if the drawings were made distinct,
if they revealed misery and rage and despair
written on the (red) faces of the condemned."

We said, "We see plainly that your God is angry
because we will neither believe nor obey him.
Ihonatiria, where first you taught his word,
is ruined, and then you came here to Ossossané,
and here too we were skeptical of your God,
and now the wolves pick Ossossané's bones,
and then you went up and down our country,
and from rising to setting sun you found none
to do the bidding of your God and bow down,
and therefore the pestilence is everywhere."

We said, "Do you believe, then? Do you repent?"

We said, "How eager you are for a humble 'Yes,'
but we know a better cure, we know a medicine
that will work more wonders than wafer or wine:
we will shut you out now from all our houses
and stop our ears when your God gives tongue,
and then, neither hearing him nor seeing you,
we will be innocent again, as before you came,
and avoid the penalty of refusing to be saved."

Our mission suffered from no lack of visitors,
for the Hurons flocked there to see the marvels
that we had wisely brought with us from France,
and in expectant silence, from dawn to evening,
they squatted on the ground before the door,
waiting for a performance of the repeating lens,
which showed them the same object eleven times,
and the magnifying glass, wherein a simple flea
became so monstrous as to overwhelm the eye,
and the mill, which they never tired of turning,
and lastly, the miracle of miracles, a clock
that struck the hours from one to twenty-four:
they thought it was alive and asked what it ate,
and when at the final stroke we cried, "Stop!"
and it stopped, their admiration was boundless.
The incomprehensible mysteries of our Faith,
the clock, the glass, the lens, and the mill—
all this served to win the Indians' affection.

They proposed that a number of young Frenchmen
should be invited to settle amongst our people
and wed our daughters in solemn and holy form,
but we said, "Of what use is so much ceremony?
If these young Frenchmen desire our daughters,
they will come and take them when they please;
they will do again what they have done before."

They led Brébeuf out and bound him to a stake,
but if they hoped he would plead for his life
(for what God gave, and only God could take away),
the red wretches were doomed to disappointment,
even as they were doomed to everlasting flames.
The priest addressed the converts he had made,
promising Heaven if they retained their faith,
thus angering the Iroquois, and to silence him
they scorched him with coals from head to foot,
and when (as if they were bound and he free)
he spoke further, they cut away his lower lip,
and they thrust a red-hot iron down his throat.
His mouth made no words now, nor uttered pain,
and they tried a subtler means to overcome him,
for they took it to be an augury of disaster
if torture failed: they brought forth Lalemant,
that Brébeuf might see his agony and cry aloud
for his brother in Christ if not for himself.
Naked under his cassock of pitch-soaked bark,
Lalemant fell to his knees, saying these words
after the sainted Paul: "We are made a spectacle
unto the world, and to angels, and to men!"
Whereupon the red devils put fire to the bark,
and Lalemant blazed up like a canoe on a beach,
but the only sound from Brébeuf was an "Ave."
Frenzied, they made a collar of hatchets,
heated till they smoked like stones from hell,
and hung it around his neck to smoke out fear,
but he was grateful, as if they had healed him,
as if it were proud flesh they had burned away,
and he gave them a prayer in payment for pain.
Then they poured boiling water over his head,

saying that the Iroquois too knew how to pay,
that their hot water was for the Jesuit cold:
"Now we baptize you, Black-robe," they cried,
"that you may be happy in your white Heaven!"
And they tore strips from his limbs and body
and devoured this unholy food before his eyes,
saying, "The more a man suffers on the Earth
(so you say), the happier he will be in Heaven,
and desiring to make you the happiest of all,
we torment you badly because we love you well."
But he sanctified their feast with a blessing,
and they scalped him and laid open his breast,
and they came in a crowd to drink his blood,
thinking thus to imbibe some part of his valor,
but he was dead, and his valor was in Paradise.

> *We do not pretend, like the people from Heaven,*
> *that each of us is a Manitou in his own right,*
> *we do not pretend that we are more than men,*
> *and being men, we endure the illnesses of men,*
> *among which we rank the sense to know a friend.*
> *You are not our friends, you people from Heaven,*
> *you are not our friends, you that speak of God*
> *and teach the Word, the word being "Mine! Mine!"*
> *You are no man's friend, you traders from Heaven*
> *that offer a word and would take our world away!*

"Which do you choose?" we said. "Heaven or hell?"

> *We choose Heaven, but not for us—for Brébeuf.*
> *He was brave, like an Indian, and in admiration*
> *we give you this gift as a shroud for his body*
> *when the time comes to send him on his journey:*
> *it is a coat of bear-skin that our women made,*
> *and in your cold Heaven it will keep him warm.*

The Black Napoleon

The Negroes lack only a leader. Where is that great man
to be found?
       —Abbé Guillaume Raynal

Had the abbé ever set foot on Santo Domingo, he might not have
asked the question. But he did his writing in France, and all he knew of
the island was what he'd read and heard. The man he sought was a slave
at the time, one of a thousand such on the Breda plantation at Haut-
du-Cap near Cap Haitien, and a slave he'd been for fortysome years.
His lot seemed to content him, for he had a master milder than most,
and he'd been allowed to marry; more than that, he'd been given *liberté
du savanna*, a status under which he enjoyed many of the privileges reserved for a freeman. Often was he seen wearing livery and driving his
master's carriage, and often too was he seen doing what few bondsmen
did—reading a book.

He read many, it's said. His speech revealed a knowledge of Roman
history, and of Greek as well, for he was no stranger to the life and
thought of Epictetus. But he had lore that he did not owe to books:
it came to him unwritten, came with his color and his blood and the
tales his people told of the shameful past. When Columbus put ashore
on Santo Domingo, there were upward of a million natives—Tainos,
Caribs, Ciboneys—on an island that he called *The Paradise of God*. But
what Negro did not know that after only two score years of Spanish
rule, that number had dwindled to five hundred? What Negro did not
know that the Spaniards had used them for sport, shooting them by the
dozen and then feeding the flesh to their dogs? What Negro did not
know that, having squandered the Indians, the Spaniards had to find
substitutes or fend now for themselves? And what Negro did not know
that he'd been brought from Africa to stand in for a slaughtered race?
No Negro knew his people's history better than the liveried slave Toussaint.

Save for his gaudy garb, he wasn't much to look at. Being short in
stature, he seemed at a distance to be unimposing, but so commanding was his closer presence that a French general was impelled to say,
Nobody can approach him without fear. And yet he must've possessed no
little charm: speaking his liquid Creole, he can only have delighted
with the Latin phrases that floated like leaves on a stream. Taken all in

14

all, though, the sometime coachman hardly gave promise of being the leader the Negroes lacked. Too plainly was he at ease with the life he'd been allowed to lead—walking to work hand-in-hand with his wife, enjoying toil and the abundance it yielded, pleasuring in his children, and thanking the Lord for His providence.

In reality, he'd never been at ease, neither with his own condition nor that of his fellow slaves. Never had he rejoiced in playing the clown on the box of a carriage; never had he relished the false freedom of *liberté du savanna;* never had he been blind to the ill-usage and degradation of his kind. A million of them had been imported from the "slave factories" of West Africa, and far worse had they fared than he. He knew of the punishments they'd been made to endure: his eyes had seen their suffering; his ears had heard their cries.

Flogging was the usual penalty for an infraction, however slight—fifty lashes well laid on—fifty!—when the very first stroke was enough to draw blood. But where the master's cast of mind was such, he'd call for disciplines so extreme that they made whipping seem a favor. On those plantations ruled by the hard heart, a slave was lucky if his balls stayed attached, luckier if he wasn't crucified (by Christians!), luckier still if he escaped being roasted over a slow fire, and luckiest of all if gunpowder wasn't rammed up his ass and made to explode. The black man in livery—he knew of these inflictions, he'd heard the pleas, the screams, he'd bled with the bleeding and died with the dead.

In letters and dispatches now and from the mouths of French sailors came word of their people rising against the established order—an insurrection of the poor commoner against the noble rich—and as the word spread like dawn over Santo Domingo, a slow fire began to burn beneath the feet of the elite, for Toussaint had risen, and the slaves of the island had found a leader at last . . . The rise, though, was through a boil of conflicting forces, a turmoil of crosscurrents and divergent aims. Blood was in collision with blood, every station was vying with every other, and divisions were divided from within. White opposed black, and both opposed the mulatto, the griffe, and the quadroon, and to confound the confusion, three nations of Europe warred for control of the welter.

Proclaiming freedom for the slaves, Toussaint fought a long fight to make it good, and he was himself proclaimed: the Black Napoleon, they called him, and he might well have been a match for the white one. General Rochambeau, commanding five thousand crack Frenchmen against him, issued a windy order to his troops: *It is only slaves you fight today—men who dare not look you in the face and who will flee in every direction. You have not come eighteen hundred miles to allow yourselves to be beaten by a rebellious slave.* Despite the order, five thousand and one Frenchmen were well-beaten that day by a rebellious slave. It was they who fled in every direction, and some may have thought the white Napoleon would've outrun them.

But there were rivalries and resentments even among the blacks, and they led finally to treachery: at a peaceful parley with the French, Toussaint was taken prisoner, put aboard the ship *Héros* (odd, the name, for in Greek it meant *protect*), and sent overseas to Brest. On arrival, he was condemned without trial—an act of the white Napoleon—and sentenced to confinement at Fort Joux in the Jura. Its stone walls were twelve feet thick.

It took only seven months for dungeon life to kill him. He died, it's said, seated on a chair in his cell, a small body from which a large black soul had just then sped. *I was born in slavery*, he'd written somewhere, *but I received from nature the soul of a freeman.* Now all of him was free.

TOBIAS LEAR, 1762–1816

Less Than Kin and More Than Minion

He has lived seven or eight years in my family as my private Secretary, and possesses a large share of my esteem & friendship.
—George Washington

He was no quill-driver in cotton hose, a scrivener who snotted his nose with an ink-smeared hand. His people were landed proprietors, a yeoman line, lower in rank than the gentry but a country mile higher than the herd. He didn't jump at the job when it was offered, fearing that he'd be treated as a menial, fed in the kitchen, and seated even there below the salt. He held a degree from Harvard, he'd sojourned abroad, and he could read and write French better than many a Frenchman. Not for him the back stairs, the fetch-and-carry, the all-hours beck-and-call.

As it turned out, he needn't have fretted. At Mt. Vernon, so far from being regarded as a servant, he was made a full member of the ménage. He dined at the general's board, he wined with him when the cloth was removed, and the two at times would play at cards—piquet, their game might've been, or quinze, or écarté—and if given to the use of *the pernicious weed*, Lear may have breathed smoke as he stared Madeira-eyed at court-card and pip. No lackey was he, but rather companion to the general and Uncle Toby to the household children.

The greats of the day were among those he wrote to in the general's name, and greats-to-be came through the door as guests, presidents in the making, envoys, lords of the land, and on terms of near equality Lear dealt with them all. But he could do more than bear himself well, hold his wine, ride to hounds, and spell correctly: he could observe and listen, he could sympathize, he could be a close-mouthed friend.

He had a nice understanding of their relation, though, and never did he presume upon it. Others, less sensitive to the general's nature, had ventured too close to him, and a few had even trespassed on his person, touching a hand, a sleeve, a shoulder, each such boor to his sorrow. The general was a commanding presence, standing several inches closer to the sky than most of any company, but when offended he seemed to expand the more. He also grew cold enough to numb the offender, to still him where he stood, open-mouthed but dumb.

For Lear, a like mistake would've been fatal, but he had neither reason nor inclination to make it. He stayed well within his proper sphere, a zone where both ice and anger were unknown. And yet, being privy to every outward concern of the general's, he could hardly have been unaware of an inner concern—a yearning that almost voiced itself at times, that took his mind off into the distance, away from Mt. Vernon and all it contained, away from his lawns and plantings, his horses, his beloved hounds, his fame, his wife, and fixed it on a certain dear face at a place called Belvoir.

Now and again, when matters of the moment had been disposed of, the general would walk about the grounds, and attended by Lear, who lagged half a pace behind, he'd stroll past the greenhouse, the dairy, the stables, the necessaries, or, more often, he'd cross the lawn, and with the tree-lined river below him, he'd pause to gaze at what he could've seen though blind—the intoxicant mistress of Belvoir. Her name, never mentioned by the general, had been Sally Cary, but longing publishes its object, and Lear must've known it (how could he *not* have?) and known too that the general had loved her on sight, loved her even after she'd married another and he Martha, and that he'd love her all his life.

Never to return, Sally Fairfax would be gone from Belvoir long before Lear arrived at Mt. Vernon, and he'd see her face and form only as fancy fashioned a fiction to take the place of fact. He'd have to imagine her voice, her ways, the color of her eyes and hair; he'd have to summon up (from where?) what the general could see in the dark and hear in a dream. But aware of the general's passion, was Lear the man to gauge its depth and extent, to measure its effect on the general and, yes, on the general's plump and placid Martha, wived for her money though his mind was then and ever elsewhere—with a dashing girl, clever, evocative, lovely as a song? Was Lear the kind to share the fascination?

More than likely not. He was possessed of higher learning, true enough, and he was a traveler who could write and sound in tongues, but nothing known of him suggests that he was profound. Schooled in words and numbers, he was simply skilled in their use, but, used, they had no meaning deeper than themselves. Thrice married, twice to connections of the general, he seems to have moved from an affinity as though its bond had failed to bind him. One such as he could hardly have fathomed the general's lifelong attachment to the mistress of Belvoir: only a susceptible heart would've served, and all he had was a sensible head.

He lived seven or eight years in my family, the general wrote of him— and what years they were for the history of the world! They embraced, those several years, the framing of a constitution for the colonial union, the choosing of a president (unanimously the general), the oath taking, and the first inaugural (*a most noble and dignified and excellent speech*, said Lear of what he may well have helped to fashion); they were years of conference and correspondence, of close association with the famous of the day and the morrow, of receptions and dinners and dancings, of sauntering the streets of Philadelphia a shade behind the general. But in ceremony and silence, did he trace the travel of the general's mind? Did he note that it always made for a place called Belvoir? More than likely not.

Lear couldn't hear what the general heard, one particular voice amid a choir, a sound that seemed more lyric than the rest; nor could he catch the soft speech of silk, the whisper of slippers on a parquet floor; and he couldn't see what the general saw, a face and figure that made all others crude, including those at home. He kept accounts for the general, he issued a blizzard of letters, reports, bills, drafts, and invitations, and he accompanied the general on his walks through the Federal city, a step behind the man but distant from his mind.

Thursday, Dec. 12, 1799—Very disagreeable weather,
snow, hail, etc. Employed all day in writing letters.
— Tobias Lear, diary

How differently the century would've ended had the general remained indoors! Instead, he rode out to his farms for five full hours,
returning so late for dinner that he chose to dine in his sodden clothes.
He was unwell on the following day, but he left the mansion to mark
some trees for felling, with the result that during the night he was badly
taken, being barely able to speak or breathe. Doctors were sent for, and
they tried their untrue concoctions, their blisterings, their bleedings,
their fomentations—and Lear was at the bedside through it all, easing
the general's position, raising his head, bathing his brow, but at last
the general murmured, *I am just going*, and withdrawing his hand from
Lear's, he went *without a struggle or a sigh*.

Mrs. Washington asked, with a firm & collected voice, Is he gone?

Lear wrote that he was unable to say the words; he had to reply
with a nod.

'Tis well, *said she*. I have no more trials to pass through.

But he may not have known what she meant.

JAMES MADISON, 1751–1836

The Framers in Philadelphia

It is of the greatest importance to guard one part of the
society against the injustice of the other.
— Madison, in the *Federalist*

He wasn't warning the poor to be leery of the rich. It was ass-end
around: he was tipping the well-off to watch out for the mob. The rag
and tag, he said, were filled with the leveling spirit, driven by ill humors,
and subject to all the follies of the bobtail mass, chief among which was
the rage to put the up-side down and the down-side up. He didn't plead
with his kind to curb their greed. Far from it: he stressed the need to
restrain the needy.

Beware of the numerous, he said, for they lust after the fruits of
their doings, and you own all but all. You have the best and most of the

19

land; you have the money and the mansions, the ships and the cargoes, the privilege, the learning, and the wit. They have the worthless warrants they got for fighting your worthwhile war; they have mean lives, lean children, broken-down wives, and lots of Continental paper for the backdoor trots.

The colonies sent fifty-five delegates to the Philadelphia convention, some few of whom, being his peers, addressed the member from Virginia as Jemmy. The rest took care to call him Mr. Madison, and well that they did, for there was no hail-fellow about him, none at all, and a bounder would've been frozen stiff where he stood. Strange, the command he had for one so unimposing. Slight of frame and less than average height, he was soft-spoken and shy, and he blushed rather easily, they say, for he was prim. But none denied that his temper was sweet and his nature generous, and all found it deplorable that his health was poor and that he'd not live long.

To Jemmy Madison, it was in no wise evident that all men had been created equal; it was evident, indeed, that they had not. If most of his fifty-four fellows were beneath him, how much more so were the ragtag in the streets! He knew the faculties of men to be of unequal weight, and since it was from faculties alone that property stemmed, perforce were some unequal in station and estate. What, though, were these faculties that Jemmy extolled—were they of base metal, or were they made of fine gold? Were they wisdom, nobility, self-surrender, were they piety, pity, and the accessible heart? Or were they cunning, love of gain, and an eye for the main chance? In short, were they powers sent by Heaven or by the prince of the lower air?

For the benefit of his silk-stocking company, Jemmy recalled a disturbing symptom that had lately appeared in a certain quarter of the colonies, an augury of dangers to come. The quarter he meant was western Massachusetts, and the symptom was the rebellion of Daniel Shays—and at the unnamed name, every man in the gathering felt the same chill wind off the Berkshire hills. And they'd be cooler still, said Jemmy, if they were ousted from their manors and shorn of their finery; if they were deprived of their lackeys, of their warehouses and wares, of their treasure in tinkling silver and ringing gold.

What befell that remote quarter, said Jemmy, was all too likely to fall closer to home. The same turbulence, the same spasms of sedition everywhere menaced the order, and what was secure today could be convulsed on the morrow—and the reason was none too far to find. Ever greater were growing the ranks of those fated to labor under the

20

hardships of life, and unceasing were their sighs for a greater share of its blessings, which only their betters enjoyed. But if they would continue to do so, said Jemmy, they must make sure that the sigh did not grow to a bellow, as it would surely do unless steps were taken to suppress it.

Indispensable to that effort, said Jemmy, was a constitution creating a central government empowered to operate not against the several colonies but directly against the individuals who comprised them. Only thus, he insisted, could overturners like Shays—let the name be spoken!—like Shays and his horde of shitten-britches be controlled; only thus, hampered by the snares and convolutions of a federal document, could the underdogs be kept where they belonged—at the bottom.

No government was worth a picayune, said Jemmy, unless it protected the permanent interest against innovation. He didn't have to construe *innovation*; the assemblage knew its meaning quite as well as he. All the same, he spelled it out for them. As the corps of rabble swelled, so too would their power, and the day was well on the way when, as a majority, they'd invade the rights of the rest. The machinery of government would become an instrument in the hands of the *desperate debtors*—as Mr. Hamilton had so piercingly put it—the ridden would be the riders, and the master would be the vassal of the slave. The rarities now relished by the few would be squandered on the many; prestige and manners would avail the gentry little and their blue blood even less: it would be a squalid world, and the base-born would rule it.

Let it be owned at once that Jemmy Madison voiced none of these things, most certainly not to the louts and the layabouts, else what was the point in excluding them from the conclave in the hall? And as for the delegates, why teach them what they already well knew—that the Great Beast had grown fractious? But what they did not yet know was how to master it, and that, beyond doubt, Jemmy *did* dwell on all through those four summer months in Philadelphia.

In his audience of fifty-four, stuck-up stiffs in fine-made stuffs and powdered wigs, there were such men of property as Daniel of St. Thomas Jenifer, and Gouverneur Morris, and William Livingston; and swells were there too, nibs like the commander-in-chief, and Hamilton, and both Pinckneys (namely, Cotesworth and Charles); and uncommon commoners were there, merchants, planters, physicians, speculators, and a shoal of lawyers—and Jemmy harangued them all, and these were the things he said:

The Articles of Confederation had been effective during the Revolution, holding the thirteen colonies together and avoiding thirteen separate wars. But with the achievement of the purpose, cohesion had been lost, and again there were thirteen separate colonies, each at odds with all the rest, each with its own laws, its own money, its own markets and tariffs, and, yes, even its own militia; debts were uncollectible or payable only in paper money (rag-money, they were calling it), and trade was falling away to nothing. For these ills, the articles afforded no cure; indeed, the articles too were ailing, and their malady was incurable. Their condition was this: they had little enough power against the several colonies; they had none at all against their citizens. The defect was inherent, said Jemmy; it could not be removed by amendment.

A new document was required, one that established a federal government for the thirteen colonies and made of the many one. That government alone would have the right and the power to maintain an army and navy, and none other would coin money, conduct foreign relations, or fix tariffs. Under this plan, presented by Edmund Randolph but authored by Madison, there would be a national legislature of two houses, a chief executive, and a supreme judiciary. These proposals and every other were greeted according to thirteen separate interests and therefore in thirteen different ways. Only in a single connection was there an absence of dispute: the new government would oblige itself to honor all debts contracted under the Articles of Confederation. Sad to say, this rare unanimity was due to the fact that no few of the delegates held depreciated paper, both Continental currency and warrants for soldiers' pay, all such bought cheap from veterans (some of them one-legged) in the hope of being paid off at par.

They were a mixed bag, those fifty-five delegates. Certainly there were honorable men in the company, but just as surely there were pettifoggers among the lawyers and slave drivers among the squires. Some of those with buckled shoes had belted souls, and behind many a candid face lay a crafty mind; and as often as not, noble words were spoken in order to deceive. The commander, being great, was above such things, and guileless too were others, but some were not so—lenders of money (meaning skinflints), merchants (meaning mongers and hucksters), shipowners (meaning blackbirders), and there were investors too, the genteel word for gamblers in land. But whatever his standing, whatever his probity, no man there was a fool, and speedily did they perceive the virtues of federation!

They might bicker about the mode of election or the terms of office, and they might turn red over bills of attainder and titles of nobility, and as to counting blacks (were they whole human beings or only ⅗ of a white?), they might even paw the ground. But ever before them was the prospect of constructing a permanent order for the new world, and its cohesive power was stronger than their divisions. To ordain stability! To frame a constitution, and with it the people! To slow change to a crawl and make it all but impossible! To ensure domestic tranquillity, they'd proclaim, but what they'd mean was that the top would stay up and the bottom down, and the Beast would always be ridden.

Jemmy Madison did not die young. He outlived every man jack in the hall.

Fling Away Ambition

By that sin fell the angels.
—Shakespeare

Go to hell! the sick man said, and they were nearly the last words he spoke, rapping them out to a servant who was merely urging him to take a dose of medicine. *Go to hell!* he cried, not knowing that if a hell existed, he'd soon be there himself, among the knaves and rogues of history. A pity, many would one day say, for his beginning had heralded no such end. In his lineage, there was clerical distinction and cultural as well, his mother being a daughter of Jonathan Edwards, and his father, he too a divine, an early president of the College of New Jersey, the original name of Princeton. Nowhere in the colonies could there have been a more favorable advent, nor did the young Aaron dash his family's hopes.

A brilliant student, he was ready for college at the age of eleven, only to be refused because of his youth. Admitted at thirteen, he led his class in literature, philosophy, and oratory, and after but three years, he was graduated summa cum laude, a proficient in Greek and Latin and so fluent in French and Spanish as to induce the belief that one or the other was his native tongue. On becoming a lawyer, he also became a dandy, a dinner guest, a ladies' man, and a crack shot with a pistol (he could stand well away from a tree, it was said, and call the leaf he meant to hit). His road, it seemed, had no turning, and he had all he needed to wend it far when he added to his natural talents the laurels won in the Continental army. Nothing could bar his progress—nothing but the sin he could not fling away.

Along with his wit, his charm of manner, his elegance, his dash and dazzle, he possessed a trait that the artless overlooked to their cost: he was slick, and he used the slickster's full bag of tricks. For all his graces, he was a double-dealer, and his way through the world was strewn with evasions, broken promises, half-truths, and whole lies. His sole aim was the high elevation of Aaron Burr, and to achieve it, he stooped low, to murder, aye, and to treason.

He rose, all right, but not to the height he aspired to, for some of those he dealt with were wary. Among them was Alexander Hamilton, no model of rectitude himself, he being quite as ambitious as Burr and equally mindful of what a skirt concealed—hardly the kind to shun glory and run from acclaim. A year younger than Burr, he'd been on Washington's staff during the Revolution; and distrustful of Burr even then, he'd disparaged him to the commander and blocked his advancement beyond the rank of lieutenant colonel. For depriving him of a sash and star, Burr hated the little bastard from St. Croix: he was the Enemy, Burr felt, oblivious of the enemy that dwelt within.

Thus, he did not, as he'd wished, become an ambassador, nor, as he'd hoped, did he become the governor of New York—and on both occasions, he ascribed the upshot to Hamilton, and not without good reason. Long had there been misgivings about Burr, but they greatly grew in 1800, when he almost stole the presidential election from Jefferson—almost, for again it was Hamilton who thwarted him. Through no fault of his own, or so Burr thought, he'd fallen short of his aim: his ill fortune, as always, had come from the calumnies of Hamilton. Hamilton had been his evil star, and it galled him that he'd been balked by the whoreson from the Caribbean. There'd never be an end to defeat unless there was an end to Hamilton, and he knew how to make the ends meet. After all, he could call the leaf he meant to hit.

Forcing a quarrel on Hamilton, he challenged him to a duel, and, contrary to the code of the time, he shot to kill, whereof Hamilton died on the following day. Unscathed, Burr would nevertheless die of the selfsame ball, though it would take him thirty more years to lie down, yelling *Go to hell!* at a well-meaning servant. To the minds of those whose opinions mattered, Burr hadn't simply been the victor in a shooting match. He'd assassinated his opponent, and what small esteem of him had remained dwindled now to nothing, to less than nothing, for he was scorned, and for Burr the bad years began, thirty of the worst.

They must've given him a taste of hell in advance. To be disdained by those of good repute, to be refused a hand, ignored in the street, denied a seat at the customary board, to find doors closed and credit suspended, to lose face and with it fortune—how heavy, such things, how hard to bear! His wit was of no avail to him, nor was he, as he once had been, at the core of every crowd. His charm no longer cast a spell, and only toadies were around those days to admire his clothes and his fluency in transatlantic tongues, of which he now mastered eight.

He dreamt of creating an empire in the western wilderness, and all it got him was a trial for treason, but having stopped short of an overt act, he was acquitted of the crime. Not of the thought, though, not of the secret intention, and even his cronies saw fit to cut and run from Emperor Aaron I. More than ever the outcast, poorer, seedier, aged beyond his age, and dunned by creditors, he was driven to using false names, dodging from mean lodgings to meaner, and daring the open air only after dark. Not even then was his real enemy plain to him, and it wounded him deeply to watch the feast through a windowpane, to see the high world from outside, and worse was it wounding that the gentry spat at the mention of his name. He'd died, it seemed, and Hamilton, killed, still lived!

It was a long hard road, though, that he had yet to go. He had to endure his daughter's drowning at sea; he had to flee bailiffs and arrest; he had to cadge meals and sponge off his son-in-law; and having lost his chattels, his standing, his pride, and his beloved Theodosia, he also had to suffer the loss of his teeth and, close to the end, a third stroke.

Were any, knowing of his plight, touched by it, were their hearts wrung by the faded plumage of the broken-winged bird? Were his virtues sung, was he praised for what he might've been, was his name bestowed on a town, a ship, a school, did his face turn up on a stamp? The answer is nay. He was made to take his medicine, and his proper place is hell.

Scenes of the
National Life, 2

Sharecropper's Bedroom*

The flooring is rough-sawn 1-by-12 planking, weathered, scrubbed, worn clean, like the deck of a ship. There are no chairs, no mats or curtains, no tables, lamps, or pictures; nothing but a bedstead in a corner and a shotgun on a wall.

An Amethyst Remembrance

The gem was gone.
—Emily Dickinson

She fell asleep, she said, with the stone in hand, and when she woke, she was alone—bereft, she thought. But the lover had left her lavender ghost to haunt the empty hand and fill the vacant room.

Blues for a Moveable and Wandering Thing

The Hudson was a colorless element once, a cold and clear, a small and falling stream. Rising in the Adirondacks, it flowed through the

*Photograph by Walker Evans.

Mohawk dominion and then the fiefs of Schuyler, Pauw, and Rensselaer, and it grew as it ran to meet the sea, and the sea did not salt it for a long way out from land; instead, it sweetened the sea. But the patroons have gone, the Kips and Beekmans, and the Mohawks too, and their river is barely fluent sewage now, inching toward the sewage sea. Beside it, where lodge and long house and manor stood, there are piers and mills and railroad tracks and the cardboard shacks of Hoovervilles.

Blues for the First Black Cadet, 1870

His name must be somewhere in the archives, a yellowed flower between foxed and faded sheets. Crispus, it may well have been, after the buck who fell in the Boston streets, or Fortunatus, or even Revels, for the sambo senator who sent him to The Point. Whatever he was called, they let him try for grades, and he lasted for all of an hour when they found that he couldn't read or write. Poor Cato, poor Scipio, they showed him the way to the ferry, the train, the road to Mississippi. What happened when he got there, got to Holly Springs, or Pascagoula, or Natchez-under-the-hill? It's something to wonder about, but the fact will never be known—still, what did he become, that sixty-minute plebe? Did he wind up a waiter, a porter, a prat-boy in a house of ill fame? That would-be sojer with the nigra name, did he end as an ornament on a roadside tree?

Message in a Bottle

Is it a come-quick call from Custer (*Two Moon's all around us, and Crazy Horse, and Gall!*)? Is it a page in a foreign language, a bill of sale, a holographic will, a sonnet launched by a swain? Is it part of a chain of seven, the one addressed to Christ, saying send seven more or die where skulls lie upon a hill? Or is there no paper scrap, no parchment scroll, no writing new or old, only a play of light on a bottle as it waltzes away with the stream?

Coney Island

What do the sea-birds make of all those lights along the shore, all those bright strands across the night where once the sand-grass grew and the reeds? Do they remember, through meat-smoke, grease, and corn-explosions, through *eatdrinkbuy* in neon pink, do they remember when there were no violations of the sky?

Only the Stone Remembers

Here lyes the body of Mrs. Margaret George, wife of
Mr. Joshua George, 1680–1735

The promised reward is carved on a shield-shaped heart lying in a field of leaves: *The Righteous Shall Be in Everlasting Remembrance.* No symbol of death can be seen—the ominous urn, the wilting willow, the Glass of Hours trickling time. Ne'er shall the Good be gone, she's promised, ne'er shall it be dust and disappear. But you know the truth now, Margaret—that not even Joshua remembers. Only the stone . . .

Two Views of a Small World

Photography is my passion. The search for truth my
obsession.
—Alfred Stieglitz

He took one of the shots on a fall evening and the other on a winter's day, both of the same still courtyard, both taking in the same walls and windows, the same catenaries of clothesline and wire. In each, fire escapes can be seen, but only in the winter print does a tree appear, only in the fall one lights, and though no people are shown in either, people seem to be near.

Fall Evening

A festoon of laundry swags across the yard, sheets, shirts, towels, and drawers, and an incandescent eye touches black and gray with white, a cornice here and there, a ladder rung, a salient of rooftop, an area of air. A hollow square of homes, the confine becomes, a common little quad where water runs and china chimes, where food is being eaten and love is being made. Beyond and overbearing, lofts fill the sky with staring floors, twos and threes and fours of glare—but they're on another planet, those things outside.

Winter's Day

Snow trims more than the tree—it decks the backyard world. It's a boa for every capstone, a crown for every post; it's piping for parapets, a filler of cracks, a collar for sills and lintels—and lines of rope are strung with pearls. No face or footprint shows, no fire or frozen motion, but many are breathing somewhere near.

Truth my obsession, he said, but what truth was he seeking in those cloistered seasons? Was it youth, you wonder, youth the soon-gone shooting star . . . ?

The Second Wife of John Brown

She was sixteen when he married her, and she bore him thirteen children in the next twenty-one years—and there'd've been more if he hadn't gotten hung for the crime at Harpers Ferry, a minor crime alongside the major one of slavery. She was a tough dame, that Mary Anne, and not just because she was a sure-fire breeder: she was tough all the way through a life that would've killed half the wives of her time. It took a hard knot of a woman to stand the news of two sons shot dead at the engine house; it took a creature made of whang-leather to out-stay the thirty-seven minutes her husband swung from a rope.

It was a rough road she'd had to travel even before that, and it didn't end when his body was brought to the Adirondacks for burial at North Elba. The family farm lay along the Ausable River, and he was put into the ground within sight of Whiteface Mountain, if only his eyes could've seen. When her time came, like as not she joined him there, and then it might've been said that, after a lifelong chase, she'd caught up with him at last.

If it wasn't a chase, what in the world was it? He must've had wheels instead of feet: it was like he ran on rails (how fitting that he wound up in an engine house!), and mostly Mary Anne ran after him through his smoke. Smoke—because there was a firebox in the man, and it was always stoked by slavery. The fire of abolition burned night and day within him; it burned no matter where he went or what he was doing—and he went far and did much. None of it came to anything; he was too transient for that, changing place and line of work pretty near at will. The fire never died, though, not even when he did.

What and where was he not in his fifty-nine years! Born in Connecticut, he seems to have started out as a tanner, and marrying a "remarkably plain" girl named Dianthe Lusk, he begot six children by her before a seventh childbirth killed her. Thereafter, he turned up as a mail carrier in Pennsylvania, a contractor for a canal company in Ohio, a speculator in land, a bankrupt, a wool merchant, and a traveler to Europe in connection with his fleeces. Where all the while was Mary Anne, and where those who were left of his begotten—how did they fare when he shot five slavers on the Potawatomie in Kansas and one named Cruise in Missouri? Who provided for his family while he was fighting at Black Jack Oaks and Sugar Creek? Who fed them, who did the grunt work, if not Mary Anne?

At the start of his rebellion, she may have tagged along after her locomotive husband, dragging one or more of his get behind her — Jason, it may have been, or Watson and Oliver, the two due to die at the Ferry. But the pace was too swift, and so also were the changes of place, and she wasn't with him for the wild moods, the night rides, the murders. She was at home in North Elba, where, while slaving for her family, she sensed and dreaded the end — the abolition of John Brown.

The Wife of John Charles Frémont

Oh, Jessie is a bright sweet lady.
　　　　— campaign song, 1856

Someone said she was the better man of the two, and the someone may have been right. Her father was Tom Benton, one of the senators from Missouri, and of his several children — two sons and four daughters — Jessie Ann was hands down his favorite. A comely sort if her portraits tell no lie, she was much more than merely pleasing to the eye. She had a mind, which Benton never had the luck to find in his sons, one of whom died young and the other of strong drink. Jessie, though, was cut from his cloth, being a reader of books, direct and free in speech, and unwavering. Less at ease with her were girls of the kind who'd been taught (worse, who believed) that their sphere was circumscribed and their proper place the home. By the time she reached the age of seventeen, Jessie Ann was being sought after, courted as a belle.

The father of John Charles Frémont was not a senator. He was a migratory and stone-broke Frenchman who ran off with another man's wife, got three bastards on her, and then wandered off to die somewhere, leaving his family high, dry, and hungry. One of these half-and-half by-blows was John Charles. His early years, all of them spent in the Carolinas, were knockabout, his mother taking in boarders and he odd-jobbing until he caught someone's fancy and was sent to college in Charleston. Proficiency in mathematics led to his appointment as an instructor in the subject aboard the *Natchez*, a naval vessel about to leave on a cruise.

Some while after his return, he found himself in Washington, and it was there that he met Jessie Ann, who, as he put it, affected him as would a rare-colored rose. *Naturally, I was attracted*, he said — naturally,

32

her father being a senator and he only a catch-colt and a topographical engineer. He was also, and so known to be, a ladies' man, and in his wake he'd left a foam of churned-up emotions: he was, by common consent, *quite simply the handsomest man in Washington*. Jessie Ann fell for him, and she fell for life. Nothing that happened during the next sixty years lessened her infatuation by a jot—and a lot happened, not all of it good.

John Charles was a rover by birth, a runaway like his parents, and following him on a map, the brain becomes footsore and the body weary. He was always on the bit, always eager to be away from the throng, as though solitude concealed him, not only from the crowd, but also from himself. During the first eight years of his marriage to Jessie Ann, he was absent for five, off in the wilds somewhere with the scout Kit Carson. Never the man to be tied down when there were new sights to be seen, when pristine vistas lay beyond the horizon, he was forever someplace else, treading where none had trod before, living in an unused world and breathing unbreathed air.

From time to time, he'd return from the forest, from the plains and the prairie, from the range of the nameless land, and he'd recite his findings to Jessie Ann, who'd phrase them nicely and write them as his report on the living things and riches that he'd discovered, timber dense as grass, veins of precious metals, buffalo herds that flowed like tides. There'd be a season then of acclaim, and he'd be called a coming man, but all too soon he'd feel the itch to roam, and the coming man would go, leaving Jessie Ann knocked up and forlorn while he sought new clefts in the Great Divide.

More than once he made his way to the Pacific, and each time he was bemused by the wealth that was there for the taking if only California were part of the Union. But when, as a mere army captain, he sought to foment a revolt against Mexico, he was commanded to desist, and on refusing, he was arrested, court-martialed, and dismissed from the service. The ragtag protested, but it was nonetheless a disgrace, one to be added to his dark beginning and the dim opinion some held of his honor. Sad to say, they thought him not quite as tall as he stood with the bobtail, being light-fingered with the money of others and loose-fingered with his own.

There were further reservations about the handsome Frenchman. He was an imposing sight, no mistake, and he cut a fine figure wherever he went, but his friends were few and his censors many, and he did himself harm with his manner. He was never a part of any company: he could be at the heart of it, indeed its focal point, and still he'd seem untouched and alone. He was known too for his silence. It was the kind usually associated with sagacity, insight, breadth of mind, and by some he was given credit for such and more. In fact, though, he was rather like a photographic negative: there was nothing behind him but the reverse of his front. He yearned for fame, but handsome is as handsome does, and he did badly whenever it bid fair to come his way. A vainglorious man, he dreamt in vain of glory. His portion was scorn, ridicule, and a seasoning of pity.

What was the portion of Jessie Ann, the better man of the two? From the earliest days of their marriage, it had been to endure the pain of parting, the longing for a form diminishing and finally lost to sight in the haze of distance. In her imaginings, she dwelt on the hardships that were only too real for him—the heat, the cold, the Indian, the ungodly acts of God. There were months when no word came from the wild, when, due to his whereabouts in nowhere, no word was on the way—and due to his schemes and dalliance, the same was true when he was in Stockton or Monterey. There were children (in time, five) to bear and rear during his truancies, and there was peril in journeys of her own, made simply to be at his side. So often was she on the go that home became a sometime thing, a momentary halt on a lifelong road.

But her trial in dispelling smear was the heaviest one of all. Rumor about John Charles was ever on the air—hearsay of an amourette here and there, of arrogance, speculation, and excessive display, of powers seized or assumed, and even of acquiring property that the grantor did not own. In none of the many instances of slander did she choose to stand aside. It was the work of her life to justify the handsome man, and she did so with a constancy so rare that scandal could never shake it.

All the same, she knew that the smoke around him came from a fire. She knew—hell, what wife doesn't?—that he'd beguiled the idle hour in someone else's bed. And she knew, being a sweet bright lady, of the shady deal he'd made for the Mariposa grant. And she knew, because she was there to see it, that he was niggardly with his miners, paying them three dollars a day to dig his gold and then soaking them a dollar a night to sleep in his cabins. He was overbearing and showy; he was comfortable with frauds because he was a false-front himself, a colorful flat of scenery; and he was also, and fatally, an injudicious ass—and she knew that too, to her sorrow.

When the war came, he was recommissioned (as a major general!) and posted to the Western Department, and almost at once he took

34

it upon himself to issue an Emancipation Proclamation for Missouri. Rebuked by Lincoln and ordered to withdraw it, he compounded his error by sending Jessie Ann to Washington to dispute the president. Though coldly received and told that she was *quite a lady politician*, she persisted, all to no avail, and not only did the order stand, but Handsome John was relieved of his command.

He was an empty man, few men more so, but true-blue Jessie remained as true as ever—and quite as blue. Others might be taken in by his heroic pose and his seeming dash (he really had the slows), others might be impressed by his bold talk and his flash clothes, but Jessie Ann had seen him in the flesh, heard his rant when none but she could hear it, known his flaws and fears, and driven off the devils that drove him: she'd seen the man undressed. She did not, therefore, settle for his image—the intrepid pathfinder, he who'd slept under the stars, survived all manner of disaster, and hacked his way to glory through the trackless. She loved the feckless Frenchman, and she took him as he was. Sweet bright Jessie Ann.

Slow-witted, indecisive, and incapable of handling a squad, let alone a division, even so he was again commissioned major general, and the appointment stirred up not a little they-say as to how he managed it. Still more was stirred up when he had the gall to try his luck against Stonewall Jackson at Cross Keys in the Shenandoah. He got a whipping, of course—Christ, Wellington would've got beat!—and for his ineptitude, he lost his commission, this time for good. Jessie Ann did not join the anvil chorus that choired his defeat. Nay, doubtless she said that, if given support, he'd've carried the day.

Some quiet years followed, the few the Frémonts were ever to enjoy. With some of the gold dug from their clouded grant (at three dollars a day, less a dollar for lodgings), they bought an estate in the Hudson River Valley. Attended by a flock of flunkies (grooms, coachmen, gardeners, maids, and a French chef), they entertained large numbers with a prodigal hand, but John Charles was not always present to receive. When away, though he may have grazed on greener grass in passing, his mind was on a new venture, the building of a railroad to be called the Memphis, El Paso, and Pacific, and for a while, the promotion went well. He sold six million dollars worth of shares to European investors, and he seemed to be en route to another bonanza.

Instead, he was riding to ruin on a railroad hardly longer than its name. Three miles of track were all that was ever laid for the Memphis,

El Paso, and Pacific before the enterprise went up the spout, leaving its shareholders holding shares in a three-mile bust. They sued the handsome man and won, and in winning, they beggared him.

Whatever he owned was sold up—the estate, the furniture, the horses, the carriages, the boats, and the glowing Bierstadt of Golden Gate—and then down and down went the Frémonts, down to little, less than little, and nothing. Gone the days of pressed duck *aux oranges;* gone the fine wines and Havanas, the jewelry, the vaulting hopes for renown. Their elegance became seedy and their quarters meaner, and they suffered once the pang of renting rooms that held a sofa that had graced their home. They were in the sunless deep now, never again to rise.

When John Charles died, in 1890, Jessie Ann had been his wife for half a century. She'd long since grown gray, her figure had lost its dales and rounds, and her skin was no longer reminiscent of the petals of a rose. She was old, and she rued it, but whenever she dwelt on her husband, he was the handsome man of a bygone time; the magic of memory had preserved him against age. It was as though they'd just met and he was not yet the aspiring nomad, the overweening incompetent, as though he were still guiltless of folly, presumption, cupidity—as though he were still innocent.

It was not that she'd forgotten his posturing, his forbidding silences, his plans that had failed. It was that, remembering them only too well, she set them aside, almost as if they belonged to someone else. She loved the man, and she would not see him as he appeared to others. While he lived, time and again she'd defended him from the world, but never had he needed to be defended from her. His frailties, his vanity, his somewhat soiled hands—none of these chilled the feeling that flowed from her to him, that flowed even now when he was dead.

She'd been lonely during his long and many absences, but what had loneliness mattered when she knew that he'd return? He was alive, and it had made no difference where, because someday he'd again be at her side. This time, though, he'd not return, and this time her longing for the handsome man would end only with the end of her life.

Sweet bright Jessie Ann.

Good-bye My Fancy

Afoot and light-hearted I take to the open road.
—Walt Whitman, "Calamus"

He didn't come back as he'd started—healthy, free, and with the world still before him: he was heartsick and footsore, aged beyond his age, and, if free at all, free only of his illusions. The long brown path hadn't led him toward ends ever-extending, it hadn't shown him the vistas he'd fancied, and he hadn't known the cheerful voices, the gay fresh sentiment of the open road; no, nor, as he strode from Paumanok, had he inhaled great draughts of space, for space, he'd found, was going as he spoke and would soon be gone. *Allons!* he'd cried, *the road is before us!* But the world he'd exulted in was passing away: no longer was it everyman's and no one's; it was owned.

He may have been thinking like an Indian; maybe he even thought he *was* an Indian—the Indian of old, though, not the wretch selling bead-and-birchbark trash at the wayside. Like the ancient, maybe he believed that the world had been created by the Great Hare, son of the West Wind and a descendant of the Moon. Maybe he too knew of the care that must be taken not to awaken the anger of the Okies that dwelt in the forest, in the air, in both still and falling waters, indeed in all things and all creatures, in birds and wolves and otters, in stones and sticks, in fish, and even in their bones. Maybe, like the Indian, he knew that these lesser spirits were easily offended; maybe he knew that it was a thin-skinned world the living lived in, and the dead as well, for their shades still hunted with shade bow and arrow and haunted still the fire . . . If these truths were known to all Indians, to Algonquin and Tuscarora alike, and to Abenaki and Cherokee, why would they not be known to Walt? Why would he be rash where they were wary? Why would he claim as his what so plainly was held in common—the world?

Forth he fared, then, singing songs of Himself, of Joys and Occupations, of the Redwood Tree and the Rolling Earth—but sad to say, he'd come too late. There was no gay fresh sentiment on the long brown path, there were no cheerful voices, faces, salutations, no spaces from which to draught pure air. Instead, there were walls and wire and signboards to warn him off: he wasn't the peregrine, the wandering minstrel young and hale and free from care; he was a trespasser possessed of nothing, not the ground he stood on nor the little that clung to his feet.

There were no limitless forests now, only burns, only stumps in the clear-cuttings and clumps preserved for shade. There were no creatures to be seen save those that slaved, and where buffalo grass had run before the wind, tracks and trains and pavement lay. Cities sprawled beside the waters and fed them their outfall, and factories stood on the hunting grounds of tribes that were no more. Everywhere the long brown path was fenced and gated, everywhere was the public realm being privately held, and nowhere was the rolling earth for the strolling player: the open road was closed.

Good-bye my fancy.

RACHEL JACKSON, 1767–1828

An Odd Little Woman from Nashville

All brides are beautiful.
—Thomas Bell

A daughter of the Widow Donelson, she lived before the day of the camera, and save for a single miniature, her likeness exists only in the say-so of the frontier. Legend has it that she was a handsome damsel with a falls of black hair, a full figure, and a manner described as sprightly. Many a maid might've been so defined—the woods were stiff with such nymphs—but since few have ever differed, it's likely that word of mouth was right for once and that the Rachel of rumor was real.

As to her looks later on, there's also broad agreement, but here the common talk, like time, turns quite unkind. With the years, it's said, her full figure grew fuller, grew fat; her skin, that health had earlier rouged, was sallow; her hair—her nightfall of hair!—was thin and grayed; her limber hands were swollen, and lively no more her feet. Graceful in youth, the story goes, she became graceless with age and dressed in homemade clothes.

Jackson was a young Tennessee lawyer and she a divorcée of twenty when they wed, and for him, thereafter, never did she change. It was as if her youth had come to stay: she was a vibrant bride and a beauty forty years later, on the day she died. He was unaware that her hands and feet were filled with fluids that her heart was unable to carry off; lamplight slid as always along braids of black hair; and she wasn't ill, she wasn't worn and well-nigh spent, she was still in his eyes what they'd

38

first beheld—a striking girl aflash with life, the Widow Donelson's girl, the Rachel of old.

In their latter days, they'd sit face to face before a fireplace at the Hermitage, each with a clay pipe (or she on occasion a cigar), and in the drifting smoke, his thoughts may have drifted too, taken him back to the stunning discovery that her husband had failed to file for divorce, that she hadn't, as she supposed, been free to remarry, and that she and Jackson had been living in sin. In time, of course, a decree was granted to the fellow (Robards, was it?), and the sin was erased, if sin it was. Forever, though, it had stained Rachel, and therefore forever it remained on Jackson's mind. Through the fault of another, she'd come to feel the spite and scorn of many, and he would not, nor could he, let her bear the shame. Any slur or slight, any reminder, even, of the hitch in their relation, and the offender was in danger of his life. There never was a day when Jackson would not have shot and killed in Rachel's name—or gotten killed himself. She was his bride and beautiful still, and she could not be made to hide her face while he lived.

What power did she possess that he could not deny, what quality that enthralled him, what held him fast for life? What in her so beguiled him that he could not see that his girl had aged, that her signs were poor and her chest pains frequent, that her state was dire and she dying even then, as they sat smoking pipes before the fire? What blinded him to the truth—or did he choose to ignore it, her pallor, her pangs, her rapid pulse? Did his mind refuse the evidence of her going?

Only too well did he know the truth, but he couldn't endure the knowing, he couldn't let it run on to the end. The end meant facing an empty chair before a fire that failed to give off heat, a cold fire in an empty room. All pleasure was still in that chair, and she'd take it all with her when she went: she'd drain life of living, leaving him only time to spend until he spent it away. He'd outlast her by seventeen years, but never a day would be passed without sorrow for what he'd lost—a young girl, eager, bright, and lively, who'd become an old woman with thinning hair and heart pain. But how good the world had been while she was still in that chair!

The Ladies' War

> She is as chaste as a virgin!
> —Andrew Jackson

There was another school of thought, and in it was taught the opposite view—that Peggy was bold as brass and free and easy with her favors—but neither view was ever shown to be the true one. If she was virtuous, how could she have demonstrated her virtue? And if she was a flip-skirt, who among the righteous had seen the flipping? It was a performance given, so to speak, to vacant seats in a darkened house; but for many, fiction was as good as fact, and they quite believed what they fancied—that Peggy was fond of lying on her back wearing nothing but a man.

Born in a village alongside the Potomac, later to be known as the city of Washington, she was the daughter of an Irish tavernkeeper, whose Franklin Hotel was patronized by the bigwigs of the new nation, among them Senator Daniel Webster, Speaker Henry Clay, and General Andrew Jackson. Much was in dispute about her, but even the censorious allowed that she was uncommonly handsome. She was more, though, than they were willing to admit: she was a tall, dark-eyed stunner with disdainful breasts and a figure like a figure-8. A turner of heads was Peggy the Mick, and she made them turn inside as well as out; at a later day, she'd've been a legend, and in song and story, Molly would've been her name.

For finders of fault, her looks alone would've made her suspect, but the breeze in her manner dispelled all doubt. Even as a child, she'd been the pet of the tavern patrons—the greats of the moment and the greats in the making—and letting her join their company, they'd listen to her comment and occasionally agree, and at times she'd be invited to sit on someone's knee. She was at home there in the taproom: she didn't mind the smells and the smoke, the inelegance of spitting, or the frequent alehouse word; indeed, she came to use the weed herself, yes, and several of the words. But what had been merely forward in a five-year-old was crass in a girl of seventeen, when, far more knowing, she was aware of being sought after not for her wit so much as for a close-up of her tits.

It was a village no more, that riverside mud-flat; it was a fast-growing town, and when men of mark came to it now, they came with their wives. Rarely did the seventy rooms of the Franklin fail to fill, and though no knees knew Peggy's weight these days (not in public, that is, said the spiteful), she was still a welcome sight in the taproom, where she flitted through fumes and commotion, took in the political chatter, and voiced opinions of her own. At length, her eye was caught by a naval lieutenant, and his was caught by her.

Their marriage in Georgetown was attended by a goodly company, among them four senators, eleven members of the House, three generals, and a commodore, but not, it was noted, by their wives. The Ladies' War had begun.

One of the guests at the Franklin was the widower John Eaton, and if Peggy's connections were high, his were higher, for he was allied with the Jackson family and himself a senator from Tennessee. It was at the tavern that he came to know Peggy and her husband, John Timberlake, purser aboard the USS *Constitution*. He found the fellow likable enough, but a do-little by inclination and something of a sot, who, when he wasn't tossing a pot, was tossing his wife. In short order, she bore him a son and two daughters, after which he sailed with his ship on a four-year cruise to Spain and the Mediterranean.

Peggy wasn't the sort to find herself a captain's walk and scan the horizon daily for the return of her man from the sea. Near at hand, there were others to beguile the lonely hour, and the most beguiling was John Eaton—who was also the nearest, since he still dwelt at the Franklin. In the long absence of Timberlake, they spent much time together, true, but nothing else was adduced against them, no crime, no unseemly behavior, and if they were ever flagrant, the fire was never seen. Evidence of fire was seen, though, all of it as insubstantial as ash, and it was of such particles that the deemsters built their judgment of guilt.

What was that evidence, what were those lightweight things? On Eaton's arm, Peggy attended state dinners and receptions, and at balls and theatricals too was the senator her squire. Often she sat beside him on drives through the town and out along the country roads, and on occasion, it was said, they alighted for a stroll in the woods, but how far and for what purpose no one ever knew. This was known, however—their custom of sitting on the tavern porch until all hours of the night and talking in low tones of whatsoever they would. None of it had been overheard, but their detractors heard themselves, which proved to be quite as good, since they knew—they simply *knew*—what the lovers had been saying in the shadows. That they *were* lovers none of the ladies doubted in the least. There in the dark, so infamously close that the woman could breathe his breath and he the heady fragrance of her hair, was it likely, the ladies asked, that they were discussing tariffs, the Compromise of 1820, or Mr. Monroe's Doctrine? Far more probable, was it not, that he was savoring recent delights and she those in store when he finished his cigar. For the accuser, surmise was the deed already done, and it was plain to one and all, as plain as plain could be, that the pair were thinking of the two-backed beast.

But had they ever made the beast? Had Eaton been ignited by her ardent beauty, and had she broken faith with her cruising sailor? Had they, on those walks in the woods, cast honor aside with their clothes and coupled in the grass? Is that what they'd done, as the ladies assumed, or had they instead merely remarked on the clouds, the birds, the profusion of flowers, the perfumed air? Which, which had come to pass among the oaks and the cedars along Rock Creek? One guess was as good as another. To some, Peggy was a spraddle-leg; to others, she was a vestal—and as they believed at the beginning, so would they believe to the end. Thus, she was both pure and impure, and the war would go on until the last diehard died.

A war it was and well under way when Lizzie Monroe wrote to say that Peggy was no longer welcome at the White House board. No less hostile, no more sparing were the other ladies, those *unspottyd lambs of the Lord*, and encountering Peggy in a public place, they behaved as though she weren't there, as though she'd turned transparent and become vacant air. But even in her social invisibility, she was a presence difficult to deny. With the unmarried and with those whose wives had been left in Vermont and Georgia, she was still thought to adorn a function; she was still brought there by Eaton, and her wit in wise company was as nimble and daring as ever before.

She was twenty-seven, and the slasher of old, when word came from Spain that her sailor had been found dead in his bunk on the *Constitution*. At once, and for all of a year, she secluded herself in her home, seeing no one—no one, said the captious, but Senator Eaton. If so, his visits were not observed, but that he made them was taken as a matter of course, even by those who were well-disposed. After all, why would he not have called, why would he have denied himself a year? He was gone on the woman; he'd been gone for a long, long time.

Greater than ever grew the ladies' hostility when, at the end of the year, Peggy again put in an appearance—not often, be it said, but only with Eaton when she did. Slander, no longer bated, was openly spoken and almost to the face. The tumult, afar once, had come near, but

Peggy, now Mrs. John Eaton, was quite able to endure it. As for her new husband, he was leading Jackson's campaign for the presidency, and when his man won, he became secretary of war and a power second only to Jackson—and Peggy was due to share his glory.

Always a favorite of the old general, she was often his honored guest, at which the outcry from the ladies reached its shrillest. A tapster's daughter, a barmaid, a flirt, a jade, and very likely worse—that such a one should grace, *dis*grace, the presidential table was an affront to the country, and the ladies would not suffer it to pass. The war was on the White House lawns now, under the portico, at the mansion's very doors.

It was fought there for two years, and it was fought as well on the Senate floor, in private parlors, in the press, and it was fought in embassies, saloons, and on the streets. Freighted with strife and spleen, the air must've seemed heavier, harder to breathe, a palpable gas. How stern, how rancorous the ladies, how indignant! And over what?—over one they saw as different from themselves, a sport, and if they'd had their way, they'd've killed her, as animals do their defective young. That instinct was equally strong in the ladies, and nothing curbed it. Many of them were married to men of importance—members of Congress, jurists, military and naval officers—but let Peggy Eaton be on the guest list at a dinner, a soirée, a musicale, and those men of importance would be sent out alone. The president was often the host, and the slight, meant for Peggy, missed its mark and injured him. To protect Jackson from further harm, Eaton resigned his position in the Cabinet. . . .

"In the end, then," Maggie said, "Peggy lost the Ladies' War."

"The ladies didn't think so. For the rest of Jackson's life, he was a friend of the Eatons, and both were at his bedside when he died. Afterward, they had other friends Tyler, Polk, Buchanan. I don't call that losing. I call it riding high. Peggy outlived Eaton by more than twenty years, and to her last day, she rode high."

On that last day, she rode in a hearse, and it took her out along what had once been a dirt road to a creek spanned by a bridge of resonant timbers. On the far side, a cemetery broke the once unbroken woods, where early birds and flowers dwelt in a late generation, and the new oaks and beech and cedars were descendants of the old. In that burial

43

ground, the box containing Peggy was placed beside John Eaton's, and then again the two were together—and again, as once they may have done, they lay beneath the trees and the clouds, while above them flowers swayed, and birds flew faint shadows through their shades.

GETTYSBURG, AFTERNOON OF THE THIRD DAY

Pickett's Charge

If I had had Jackson . . .
   —General Robert E. Lee

On an earlier afternoon, you and Maggie had been atop Lookout Mountain, gazing down at the town of Chattanooga across a bend in the Tennessee. You were fifteen hundred feet above its sound and motion, and from there, all seemed still and quiet below. Not even in fancy were Federals storming the cliff, nor was a plunging Rebel fire on its way to meet them. There was no tumult that day, no rising tide of blue from Chattanooga, there were no explosions great or small, and no smoke lay on the air. A few fieldpieces, their carriages chained to the parapet, stood mute.

It was otherwise at Gettysburg.

The woods at the foot of Seminary Ridge screened a long line of artillery, 137 guns in all, each of them trained on the Union center a mile away over stands of wheat and rye, and for two hours they spoke without a stop. For two hours, firing at a wall of rocks on Cemetery Ridge, a gun a second could be heard, and sometimes more than one—two hours of flash and smoke and shatter—and when at last the cannonade was broken off, dazed and deafened gunners fell beside their trails and limbers and lay as though dead. Nearby, among the forty-two regiments forming up for the charge against the wall, there were many who within the hour would verily be dead.

It is not so hard to go there. The trouble is to stay. The whole Yankee army is there in a bunch.
   —Brigadier General Ambrose Wright

The order to move out was long in coming, and the men spent the time in various ways. Some wrote letters; some lay staring at the trees, the sky, the birds, or at nothing visible to the eye; some were certain that their hour had come and awaited it resigned and numb; some showed fear and seemed ready to run (play-outs, they were called); and some simply suppressed thought and feeling and sat chomping a cold cigar. But all, at the command to go, went (even the play-outs), and you watched fifteen thousand men flow toward a mile-away wall.

> Great God, General Lee! We'll have to fight our infantry against their batteries! We'll have to charge over a mile of open ground under their shrapnel . . . !
>   —Lieutenant General James Longstreet

> The enemy is there, General Longstreet, and I am going to strike him.
>   —General Robert E. Lee

The fifteen thousand were blind to changes made in the terrain. Footpaths crisscrossed it now, and pavement had been laid for motorcars, but the forty-two regiments were unaware of their existence, nor were they deflected by statuary, 12-pounders, pyramids of shot, or areas fenced against trespass: they simply filtered through all such things as if they weren't there. Beyond the Emmitsburg road, they entered a pasture creamed with clover, and here they were put to a pour of canister that tore huge holes in their formations, but still they kept coming on. Behind them by the hundreds, though, lay sacks of soiled clothes.

> Dick Garnett did not dismount, and he was killed. Kemper, desperately wounded, was taken prisoner. Armistead was mortally wounded at the head of his command. Seven of my colonels were killed and nine of my lieutenant colonels. Only two field officers came out of the fight unhurt.
>   —Major General George E. Pickett

One of the two was he—due, some say, to having posted himself behind a clump of rocks.

Partly sheltered by the wall along Cemetery Ridge—*the whole Yankee army is there in a bunch*—the Federals now went to work with their Springfields, and down across the cloverfield they sent shots in sheets like driven rain—a most withering fire, Pickett would call it, but a few score of his men (without him) managed to make it to the wall. In the melee, none of them took notice of the granite monument to the

High Water Mark, none saw the plaque on the plinth, none read the names graven on the book of bronze. Just there where that reminder stood, they fought the Federals hand-to-hand until they were captured or dead.

If I had had Jackson, Lee later said.

The memorial had been placed in a stand of trees near the stone wall, and through them, the long downslope of grasses could be seen, open ground ending at the foot of Seminary Ridge. No cannonade came that day from Confederate guns emplaced in the woods: those that remained were still trained on the Union position, but they'd never fire the cans of case shot, fused together, that lay beside them. Of the fifteen thousand men who'd made the charge, not some but all were now dead and gone, save for such vestiges as might yet be found in that mile of open ground—a belt buckle, a button, the bones of a leg or arm.

"Suppose he'd had Jackson," Maggie said. "What would've happened that didn't happen?"

"He'd've been killed here instead of at Chancellorsville."

You watched a sightseer wander among mementoes of the charge—an obelisk, a cross, a block of marble—and when you saw him stoop to pick up an object, you took it that he'd chanced on a prize, a regimental numeral, possibly, or even a minié ball. But after a moment's inspection, he cast it aside, dusted his hands, and moved on.

"You don't think Jackson would've made a difference?"

"He was a great commander, in some ways greater than Lee, but no one could've brought off that charge. It was a mistake to order it."

"People don't usually say that about Lee."

"He did what Burnside did at Fredericksburg, and he got the same result. A worse one, because Burnside lost only a battle, and Lee lost a war."

"If he'd had Jackson," she said.

You gazed down the long slant where clover once had been, and you tried to imagine a comber of Confederates coming to a crest at the wall. You could almost hear gunfire, you could almost smell smoke and almost see men fall.

"It was more than a mistake," you said. "It was sinful to send out thousands, knowing they'd never come back."
"Every general knows that."

Drifting toward the Taneytown Road at the Federal rear, you could see the cut-stone cowl over Spangler's Spring, where the wounded of both sides had come to drink. Two boys were engaged now in pitching pebbles at the basin, in which the water had once been as red as wine.

"Yes," you said, "but knowing it, not every general can give the order. Longstreet couldn't, and he wasn't nearly as knightly as Lee. How could so stainless a man kill so many in so mean a cause?"
"I never understood that he was fighting to keep slavery. He was fighting for his country—Virginia."
"They had many countries—Alabama, Mississippi, Carolina—but deep down, they were all slavers."

Along your way, you saw commemorations of the 29th Ohio Infantry and the 7th Georgia, and then you passed a metal General Meade on a metal charger. Across the pedestal of this last, someone had chalked *nigger-lover.*

"In one of your books," Maggie said, "you wrote that at Cold Harbor, Grant lost five thousand men in eight minutes. I wonder how he felt, losing six hundred men every sixty seconds."
"The way anyone would—the way Lee did. But Grant's cause was the better one."
"Cold Harbor," she said. "The name weighs on me."

47

Occurrence on the Hill of Bells

I am a son of the people, and I shall not forget it.
   —Juarez

He is very homely, but very good, said his wife of her full-blooded Zapotec, and as to his phiz, few disagreed with Doña Margarita: he was indeed an ill-favored Indian, and photographs prove it. His face was rather like a bronze medallion, each of its features in low relief and all of them impassive except for the eyes, black as the clothes he wore and mourning with the sumless sorrows of his race. Very homely, yes, but that he was also very good, as asserted by the *señora,* was far from clear to the *gachupines,* the booted and spurred who owned half of Mexico; nor was it clear to the Church and the *clericos,* owners of the other half; and least of all was it clear to the gringos and the high-and-mighty French. What they saw in Benito was no mere five-foot *indio* dressed in black: they saw Mexico, somehow out from underfoot and bidding fair to tread on them.

An unhandsome man, with the flat façade of a newborn child, he was more than seemly in his ways, being modest and soft-spoken, a good listener, and deferential to *magnífico* and *peón* alike—and, further, he was abstemious save in the fathering of a family of twelve upon his wife, but that simply attested to a benedictine life. The private person, then, was stainless. As a public official, though, he lacked the cardinal virtue of being corrupt. In a time when a man's price was posted on his door, Benito's honor was absolute, which, for the *hidalgo,* the *caballero,* and the rich, made dark the day when he became *el presidente.* To the *Inglese,* who held Mexican bonds, and to the moneylending and dunning French, their bloodsucking seemed to end when he suspended the payment of foreign debt—aie, and the ticks were not yet full! To compel resumption, Napoleon III sent over an army of occupation thirty thousand strong and, for good measure, an emperor to rule the country properly—a Hapsburg fop named Maximilian, a now-and-then student of botany.

Not unexpectedly, he was well received by the swells, and so too by some few Indians, to whom he appeared to be the blond and bearded god foretold by Quetzalcoatl. In truth, he was not an evil man. On the contrary, he was a gentle one and harmless, and being much taken with the beauty and flora of the land, he found its people likewise agree-

48

able, enchanting, even, with their natural dignity and the music of their speech. Moved by their history of agony, he resolved to assuage them with a reign most benevolent: *We Mexicans*, he was often heard to say, and he quite believed he was one of them. He'd made scant study of their language, though, and he failed to grasp their comment as he passed among them sporting a sombrero and all ajingle in his studded charro pants. A fool, that Maximiliano, but, *señoras y señores*, fools entertain.

There was a certain difficulty, however: no one of the Mexican many had requested his presence: their *casa* was not his *casa*. As a self-invited guest, he was a trespasser—worse, with thirty thousand troops clearing his way he was an invader, and as such he was greeted by all but the bon tons he regaled with banquets, balls, receptions, and a cataract of wine. His vanguard overran much of Mexico almost as it pleased, and the tricolor flew in the city of Mexico, and in Puebla too, and in Tampico and Monterrey. But thirty times thirty thousand would not have made the gains secure. The French held only what they stood on, and they died in numbers whenever they tried for more.

If Maximilian wasn't aware of being in the wrong place, others were, among them Napoleon, who ordered his army to withdraw and return to France. The botanical student was urged to pursue his studies elsewhere, to go while the going was good, but he must've been bemused, must've fancied that he really was an emperor, and he dreamt not of quitting his dream-dominion but of extending it—to Panama, perhaps, and, wherefore not, to Patagonia!

Ah, but his empire did not expand. Rather did it contract, dwindling in the end to a small domain in the hills of Querétaro, where, amid a nondescript retinue, he was surrounded by the *Juaristas* and forced to surrender—himself, his benighted retainers, and the last square yard of his shrunken realm. Tried by court-martial, he was found guilty and sentenced to be shot.

No sooner was judgment pronounced than worldwide appeals were made for mercy. The royal houses of Europe applied to Juarez for a punishment less severe, the nonesuch Victor Hugo sought the same, and so too that *uomo del popolo*, Garibaldi. To *el presidente* at San Luis Potosí came petitions, and letters arrived by the cart-load; and prayers were offered up by the clergy, and stories were told of anguished women casting themselves at Benito's feet.

Was the Zapotec swayed by the pleas, was a milder fate weighed for the false white god from overseas? Did they reach his heart, those supplications, or did they rebound, as from a wall, and fall to the ground unheard?

Once, before his fool's errand to a fool's paradise, Maximilian's passion for plants and flowers had taken him to a real paradise, the rain forests of Brazil. Better by far had he stayed there. He'd've had a good life, a life of color and quiet and perfume; he'd've lived out his days amid the laurels and euphorbias, the mimosas, eugenias, and jacarandas, yes, and the cashews and the mangoes and the ilex trees, all these afloat in flowers plied by flowers of the air—the rarest of butterflies. But he did not stay there: he came instead to Mexico, and when he stepped ashore, he was only four years away from the grave.

In San Luis Potosí, barely a hundred miles from Maximilian's cell in Querétaro, Benito sat in a cell of his own—a suit of black broadcloth, a starched shirt, and a hard collar that constricted his throat and reddened the more an already ruddy face. He gave no thought to Querétaro or to the fatuous dandy in his frogged uniform with its fringed epaulettes, flashing a sash of gold and an Order of the Golden Fleece. The town, the man, the regalia did not exist, for the Indian wasn't thinking; he was enduring all that his race had endured since the coming of the people from Heaven out of the east, but not with love, as foretold, save for the love of killing and gold.

The Indian may never have read, may never even have heard, of the *Brevissima Relación* of Las Casas, but he had no need of the account given by the good friar, for whatever it contained had come to him by inheritance, and he knew it in his being. Off there in San Luis Potosí he might've been sitting in a chair and staring at a wall, or he might've been at a window that gave on a garden, or he might've been out-of-doors and walking in the glare of a sunstruck street. But in truth he was in none of those places and doing none of those things: he was suffering the bloodstained past as though the blood had not yet dried . . .

—With great joy did we greet them as the gods we had been promised, and having strewn their way with flowers, we brought them feathered gifts and things fine-wrought of silver, and then we came with food and served it.

—They requited our kindly reception with acts of savagery such as we savages never dreamed of.

—They had arms and armor and terrible four-legged beasts, and they used them to subdue us, and then for amusement, they set their dogs upon us and pleasured as they tore us to pieces.

50

—They flogged us and beggared us, and having devoured our harvests, our very substance, they might have devoured us as well, for we'd all be dead within the year.

—They enslaved our women and fed them so poorly that their milk dried up, and their sucking children died.

—They forced us to carry them in their hammocks, a burden so heavy, what with their gear, that we broke down under it, whereupon we were broken still further—meaning beaten to death.

—They raped our women and made us watch.

—They tied us to stakes and lit fires at our feet, demanding gold, gold, and when we had no more of it, they let the fires burn until the marrow boiled from our bones.

—To feed their dogs they cut off the arms of children, and when the dogs had eaten these, they fed them the children.

—They commanded a certain boy to go with them, and when he refused, they cut off his ears, and when he refused them again, they cut off his nose, and then, still refusing, he was killed.

— One of their heavenly delights was tearing a child from its mother and dashing its head against a rock.

—They made wagers with each other as to who, with a single stroke of the sword, could cut off a head or split a body in two.

—They killed us as they willed.

—We were less to them than shit in the public square.

All these severities, and all the agony and despair attending them, had devolved on Benito, as though he were the one on whom they'd been inflicted through the centuries: it was he who'd been enslaved and overburdened, he who'd been mutilated, his the arms flung to the dogs, his the body cleft in twain for the gain of a copper coin.

To the very last, appeals were made for the life of Maximilian. From near and far they came; by word of mouth and pack-train, testimonies, memorials, round-robins, and prayer clogged the mile-high air; and women still fell at the Indian's feet. They rose, though, with melted marrow on their garments, and on the Hill of Bells in Querétaro, the Emperor of Nada was shot.

The Mighty Fallen

He offered to bet that he could fall it with an ax in thirty days or better—a month's pay, he said, for a month's work—and he was covered. The stake didn't come to much, a hundred dollars maybe, give or take, nor did the parties in their persons make the little seem a lot: to tell the truth, nobody ever rightly knew their names. What sweetened the pot was simply the size of the tree.

It grew near Dinkey Creek, a tributary of the North Fork of the Kings, and it'd been growing there since the Year One, meaning the one in 1 A.D. At the rise of Christ, therefore, it had thirty-three plies, and it comprised seventy-nine for Pompeii. Fire scarred it when Roland died, betrayed on the Pampeluna road, and drought and flood tried it, and heat and freeze; and it stood off moth, disease, sapsucker, and the pest that fed on seed; and it lived through lightning, fork, sheet, chain, and ball, and through wind and rain and all the crescent hazards of age. So tall was it, some swore, that it touched the face of the moon, and to band the base, it took a ring-around of twenty men. *The Old Gentleman*, the stick was called, a good deal of wood to bring down in thirty days.

Three feet thick, the bark was, but like a sponge, and the blade bit it free in henna chunks, and then the cambium layer went, showing the alburnum, after which the going got harder. In a week, though, there was a knee-deep rut in the chips about the tree, and in two weeks, the bole appeared to rare up from a pit of old-rose smithereens: the man himself was out of sight. All day and part of the night, flakes of history flew, and time ran backward as the evergreen's time ran out. Oolong steeped in Boston Bay, and the Maid became a saint on a spit. King John signed a screed in a Surrey meadow, a Crusade began and failed, and heartwood grown when Rome was sacked scaled through later air. The wafer was taken by Constantine, and seven miles from Naples, a spew of cinders, stone, and ash . . .

The tree went down as the fourth week ended, crown, trunk, butt, and all. At the core of the stump, a sliver was left, a spicule as old as the Calvary cross. In a moment, the man would break it off and use it to pick his teeth.

"That's from 'A More Goodly Country,' " she said.
And you said, "Word for word."
"I've always liked the piece, especially the bitter end . . . But for
a new book, why not a new piece?"
"I didn't think I could beat the old one."
"That doesn't sound like you."
"The base uses of man. No matter what I say about them,
Hamlet will always say it better: Imperial Caesar, dead, and
turned to clay, might stop a crack to keep the wind away."
"All the same," she said, "I wish you'd try."

It was a seedling when the sun, as men still thought, spun once
each day round the earth, when Canaan had yet to be seen from Pis-
gah, neither had the Indies been dreamt of, much less found. It was
a half-grown tree when Jesus walked the Way of Light, and He may
have known of its blue-green hue, caught sight of the gem-like cones it
wore, its studs of precious stones . . .

"Well," she said, "go on."

WILLIAM BONNEY, 1859-80

Billy the Kid

No matter what he did, he always smiled.
    —Sheriff Pat Garrett

In lyric and legend, only the fabulous Billy, the baby-faced innocent, wide-eyed amid the marvels of the world. Eager, soft-spoken, and
serene, he wends his way unsullied through the soiled. It's only when
he's tried beyond endurance, only when his honor is impugned or his
courage questioned, that the youth shows his mettle. And twenty-one
times he'll be forced to show it before he's twenty-one years of age.
That year is his last, for he dies of two dastardly shots in the dark.

Only a single likeness has outlived him, a photographic image far,
far from the sung and storied Billy, artless sightseer among the wonders of life. Rather is he shown to be a slipshod lout, a jimber-jawed
dunce with a slack mouth and a lack of expression, not even the ever-

53

present grin reported by his killer. His clothes are a poor fit, as though he'd climbed by mistake into those of someone else, but the pistol at his left hand and the carbine at his right seem to suit him quite well: he's a rough-and-ready dead-eyed thug.

As his thin story goes, he was born in 1859, or thereabouts, in a New York slum. Of his father, nothing is known that matters, and of his mother little more than this, that she died in New Mexico when Billy was rising sixteen. Soon thereafter, he had his first tangle with the law. Accused of stealing some clothing from a Chinaman (the outfit he posed in?), he flew the coop to Arizona, where one E. P. Cahill crossed his path and wound up on the floor with a socket instead of an eye— and now Billy was on the road to killing twenty more. Did he smile all the time, as Sheriff Garrett said? Was he still smiling when he himself was dead?

Scarcely was he cold when fancy began to embroider fact—and Henry McCarty (or Henry Antrim, or William Bonney, or whatever handle Billy chose to go by) entered the realm of myth, a very Siegfried of the newcome age. It made no neverminds that the dragons he slew were vermin—a blacksmith, a cardsharp, a bookkeeper named Bernstein (*he never did like a Jew nohow*), a marshal, a deputy, and numerous small fry, among them a Jimmy Carlisle and a Bob Beckwith and a Buckshot Roberts . . . But why go on? The list is as long as the last liar made it—and besides, no count was ever kept of the no-account, the redskins and the Mexes, those that Billy killed to hone his skill. To the inkslinger, the balladeer, and the teller of tall tales, he wasn't a kid anymore: he was a saga all by hisself.

It was the real kids, the would-be Billies that he appealed to at first. They heard the lays that issued from saloons, they read the printed ten-cent word, and in dreamland they drew their whittled guns; and dreaming still, they killed their man. For some, it was not enough to dream—no blood was spilled in sleep, no fear was inspired, and no respect remained on waking—wherefore steel took the place of wood, the fake gave way to fact. There was blood aplenty now, in ditches and barns and on kitchen floors, all of it shed in sudden encounters, random and impersonal—a quarrel over a whore, a boundary line, a barking dog, a debt denied.

There were wiser Billies, though, and they had longer views. When they killed, it was for more than a pair of tits or an overdue dollar. They killed for power, for the effervescent thrill of command. They killed for Chicago and the title of Number One.

54

The Purest Man of Our Race

El hombre más puro de la raza.
  —Gabriela Mistral

He had a sad face, they say, but if so, it wasn't due to his constant bad health. Rather did it bespeak his sorrow for the *patria*, for Cuba his homeland three centuries under the rule of Spain, a dominion blind to the plight of the people and deaf to their cries of pain.

To be the horseman, he'd write one day, *and not the steed.*

His father, a one-time sergeant in the Spanish army and now a minor official on the island, was all his days ardent in his loyalty to the Crown, and his sympathies, so far as he had any, lay with those that the stars had placed above him—with the riders and not with the ridden. Had his strait views governed, the son's schooling would've ended early, for what need had he for learning in the life he'd have to live? But it was the wife who had the final say, and at the school she chose for the boy, his showing proved to be so exceptional that he moved with ease to a higher stage, the Escuela Superior in Havana. There he soon came to the notice of its master, the poet Rafael Mendive, suspected by many of being a revolutionary. The suspicion was well-founded: he *was* a revolutionary. To the ex-sergeant, that was a sin; to his son, it was the Way.

To be the hand, he'd write one day, *and not the pounded dough.*

He was only twelve at the time, but he was dead ripe for such a one as Mendive. Youthful though he was, already the boy had been a witness to much and given thought to what he'd seen, and it was as if he knew even then where the road would take him. He never sought another.

A rebellious person is worth more than a meek one, he'd write. *A river is worth more than a stagnant lake.*

Mendive must've sensed the advent of a rare one, rarer than a merely bright pupil, rarer than the master, for quickly did the elder find that he was learning from the boy. There must've been wonder in the man's mind, as though he'd come upon a being not altogether of this world, like the luminous creature once seen in a manger, and in fancy he may have dwelt on the coming of a second Son. But whatever else the youth's presence may have conjured, he left no doubt of his purpose on earth: he meant to do what Bolívar had done in Venezuela, in Ecuador, in Colombia and Peru—he aimed to set his country free.

In the poem of independence, he'd write, *a stanza is missing.*

55

To Mendive, and to many, it must've seemed strange that he who'd eaten suffered for the hungry, that he flinched with those who'd felt the lash, that he was in thrall because others were bound. It was more than strange; it was saintly. Saintly, Mendive must've thought as he brought the boy along, saintly, as he watched the fervor grow. In time, though, saintly must've seemed too weak a word to embrace the nature of the boy. Purity, piety, virtue—he possessed them all, for they were human qualities, but those that Mendive began to perceive came from another realm; they were, he found himself thinking, very near to being divine.

From the earliest times, Cuba had been an uneasy possession, a motley of fiefs lorded over by proprietors born in Spain, *peninsulares*, to whom the creoles were of small importance and the blacks and mixed-bloods none at all, and from the beginning, therefore, the island had been unstable, as if its entire seven hundred miles lay along a fault. Over the years, upheavals had occurred, but spontaneous in the main; they'd been mere local commotions, escapes of steam, and speedily had they been suppressed, always with brutality and often with death.

A sincere patriot should sacrifice everything.

Martí was seventeen when he composed a letter of protest against an oppressive act of the government. Tried for treason, he was convicted and sentenced to six years at hard labor in the political prison of San Lázaro, but he'd hardly served a year when the authorities deported him to Spain, a serious blunder. Whatever he might've been when he began to split rock, he was a damn sight more so when he stopped, and straightway, on reaching Madrid, the boy (say, rather, the man, since he was beyond twenty) published a pamphlet in which he condemned political prisons, and in particular the one called Cuba. No longer was he the mere humanitarian, the compassionate writer of letters of protest: he was a revolutionary now, bent on bringing down the order. Worse, his aim was to build a new one, a regime wherein there were neither steeds nor horsemen, wherein no one rode and none was ridden. It was a new world that he had in mind for the New World.

He was no combustible insurgent, though; he was something far more dangerous, a student of insurrection; and it was on the peninsula and among the *peninsulares* that he earned a degree in civil and canon law and another in philosophy, and with these, after travel in Mexico and Central America, he returned to Havana and applied for permission to pursue his profession. It was denied him, whereupon, in both the written and spoken word, he assailed Spain for its wrongful sway over Cuba. For such calculated activity, he was charged with conspiracy and once again deported to Spain. He did not stay there long: the missing stanza was still missing.

Only twenty-seven when he arrived at New York, he was even then acknowledged to be one of the leaders of the movement for Cuban independence. He was its designer, its voice, its embodied spirit, and all through the next fifteen years, most of them in the States, never did he cease to fashion and expound the conditions he regarded as indispensable to triumph. The revolution and his life had become one, and he gave to it all that he possessed—his wife and child, his sources of income, his days and nights, his well-being.

A sincere patriot should sacrifice everything.

Small wonder, then, that as with his mentor Mendive, intimations of his divinity should begin to murmur in the *compañero* mind. *Jesus Martí* was said without speech, and *The Redeemer,* and *The Bright and Morning Star,* and deeply did those who so thought believe. To be in the man's presence, that alone was enough to inspire devotion to him, but to witness his dedication to the Cause, his zeal, his constancy, his passion, was to feel that he was more than mortal, that truly he might be Him who bore the burden of the Cross.

In his thesis, the Cuban revolution was to be unlike any other. It was not to be an uprising of the oppressed against the oppressors, the deprived multitudes against the privileged elite. Neither, he said, was invariably in the right. Instead of a violent overthrow, which would result only in a new domination, he sought equality of all kinds, racial, social, and intellectual, and he took it to be certain that, once Cuba was free of Spain, the spirit of the people would flower and fill the *patria* with its perfume. It was an ideal world that he foresaw, one in which man's better condition had made him a better man, improved his very nature until he'd become as he was in the long-gone beginning, selfless, not-yet fallen, new—and Cuba the beloved was the Garden, not as before but forever.

It is a case of changing a nation's soul, he wrote, *not just its clothes.*

And now, the time to strike having come, he set sail for Oriente Province to lead the waiting *compañeros* to his Land of Dreams. He came ashore, it's said, in a rowboat, and from that hour, he had one more month to live: riding a white horse into battle at Dos Ríos, he was shot dead. *The missing stanza,* he may have thought just before he died.

All the glory in the world fits inside a kernel of corn.

Sixty-five years later, the missing stanza would be supplied by a disciple of the Savior, a man named Fidel.

After the piece had been read to her, Maggie said, "In a way, you and Martí are alike."

"You'd better not say that when a Cuban is around."

"He had faith in people, and so have you."

"That doesn't make us alike," you said. "He was a great man, and alongside him, I'm nothing. You slight him by comparing us."

"That's far from what I mean to do. I'm only saying you have something in common with him. I don't know any more about him than what you've just read, but I know all about you. You have the same wide-eyed look that he must've had—and you ride a white horse too."

"You think I'm a Simple Simon, don't you?"

"I like the Simple Simons. God save me from a man with a cold eye."

"My father used to warn me about that kind," you said. "But that kind rules the world."

Your mind strayed to a 700-mile island in the Caribbean, to the coast of Oriente Province, to an *insurrecto* stepping ashore from a row-boat. Had he been alone, you wondered, or had a companion been at the oars, and had he come in the dark or the daylight, and who'd greeted his arrival, and from whom the white horse? The image was slow to fade—an old young man riding to his death astride a white horse! It was as if he were acting out the end he'd written of: a sincere patriot should sacrifice all.

"The white horse," you said. "He was giving the enemy something to shoot at."

"You do the same," she said. "Your white horse is your writing . . . And don't ever think you're nothing!"

The Atheist

Robert Ingersoll died yesterday. Perhaps he knows
better now.
—*Charleston News and Courier*

In his later years, angina stinted his stunts at the board, but in his
prime, he'd weigh 280 when he sat down to dine and 5 pounds more
when he rose. Untold the raw clams he inhaled for breakfast and the
midnight oysters fried; the timbales he consumed were as the hairs of
the head, and so too the sweetbreads, the fritters, the pies, the cream he
swigged by the glass. Ah, how he loved this pea, this pearl the earth!—
and he laid a red and gold swirl across it, like a royal flush called.

He was at the heart of every crowd—he *drew* the crowd; it was a
crowd because of *him*—and he relished the cigars, the six-figure fees,
the applause, the palace cars, the breeze he could raise with words, the
blood sped by fame and whiskey (there was no *bad* whiskey, he said, but
some was better). All the same, he always knew that the highs and lows
of life were merely elevations on a map. There was no heaven, he declared, and there was no hell, and when you fell, you were simply dead.
There was only this, the world of jugged hare, smothered pigeons, and
Havanas rolled in bond—and a crowd to stave off the cold. Life was a
lifelong good-bye to the things and those you loved.

Some were sure he'd hedge at the end, on his last day, say, and
with his last breath—but if he ever changed his views, he did so after
death . . . *perhaps*, as they put it in the *News*.

Full within of Dead Men's Bones

The *Maine* was sunk by an act of dirty treachery on the
part of the Spaniards.
—Assistant Secretary of the Navy Roosevelt

I was commissioned three years earlier, in 1895, and even by the
standards of the time, I was no thing of beauty, having two black stacks
standing upright amidships, a junkyard of clutter on my decks, and
masts that looked like Maypoles, what with their streamers of stays.

I did have triple-expansion engines, though, and with all my boilers fired, I could steam at seventeen knots.

I was riding at anchor near Key West when Captain Sigsbee was ordered to pay a call on the port of Havana. It was to be a friendly call, but designed, I gathered, to remind the governor general that the world was concerned for the *reconcentrados*, the Cubans dying of hunger and disease in the Spanish camps. Havana lay almost due south of me and only ninety miles away. It was the last voyage I ever made under my own power.

Three weeks after my arrival, while moored to a buoy in the harbor, I blew up and sank in thirty feet of water, taking with me more than two-thirds of my complement of 354 officers and men. In all forty-five states of the Union there was hell to pay at once. The navy ordered a court of inquiry, and the officers to serve on it, named by Admiral Sicard, were Captains Sampson and Chadwick and Lieutenant Commander Potter, and appointed judge advocate was Lieutenant Commander Marix.

At the hearings, which spanned more than a fortnight, testimony was heard from survivors of the wreck, from engineers, a ship architect, navy divers, and witnesses on shore. Questions were asked about the condition of my hull, about the position of the powder magazines in relation to the coal bunkers, about the apparent force of the explosion (was it from the outside in or the inside out?), and were there derelictions on the part of officers or men? All this gas, mind you, while I'm lying in thirty feet of Havana shit!

Aboard the USS *Iowa* at Key West, the court of inquiry held its final session and arrived at a verdict: my destruction had been caused externally by a submerged mine.

The court was wrong: I blew myself up.

Bunker A16 had been filled at Newport News three months before, and it was still full when I reached Havana. By then, it was old coal, old in the sense that it was evolving heat from its own chemical action—and at a certain hour of a certain evening, enough had been generated to pass through a metal bulkhead and touch off a store of six-inch ammunition. The testimony given to the court was so much jibber-jabber, and everybody knew it, no one more surely than I. The fact is, the jingoes wanted a war, and a war is what they got. They also got Puerto Rico and the Philippines, and though they didn't own it, they sucked blood from Cuba for the next sixty years.

60

. . . The available evidence is consistent with an internal
explosion alone. The most likely source was heat from a
fire in the coal bunker adjacent to the 6-inch reserve
magazine. . . .
    —report of Admiral Rickover, 1976

I'd known that for seventy-eight years.

MARCUS ALONZO HANNA, 1837-1904

The President Maker

Don't any of you realize that there's only one life between
this madman and the White House?
    —M. A. Hanna, 1900

The madman he meant was Teddy Roosevelt, and in the hotel
rooms of Philadelphia that summer, there was a spate of talk about
making him the second-term running mate of McKinley. The notion
alone was enough to give Hanna the flit-flats, and he denounced it
roundly, thereby adding his own heat to the seasonal heat, which had
already brought on the hives. Nettle rash, his physician had called it,
but if so, Teddy was the nettle, that crazy-ike Teddy: he'd caused the
itch that Hanna couldn't get at. *Don't any of you realize?* he cried to the
delegates; but though they heard, they failed to heed him: they were
dazzled by the squat roly-poly who'd beaten Spain all by himself. *Don't
any of you realize?*—but Hanna was the only one who did.

Those hot rooms must've stank, what with the whiskey and the
cigar smoke, the dank collars and the sweat-soaked broadcloth, but
nothing—the swelter, the rank smell, the warning given more than
once—nothing swayed the Teddy-lovers, and in the end (*Don't any of
you realize?*) they had their hearts' desire, and Teddy was on his way . . .
But to what? Hanna may have reflected. After all, there *was* a life that
blocked the road to the White House—Mac's—and Mac, put there by
Hanna, was Hanna's man. So much so, some said, that it was Hanna
who'd been nominated and ponderous Mac who ran.

Hanna was weighty too—who was not in those fill-belly days?—
and in the cartoons of the time, his paunch was pinked with dollar signs.
Justly so, for with his holdings in coal, oil, banks, traction, and shipping,
he was no common wire-pulling fixer: he was an Eminence, and he was
pissy-ass rich. He was not, however, a mirror of his kind. He scorned

61

their ways, he had no style, no class, and he made no crass displays; oddest of all, his only potion was mineral water, for the iron or the sodium, it was supposed, or simply because he had no fine feeling for wine. His laugh, they say, was rather like a snort, and he was given to strong language, in no way weakened by the sweets he sucked all the day long.

But whatever he may have lacked in the graces—the courtly bearing, the art of genteel conversation, knowledge of the difference between a Tintoretto and a Steen—he more than atoned for with his views. There alone did he see eye to eye with the swells, for he was sweller. He owned all of Cleveland and half of Ohio, and he was so flush that—great God!—he even gave money away. All the same, he believed, as Wall Street did, in a high protective tariff, the gold standard, and the right of the rich to rule the rank and file—and of course he believed in McKinley.

With the defeat of Bryan four years before, Hanna's creed had been made orthodox. But unspoken of as yet, scarcely so much as dreamt of, was an article of faith that he had to keep private for four years more: he hoped to be his party's choice when McKinley finished his second term—and wherefore not? So often had he been at the White House that he'd come to feel it his home, a resident rather than a guest, and at times, from his seat in the Senate, he'd let his fancy bear him away to the rarer air of the Mansion. Faintly, through the involutions of the vision, he saw himself in McKinley's chair, heard the music of office, felt the elevation, and now and again, when the roll was called, he'd forget that he was the gentleman from Ohio, not the twenty-sixth president, and he'd think in vetoes instead of ayes and nays.

There was a certain substance to the dream, though, the fundamental McKinley, and it was on Mac that Hanna based his chance of achieving the chair. But alas for the muted hope, the beatific dream! Mac never did serve out his second term: at an exhibition in Buffalo, he took two bullets in the body, and they moved him out of the White House and moved the madman in. Dead Hanna's hope now, dashed his dream! Teddy might've been a madman, but he wasn't quite mad enough to condone the epithet, and as if to spite Hanna, he finished the McKinley term so full of foam and faunch that his party thought him worth a term of his own.

Wall Street tried to push Hanna—Dollar Mark Hanna—but he knew better than the bigwigs that the jig was up, and he turned away. Strangely, it didn't matter as much as he'd feared: he was still the gentleman from Ohio, and so he'd be till the day he died. As it befell, that day was none too far away. For some time now, he'd been failing, and he had little left but scorn for such plutes as "Palace-car" George Pullman and "Coal-king" George Baer. Typhoid took him a few weeks before Teddy was sworn in.

Hanna would not have wished to see it. He'd made one president— made two, in fact—but he couldn't make three, and he was better off dead.

ÉCOLES DE PEINTURE

J. A. McN. Whistler

A great painter, but there are many of his works for which
I do not care.
—Thomas Eakins

Which? The midget panels that shrank the seas to pint-size waves, or did he mean the *crêpe de Chine* concealments of the Thames? Were such the kind he had in mind, or was it those with high-world *femmes*, adventitious leaves, butterflies affixed to space, lights dispersed like unstrung beads? Or was he cool because the low world had been left outside the frames, because the stones had been denied . . . ?

Did they ever meet, the silk-lined nob and the grind who ground in his underwear? Did they ever pass in the street, one with his washed-out wife and the other with his redhead mistress Jo? At a salon, say, at a vernissage, did they graze and speak for once, or did they merely stare down from their places on a wall? Or did their ways never cross at all, did one never greet his fellow, were hands never offered, hats never raised?

Works for which I do not care, said the one, but which of his own would the other have frowned on? The rapt contraltos, ungainly, badly gowned—those? Or would he have shied at heavy-minded men, turned his back on scullers and *monsignori,* pale pugs, draining cadavers and gory lancets, fowlers pushing for rail? Would he have found the lackluster wife ill-made, undetaining, with a head too big and breasts too small, mere ounces, really, against the pounds of vivid Jo, and would he have said . . . ?

63

A "Boston Marriage"

> Her personal metaphor, the daisy, is one of the most
> obviously symmetrical of blossoms, and the loss of even a
> single petal spoils the loveliness of the whole.
> —Paula Blanchard*

She saw Sarah's likeness, then, in a weed—a comely thing, but none-theless a weed. In the way it grew, one among many, a self among simi-lars, she found in nature a figure of speech for Sarah's essence, found it everywhere, at roadsides, in meadows and dooryards, on the lawn of a courthouse square, a private thing on public view, a symmetrical thing. Rather like a woman, she must've thought.

Attachments to other women became more powerful as she grew older. There is no sign that she was ever strongly moved by a man.

She betokened the preference early in a series of "crushes," four or five at least, and each, however brief, was an intense and consuming experience—but once it ended she began another with equal passion and equal purity. None of them long endured, none ever ripened into an attachment. She was twenty at the time of her meeting with Annie Fields, a married woman some fifteen years her senior, and soon after the death of Annie's husband, a connection began for which attach-ment would've been a misnomer: it was a "Boston marriage," and it lasted both for the rest of their lives.

She was not, in the strictest sense of the term [a lesbian].

What was she, then? A consolatory caller at the house on Charles Street, a bright particular guest on Annie's afternoons, a confidante dependably discreet? Was she the good companion, droll, willing, and tireless, was she a wise counselor, was she rigid about paying her way and never accepting a treat? Was she the quiet sort and quietly dressed, was she fresh and fragrant always, and did she grasp the unspoken and reply in kind? Was she, in fine, the rare, the indispensable, the ever-bearable friend?

She was not, in the strictest sense . . . but when Annie, widowed, in-vited her companion, her confidante, her aromatic friend to join her, she moved into the Charles Street house, and there she dwelt for half of each of the next forty years. It became her home, and so it remained for as long as she lived. She wasn't the advisor, the decorative guest,

*In her biography of Jewett, 1994.

64

the repository of secrets: she was part of the establishment, she was ensconced, she belonged. *In the strictest sense*, though . . .

No hint has been given of the household arrangements. It isn't known which were the common rooms and which, if any, were reserved, and never will it be known whether they slept sequestered or whether they shared the sheets of the self-same bed. Forty half-years were they under one roof, dressing there, dining, receiving the cream of New England, and then retiring to yearn for what lay beyond a wall, if that's where it was, or merely to reach for the near-at-hand. Only they know; only the twain can say.

They did much traveling, both for pleasure and for health. They were at St. Augustine and Richfield Springs and Raquette Lake, they summered at the beach, and thrice they sailed for stays on foreign strands. Again, no light is shed on their personal dispositions, the placing of one in relation to the other, and it can't be said with certainty whether they put themselves together or chose to be apart—but at home or abroad, could they have denied the urgent heart? Many the times when the two were alone, times when it was raining, snowing, gray outside, when the lamps were dimmed, the blinds drawn, the doors locked, when in the stillness their thoughts could be heard—and then, wordless, might they not have risen and gone hand-in-hand toward the stair?

In the strictest sense, she was not . . .

Had there been nearness only, near they'd've lived their lives and never come nearer, but they were more than occupants of adjacent spaces. Was there not a force at work between them, a centripetence that drew the two closer, and did they not then sometimes meet? In their comings and goings through corridors, doorways, rooms, did they not brush one against the other, an arm grazing an arm, a hand that somehow found a silken swale or round? And were there not occasions when a service was required, the buttoning of a button, the hooking of an eye, and were they not then in actual contact and breathing the same air? And what of their dressing and disrobing—were they performed in privacy, or were their bodies revealed until clothed and clothed until revealed?

In the strictest sense . . .

Did not each of them brush the other's hair, wash it, even, stand swathed in its steaming perfume? Did they not ease each other's pain, massage a brow, a wry neck, a rheumatic shoulder, and did they not forget the ache and let the attractive force take them where it would?

She was not a lesbian . . .

That she was never strongly moved by a man doesn't mean that she was never strongly moved; she was, and she proved it with forty half-years of Annie. She didn't spend them sipping tea with the literati; she didn't traipse the globe simply to say she'd seen the sights; she didn't fret over what to wear, because she didn't much care about being in style; she didn't make small talk, and often she made none at all. But she was a presence wherever she happened to be, in the reception room on Charles, in an Adirondack lodge or the Colosseum, on the deck of a ship. And in each of many places, she was strongly moved by Annie; Annie moved her strongly all her life.

She was not, in the strictest sense of the term, a lesbian.

But what if she *were* so inclined, what if only her own kind drew her—and of that kind only the dear one she'd known and loved from near and nearer through a span of forty years? What if men never entered her mind, save as the half of the world that repelled her—a teeming slum, it might've been, a Bombay? What if she were at home in the dales and swells of Annie, welcome to savor her flavors, inhale her fragrance, and sleep upon her breast?

Nothing would change, nothing at all. She'd still be a daisy, symmetrical and lovely. Not one of her petals would she lose, not a single one.

66

Scenes of the National Life, 3

They Promised You Liberty

> Where is the liberty?
> —Bartolomeo Vanzetti

It wasn't his question that got him two thousand volts in the chair. We fried him for his answer: there's no liberty for the poor man, he said; the poor man is a slave. He didn't mean the Dixie kind, where they paid for your life with a sack of beans, a dirt-floor shack, and Sundays off. He meant our kind, where we sweat you for a wage, and a wage is all you get—no food, no roof, no jeans, no nothing but what you scrimp to save, which usually amounts to carfare to the grave. Liberty's for the rich, he said.

For stiffs like you, it's a word on a coin, a bill, a bell in Philadelphia. You're free, he said, but only to eat the smell while we eat the meat; you're free to walk and watch us ride, free to fight the wars we cause, free to obey the laws we pass to keep you off our grass. You're free to drudge your years away for such pistareens as ball games, beer, and shadows on a screen, and if you balk at the speed-up, the pay cut, the rule against pissing on company time, you're free to strike and piss on your own—and there'll be lots of it, because we'll never take you back.

We own the earth. All you own is you, and you're free to do with yourself as you please, which is to say you can live on your knees or die

67

in a ditch. Free? You're as free as a corncob in an outhouse. Only the rich are free, and that's what the wop was telling you when we choked him off.

A Pale Yellow Trifle

Inching through the tailrace of the mill, the thing might've been an Indian bead, a snail shell, a flake of mica brought by the current from Slab Creek, say, or Tells, or Whaler. Flushed from between two pages of slate or some vein of quartz and buffed by sand and gravel, it'd been borne by slow water and spate to the mill wheel and the spillway, and soon now it'd rejoin the main stream, the South Fork of the American.

A man stood on the near bank and gazed at the far, where brown hills grazed and drank—or was it a strew of *robles* that he had in view, or magpies and other-colored jays, or, if none of these, was he mulling over the mill, which he'd built to suit a Switzer who was less than easy to please? What was he thinking of—whether the bypass would work at high water? whether the flume would choke itself or flush itself clean?—when he saw the sun blaze on the bead, the stone, the shell of a snail.

The man reached for the pale yellow trifle, polished for ages by granules of sand and untouched as yet by a hand, and in its last immaculate moment, it shone.

The Unendurable Here

Some, like redmen, wear headbands; and some appear in Reb regalia, aflash with sash and epaulette; and still others shave off their hair or give it dyes of vivid hues. A few affect the corsair garb of illustration, eyepatch, cutlass, and all; but many, alas, many choose the shot in the arm, the intravenous hegira, and, sad to say, flight fails them: they merely flee to another *here*.

The Party of the Master Class

> This government cannot endure permanently, half-slave
> and half-free.
> —Abraham Lincoln

In due time, the Republicans took care of that: they got rid of the half that was free.

The Films of Frank Capra

> fairy tale: a simple narrative told for the amusement of
> children
> —*Webster's International*

That's what they were: tales for children at every stage of childhood, from fitful youth to fretful age. His personae, though, were personifications: they moved and spoke as the mundane might, but people they never were, only vehicles for conveying the illusion that the trials of life had happy outcomes—the *de*lusion, really, for Frank the Magician knew (and who better?) that his Common Man was due for the common end. At what time and what place did the hard heart soften? Where and when did worth prevail? Only in miles of celluloid, Frank, only in the reels of unreality unwinding from your mind.

Black Is White

> It was the proper time for one of the lunatics in a New
> England asylum to cry out that he had it, he could solve
> the slavery question. "Let the niggers be whitewashed."
> —Sandburg's *Lincoln*

But there was dissension even among the lunatics: some wanted to blackwash the whites.

King of the Kindergarten

> I have my own world.
> —Lionel Feininger

Colonora, he called it, and a teeming little round it was, nowhere to be found save inside his head. A place of tall people, he made it, and fiddlers dressed in red played its deep and crooked streets. His yachts were steepled, and his cathedrals raced, and his cardboard towns, it seemed, could be folded and stored away. He drew isosceles clouds, buildings leaned, crowds hurried standing still, and jaded locomotives slept on oval feet. No wars were fought in his realm, that is, none but those he staged, controlled disasters, they really were, shows of force that came to naught. Nor were acts of God suffered to happen in that dominion, that kingdom contained in a sandbox, and only one child would die there after a long life of play.

The Topless Towers of Chicago

> What the people are within, the buildings express without.
> —Louis Sullivan

And so he still believed in his stale hotel room while he waited for them to commission another Auditorium, another bank, another Golden Door, but the Maestro was slow to understand: they didn't want him anymore. What they sought for their money-changing was a temple that would escape the notice of Christ, and the kind he designed merely drew it—wherefore, while waiting in that stale hotel room, one day he'd die.

Frank Merriwell

> All stories, if continued . . .
> —Ernest Hemingway

We're half salamander and half sidewinder, we cry, we're half man and half highbinder—we're four-half wholes, fresh and special souls who piss once a year, and that one time champagne. We're rip-stavers and jim-dandies, slick and natural, swift and pure, the crème of the cream, the first-water gem, the Cracker Jack prize, and we're mean, like bees in a bag, and our spigots come in one size only: big.

Don't say that we were always afraid of the dark, afraid from the start, when we prayed on the beach. Don't say that the end appalled us and that we chased the sun west to make it last all day long. Don't say that on the way we dealt out death as though we hoped to run short, leaving none for us when our turn came.

The Last Freedom

Speed . . .

Though we have no place to go, we have to know we're in motion, but not, as in space, from the dial's indicative hand. We have to know it with the scalp and fright-wig hair; we have to sense it in the freeze behind the navel, apprehend it with tightened scrotum and loosened knees. Otherwise, we'd be standing still, and Time, on the move, would kill us *here.*

Speed.

The South Fork Hunting and Fishing Club

Its object is the protection of game and game fish against
the unlawful killing or wounding of the same.
—from the club charter

The club was the private preserve of several score of Pittsburgh
rich, and it embraced some two hundred acres along the shore of a man-
made lake in the Alleghenies. Decades earlier, a canal company had
thrown a rock-and-fill dam across South Fork Creek, impeding its flow
until it backed up into the coves and concaves of the all-surrounding
hills. The body of water thus formed was nearly three miles long, and
it became known as Lake Conemaugh.

Once the property had been acquired by the club, its members
began the construction of their retreats from the furnaces, the smoke,
and the din of the city, the hell from which they drew their wealth.
And wealthy they were, those clubmen—what else, with such names as
Carnegie, Mellon, Frick, and Phipps?—and had they been so inclined,
they could've been just as *kiss-my-ass* as their eastern brother with that
shanty of his in the Smokies (damn the man for a pile that was four
blocks long!). They were not so inclined. They were too wise to show
off for the puddlers in their foundries and the pit-men in their mines.
Why, Christ, the dollar-a-day Hunkies would've asked for a raise!

They were made of money, those plutes from the Golden Triangle,
and with more to be gotten, always more, they knew better than to
fly their plenty for all to see, like the sheets and shirts of the weekly
wash. Nay to that: no pleasure domes for such as they, no parks the size
of fiefs; instead, they'd be content with mere cottages for "the heated
term," their fancy phrase for the summer months. Nothing else was
fancy about the South Fork Club. A prying eye would've found modest
quarters quite in keeping with the claim in the charter—that the pres-
ervation of Nature was the membership's aim.

Gabled and dormered, their cottages were built of frame, and with
their fish-scale shingling bravely painted, they looked as they'd been
designed to look—rather like illustrations in a book of fairy tales—
and they gave no offense to an easily offended world. Ah, but what lay
within, beyond the reach of the curious eye? Was it as humble there
as the outside suggested, or, hidden from view behind closed door and
drawn blind, was luxury enjoyed in private by the few? Who can say?—

72

certainly not the nobodies in Johnstown, eighteen miles away and five hundred feet lower than the level of the dam. Odd, though, that little was made of the steamboats freighted through the streets and hauled to the lake; odd, so little wonder whether life at the club was as simple as it seemed.

Up at Conemaugh, the sky was a blue long forgotten in Pittsburgh. At an elevation of fifteen hundred feet the air was rare, cool, free of fumes, and almost effervescent, almost a sparkling wine—and, like wine, it fed dreams, of girls and boys among the youth and of gain among their elders. For hours less ardent, there was boating and bathing, there were waltzes, archery, and musicales, and there were charades and whist for the rainy days. For all days, though, there was ease, with bells to ring for service, and thus was many a summer spent, thus was many a heated term whiled away in flirtation and schemes for adding still more to much.

The opening of the season of 1889 was still some three weeks ahead when a handful of clubmen put in an appearance, possibly, in conformity with the charter, to give comfort to the animal life of the region. Far more likely, they were there for the quiet, wherein they might pull a cork, smoke a Havana, and play poker for stakes that would've enraged the Bohunks who tended their coke ovens and smelters. But even had they been inspired by the purpose of the club, even had they desired to commune with game fish and game, they'd've been balked by the phenomenal rain that was falling. Never had western Pennsylvania seen a spate to match it, in some places eight inches in twenty-four hours and in some as much as ten.

South Fork Creek wasn't the only stream that flowed into Lake Conemaugh. So did Toppers Run, Yellow Run, Muddy Run, Trout Run, Clapboard Run, Fallen Timber Run, and all the rills that ran into those runs, and added to these were the freshets now pouring from every fold in the ring-around hills. Whatever their intention, the clubmen, those friends of fish and game, were held indoors by the weather—and indoors would they not have pulled more corks, burned more tobacco, and drawn to more inside straights?

None of them seemed concerned about the ever-rising level of the lake, assuming of course that they knew it was rising, and none was troubled about the condition of the dam. If doubts ever fogged their minds, however, they were dispelled by past reports that had certified the dam as safe, though the reports were now long out-of-date, and, worse, they'd been made by inspectors nowise safe themselves. So unqualified were they that in some engineering whim-wham, they'd called for the removal of the drainage pipes at the base of the dam, making it impossible thereafter to lower the water level and prevent an overflow.

Seated in a circle around a card table, the clubmen may have been unaware of what was in the making out-of-doors. They need only have risen from a chair and gone to a window, but they may have been comfortable where they were, dulled by the bottle, dazzled by pips and court cards, and lulled by the sharps and flats of chips. The rainfall, the risen lake, the riprap dam—all were far away, and farther, even, were the butchers and bakers of Johnstown. What were they to the clubmen, and what were the clubmen to such as they?

The South Fork Dam impounded 78,000,000 tons
of water.
     —American Guide series

The rock-and-earth embankment was 1,000 feet in length, 110 feet high, 90 feet thick at the base, and 25 feet across the crest. In earlier years, the spillway had been screened to prevent the escape of trout, and debris now clogged the mesh, shutting off the escape of water. Lacking an outlet, it kept on rising until it brimmed over the top of the dam. Little by little, it ate away at the fill, and then more and more, and finally the whole middle third of the dam broke out, and a wave weighing 78,000,000 tons rammed into the valley below.

The distance of 18 M. between Johnstown and the lake
was traversed in about 7 minutes.
     —Baedeker's United States

It left almost nothing behind but the valley itself. Tree stumps, crumpled machinery, strange ladders of ties and twisted rail, these remained. All else, every house and barn, every school and church, every wall, bridge, privy, and fence, was smashed to flinders and flushed away, together with livestock luckless enough to be caught by the monumental breaker—horses, cows, goats, dogs, cats, and man. It took only seven minutes (did someone time it?) for 78,000,000 tons of water to scour the valley of the South Fork and dump 18 m. of trash on Johnstown, where it drowned 2,000 (some said more) butchers, bakers, candlestick makers, children clutching dolls—nobodies. It took seven minutes!

Were they still befuddled at the club? Were they still shuffling,

74

dealing, jiggling chips? Were they still in the dark about the dam, still dead to the mud flat where the lake once had been? Careful of fish and game, were they still careless of people? And when at last they learned that their lake had gone (letting loose the trout they'd stocked it with), did they rue the day or merely sigh and say, *How provoking!*

Never a dime did they pay for the damage done by the broken dam; never a cent were they soaked for the loss of life. They *were* put to some inconvenience, though. When the club cancelled the season of '89, they had to change their plans and summer at White Sulphur. *How provoking!*

Once upon a Time in Watercolor

It is a gift to be able to see the beauties of nature.
—Winslow Homer

Already when he was born, the wilderness had begun to go, and by the time he died, it was nearly gone, but what he'd known of it he preserved in tinted wash. He left to others the majesty of mountains and the splendor of exploding suns; what he kept for himself was the forest at close range, dense, deep, and silent, as in the days before the invasion of streets. Seldom do people appear, and when they do, they're shown in motion: they're guiding a canoe, they're casting a fly, they're being blown on, like a stand of grain. Thus they seem to become part of the motion, to be one with the rod, the stream, the leaning grass, the wind. A pass of the brush, and trees grow in its wake, and thickets, and scraps of sky, and deer are made to peer through the leaves. So fine as to be almost invisible, a line curves in a flawless arc against the dark woods and lays a Silver Doctor on a pool.

He had the gift, and he must've rued the day when only his dispersions of pigment would be left to evidence the beauties he'd seen—a log fallen partly submerged, brash on the forest floor, a hooked ouananiche leaping, slashes of shadow on the surface of a pond. How he'd've regretted living into the age of streets!

Mexico, Stepmother of Mexicans

The people have been mocked in their hopes.
  —Zapata

He was born at Anenecuilco in Morelos, and though need took him afar, he never left there in his mind. Always he stayed one of the pueblo, a villager like the rest, and save for the silver buttons on the seams of his pants, he dressed much as they did, part peasant and part *ranchero*. You'd not have guessed him a *revolucionario* unless you got in the way of his eyes—Mother of God, they took you back to the day of the Feathered Snake! They were black holes of Indio grief and rage four centuries deep, and in them was every loss suffered to the Spaniardos and the vultures of the Church who came with the Cross . . .

The *zopilotes!* High above, they do their balancing-act on a mere sigh of wind. Moving no more than the fringes of their wings—their fingertips—they float overhead tied to the earth only by their lines of sight. They can see their prey, living or dying or dead, from better than a mile away. The *zopilotes!*

Looking at his photos (confrontations!), you wonder whether ever there lived an *hombre* as striking as he. All show him in those tight charro pants, a bolero jacket, and a shoulder-wide sombrero much whiter than his face: in some, he's seen with an X of bandoliers on his chest; in others, he wears a pistol and a cartridge belt, or he brandishes a .30/30 at the skies; and once only does he pose with a saber at his side. But how unwise, they who note the weapons and overlook the eyes! They're neither meek nor resigned—Cristo, no!—nor are they cast at some *hacendado*'s feet, and if any mistook him for mild, it was the mistake of their lives, and the last.

The lament of his people was a soft sound, but it was always in his ear, a constant that he could hear through music, laughter, love, and brandy, through thunder and gunfire, and even during sleep. It was a sound he must've heard before he saw light; he must've known in his blood that, soon with his Indios, he'd be mourning for a land they did not own . . .

Name of God, but they'd owned it all once, all that lay between the two great seas! The Sierras had been theirs, and theirs too the tierras calientes, where the wild orchids grew. The Smoking Mountain had belonged to them,

76

and the one named White Woman, and those that some chose to call Ori-
zaba and the Volcán de Colima. But no matter the designation: they'd all been
part and parcel of the Indio domain. And so had the trees of the forest, and
these as well, the rare myrtle, and the palo blanco, *and the brazilwood that*
they used in the making of dyes. Theirs the myriad fowls of the air, among
them the macaw and quetzal and that dazzle of iridescence that was ever on
the wing—the flower-kisser!—and what of the floral plumage, the blossoms of
every hue with their intoxicant perfumes? All, all were appurtenant to that
land, as were the beasts of the field and the jungle and whatsoever the land
would yield, its grasses and grains, its tamarinds and limes and granadillos,
its plantains, plums, and tomatillos. In God's truth, all these things had been
Indian once, all between the two great seas.

Sad to say, they were the Indians' no longer, nay, nor had they
been since the horse-man creatures came in their Houses of the Water.
These, seeing the magnificence of the gifts that were brought them,
yearned for still more, and most did they long for what to the Indios
was only the shit of the gods—a heavy metal substance that the Spaniardos called *oro.*

Be it remembered that upon his departure for Tlapallan, the land of
legend, their god Quetzalcoatl had promised the Indios that his brethren would one day return to rule them. They would emerge from the
eastern seas, he said, and they would be bearded and white-skinned, as
he was, and their teachings, like his own, would be of hatred for violence and war. These Spaniardos, then, thought the Indios, they must
be the promised brethren of the Plumed Serpent—and they welcomed
them with food, and with a profusion of flowers, and with gifts that
their artisans had wondrously wrought . . .

They brought collars of gold and precious stones, and they brought a sil-
ver wheel weighing forty-eight marcos, *which is to say fifteen pounds, and*
they brought bracelets and shields and leaves, all these too of silver, and they
brought a plate of gold five pounds in weight, and they brought a golden wheel
of three thousand eight hundred ounces, and they brought fine embroidered
cloths and featherwork and things of leather, and they brought . . .*

But all this and more would not have been enough: the Spaniardos
wanted all. Soon, only too soon did they betray that they were not the
brethren of him who had sailed away into the dawn. These might well
have come from the pages of their own Book of Books, wherein they
were shown as horses with breastplates of iron, out of whose mouths

*Bernal Díaz, *Historia de la Conquista.*

77

issued streams of smoke and fire. These Spaniardos and their birds of black feather, they came bringing no instruction in the arts of benevolence and love; they came instead with the Cross and death.

And alas, they'd never left. Indeed, as the years passed, they'd arrived in ever greater numbers, avid for riches all and none scrupling as to the method of acquiring it, be it by trickery, theft, murder, or enslavement. In the beginning, slavery seemed to serve them best. It cost them nothing to drive the Indios into the mines at Peñón Blanco and Guadalcázar, where, six hundred feet down, they toiled in the heat and damp and candlelit darkness for twelve hours a day on a ration of a pint of maize, after which they were required to carry the ore to the surface on their backs, often being sent down again for having brought up too light a load. None, were he ever so strapping, could survive more than four or five years of such labors, and mothers were known to kill their children rather than see them consigned to the mines.

True, that great was the treasure to be found in the depths of the earth, but on being removed, it could not replace itself; it was forever gone from where it had been. But the *surface* of the earth!—there and there alone would wealth grow where wealth had been taken away. It was self-renewing without end, wealth that one might spend or squander and then watch it most marvelously reappear. Against such riches—against sugarcane, say—what did silver count for, what did lead and cinnabar, and, yes, what even gold?

Cane, a member of the grass family, would thrive in a warm, moist climate, and that of much of Mexico suited it well. Accordingly, it was planted on the land of the great *hacendados* wherever it was level enough for irrigation. They grew it in the bottoms and the basins and over the savannas; they grew it in their pastures and out across their range; they grew it on their very lawns and all along the roads to the pueblo walls. And wherefore not? They owned the world between the two blue seas.

Left to the peasants were only the few acres of their *ejidos*, the village commons, where each of them had the use of two or three furrows (furrows!) in which to raise his family's supply of beans and maize—and now even that little was being reached for by the *hacendados*, eager to add to their superabundance. Lacking the yield of his minute share of the earth, the peon and his family would have to quit the region or be buried in it, dead of starvation. Let him protest the seizure and his fate would be equally hard: he'd be forced into the military or be made to feel the weight and cost of the law. What he was doomed to become, therefore, was the slave of old, not now for the *conquistadores*, but for the latter-day lords of the land—and lords indeed they were . . .

Three thousand of the hacendados *owned half of Mexico's five hundred million acres. In Chihuahua, thirteen million were held by the Terrazas clan alone—twenty thousand square miles—a dominion nine times greater than the entire state of Morelos—and though full as ticks, they thirsted for still more —for the peons'* ejidos, *ever shrinking even as their despair ever grew.* Death to that! Zapata *said in that soft voice of his that some likened to a woman's— but woman's or no, it carried far. It was heard without difficulty in his pueblo of Anenecuilco, and it was equally heard in Cuautla eight miles away; it was heard in Jojutla and Yautepec and Cuernavaca, and, still quite distinct, it reached the Distrito Federal and was heard there in the bancos and paseos, in the bon ton salons and on the bridle-paths of Chapultepec Park; and, little diminished, it crossed over into the land of the gringos, where it was plainly heard in the street that was known as The Street. To the magníficos, it meant an end of splendor, but to the peons, it meant the beginning of liberty, and when Zapata, being one of them, said* Vamonos, compañeros! *they went . . .*

He was reserved, some said, self-effacing, even, speaking little when he spoke at all, and it was said too that he had an eye for the *muchachas*, which was no more a vice than his liking for cigars—and when his mild voice was called to mind, you knew nearly all of the manner of the man. The man—him you'd have to find in his photos.

Regarding one in particular, you feel as you always do when you see it—that in its contrast of light and dark is the history of his people in collision with the white. The festering rage of centuries, the age-old inflammation of fury—all of it shows in his eyes. Black brows over-hang their glow of anger, and no more is the shy *hombre* a peon and a breaker of horses. In that broad sombrero and that embroidered charro costume is the one true revolutionary upthrust by Indian agony under the rule of the Spaniardos and their *maldito* priests. Here was no stoop-ing servile pleading for a fraction of the earth; here was the *verdadero rebelde* demanding—and what he demanded was all!

When it was denied, he and his *zapatistas* set out to take it, and though they took much, they could not take enough. They took Jalisco, and they took Guerrero and Puebla and the Federal District, and of course they took Morelos, the state from which they'd started. Díaz the tyrant went, and along with him went his gang, and a new *presi-dente* came, more than one, each of them promising land and delivering dust, and after years of fighting and dying, the rebels had only a tenth of Mexico to show for it. The rest was still in the grasp of the generals and the bankers and the grandees, they whom vassals addressed as Don.

Ill-served and deceived by the politicos, Zapata wrote to Carranza (or someone wrote for him) to remind the president of promises again and again broken. The revolution, he said, was not for the benefit of the old *hacendados*, and much less was it for the benefit of the new, the suckers of blood from the *Estados Unidos del Norte*. Mexico was for the Mexicans, he said, for the multitudes who dwelt in its sixty-four thousand pueblos, for the insulted and injured, for the dispossessed. *The people have been mocked in their hopes*, he said, and therefore, though many were already dead, the revolution would go on until it was won.

He received a reply that lured him into an ambush, and government forces shot him to rags. The charro suit, the white sombrero, the small and fine-made man—shot to raddled rags.

Again you address the photo,* and this time you take note of his left hand, the only one visible in the pose. Its dark skin, its long limber fingers, its grace even at rest—how beautiful it is . . . !

PORFIRIO DÍAZ, 1830-1915

The White Indian

Power tends to corrupt, and absolute power corrupts absolutely.
 —Lord Acton

A *mestizo* with a drench of Mixtec blood, Díaz was born in Oaxaca to parents who kept an inn frequented in the main by mule skinners. The family was always short of money, and never more so than after the father's death of cholera when the son was only three. As soon as he was old enough to pitch in, he odd-jobbed at whatever would yield a centavo or two, and the need was so great that, according to legend, he made his own shoes. Brought up in the Catholic faith, he seemed to be bound for the priesthood, but he had little liking for the seminary life, and it was early evident that he'd end somewhere else. It proved to be the military, and most marvelously did the trade suit his nature: he was made for the sword.

He was barely thirty when the French imposed the overweening Maximilian on Mexico, and by the time the invaders were driven out,

*A print by Tina Modotti, photographer unknown.

80

he'd emerged as a bold, brave, and cunning warrior, and he'd risen—say, rather, soared—to the rank of General of the Army of the East. He was that rarity even among the rare—a commander who'd come from the poor to fight for the kind he came from, a people in cotton pajamas and one-thong sandals.

But ever at work in him, the worm, a creature gorged on his triumphs in the field, and it became clear before long that he coveted far greater glory, the *presidencia*, presently being enjoyed by Juarez—by another Indian! The people, though, *péon* and *campesino*, did not gratify his yearning and voted a further term for the incumbent, his fourth, but the worm was imperious, and crying, *No re-election! No dictatorship!* Diaz rebelled.

What fresh afflictions did not then befall that lovely land of flowers, of iridescent birds and snow on burning mountains! What new miseries for Job!

Squalls and convulsions befell it, sudden shocks and falls from power, loyalties sold in the streets and squares, walls pocked with bullet holes and polka-dotted with brains, and all across that priest-smothered land, the blackrobes schemed to retrieve their share of it—half! half of the land of the musical name—and in Tenancingo, in Mezquital and Zacatecas, in Miquihuana and Michoacan, gunfire was heard in the daylight hours and screaming in the night, and there were rebellions within the rebellion, revolts put down with bribery and betrayals, with amnesties, with flights and pursuits, and invariably with death.

And then Juarez died, of heart failure, it was said (and it was also said of poison), and he was legally succeeded by Lerdo de Tejada, against whom the rebellion continued. Beaten and forced to run for it, Díaz saved his skin disguised as a padre, a groom, a stevedore, a medico in a wig and a make-believe beard, but though chivied and chased and gone to ground, the General of the Army of the East always came out for more (the worm lived!), and in the end, it was Lerdo who ran, all the way to an obscure death in Nuevo gringo York. But long before that day, Díaz had made himself *el presidente*, and his Indian blood had begun to thin.

Turning off his clamor against absolute rule, he became what he'd decried, a dictator, and for more than a third of a century, he was Mexico's master—*el presidente permanente*. It was nothing short of a reign. Re-elected time after time (without fraud, of course, without intimidation, without murder, or worse, a stay in the dungeons of Belen), he held sway over the twenty-odd states of Mexico as if they were his fiefs—and indeed they *were* his fiefs, ruled by him as he willed. Their nominal governors, hand-picked and beholden, were subordinates all, vassals like the vassals beneath them, and the commands they gave were the ones they'd been given. His was the one and only word, and woe to him who contravened it. Of his henchmen, he trusted none, for none was worthy of trust, but their fear of him was greater than their greed, and amid his rogues he was perfectly at ease. And rogues they were— liars, bullies, extortioners, rapists, assassins quick to kill on order from Díaz. If told, being venal and craven, they'd've eaten his shit and said *gracias.*

He knew they were thieves, and he let them steal—and they stole as if promised elevation for stealing the most. Having the unremitting itch, all week they stole from the people, and on Sunday they stole from the plate, they picked the pocket of the Lord. Compared to Díaz, though, they were simply children swiping fruit. He was the very Prince of Thieves, and had he been in Bethany, he'd've made off with the Last Supper. As it was, he took Mexico; it became his, from Yucatan to the Rio Grande. The Mixtec in a silk hat, the white Indian—he owned it all.

The Congress, both the Chamber and the Senate, was hand-picked by Porfirio, and the measures he desired were enacted in a trice—and why would they not be? Why, when its members were also members of his family, when they were one-time comrades-in-arms, when they were hangers-on, spitlickers, the vacant sons of servile governors, when— Cristo!—they were his doctor and his dentist.

As for the judiciary, *his* judiciary, it was elected by a single vote, the one cast by Díaz, and no decision was rendered that failed to reflect his wishes. A *campesino* with the temerity to sue a *hacendado* stood to lose his case, his savings, if any, and sometimes his life: the rich were never wrong. No Mexican could win a lawsuit against a foreigner: foreigners were never wrong. And no legal action, whatever its nature, received more than a five-minute hearing, not even the appeal of an innocent man mistakenly sentenced to death: the appeal was denied. Díaz, stepfather of Mexicans.

Truth, a disease spread by the word, was cured by the infliction of pain and penalty, and especially liable to retribution was the scribe. Dispraise of Porfirio, opinions at variance with his, protests, exposures of wrongdoing—all such met with merciless reprisal. The lash was well laid on, ruinous fines were levied, and a stay in the cells of Belen would follow. For a journalist named Ordonez, these visitations were omitted: he was merely shoved into an oven.

82

Juarez was a Zapotec to the last. Porfirio, fifty-one, married the beautiful Carmen, who was some thirty-three years his junior, and thereupon fell to using cosmetics in order to bleach his skin to the whiteness of hers. The creams and lotions failed him, and he had to be content with being white inside. Two Indians, one of them taking pride in his blood, the other eager to hide it.

Eight times would Díaz falsify elections and make himself president (*No dictatorship!* he once had cried), and he'd hold office until 1911, when the Madero revolution flushed him out of the country. During his long dominion, he couldn't bleach himself, but poor Mexico!—he and his leeches bled it white. For his services to Europeans, he was made a Commander of the Bath (Maltese cross with four lions, rose, thistle, and shamrock, *tria juncto in uno*), and he wore the decoration along with the many—verily a breastplate!—bestowed by grateful *hacendados*, to seventeen of whom his government had sold ninety-six million acres for ten cents an acre.

At Paris in 1915, he went the way of the numberless he'd starved, strangled, robbed, poisoned, and shot to death. In that land of face creams, his skin was still red when he died.

ROBERT TODD LINCOLN, 1843–1926

An Apple That Rolled

Robert Lincoln, a distant relative of Abraham. . . .
— Brand Whitlock

He lived to be six days shy of eighty-three, but he could've lasted twice that long and still fallen short of Abe. He was the wrong sort for a Lincoln, hardly a Lincoln at all: he was five-foot-ten of spit and spite and quite as cold as Mother Todd's middle tit. He'd rolled, that apple, far from the Lincoln tree.

He was nothing at Harvard and nil in the war (an aide-de-camp who showed old ramparts to guests of Grant), and he was nowhere near for the shot at Ford's. He liked money, a Todd rage, and getting some at an early age, thirty thousand from Abe's estate, he ran the five figures up to seven, maybe even eight, before he died and warmed up to room temperature. Between times, he had Mary declared *non compos* for caching her cash in her underwear, and then and there his magic name became unmagic mud. He didn't mind that overmuch, not with such friends as Marshall Field and the Illinois Central. He'd rolled, that little apple.

He had another friend, Pullman the strong man of Utopia, and for him he lawyered so long and well that he wound up heading the board, boss of the company town, the company car-works, the company store, and that God-damn company library of 8,000 volumes. He also slave-drove a corps of nigger porters, and it was a hard thing to see, the way he bled them white for a dollar a day: it was as if the war had been fought to give him the right. That sour little apple, how far he'd rolled before his rolling ended!

WILLA SIBERT CATHER, 1873–1947

Agony in a House of the Lord

A friendship so fervent, the ruling passion of her mind.
—William Godwin

In three early photos, all of them taken in Virginia, a blurred child appears, ill-favored, wild-haired, and staring at some monkeyshine behind the camera. In a fourth, there's definition, and a round face gazes out from under bangs, not at a picture-taker's antic, but at the world beyond the tripod and the lens. She's Willa in small—steady-eyed, grave, and not wholly satisfied with the shape of what she sees. She's still the plain little girl, but she gives promise of being comely enough in time, and the promise might've been kept if, as a young woman, she'd fought off the notion that she'd look better as a man. At college in Nebraska, she wore a fedora and went about in a Norfolk jacket, a high collar, and an ascot—and to carry out the illusion, she called herself William in lieu of Willa, thus embodying the only man who ever knew her.

Her looks weren't improved by the masquerade. She lacked a figure for the garb, and she lacked the proper bearing, each lack costing her a measure of what looks she had, and she gave the impression of having been gotten up for a role she was wrong for. It wasn't long before she went back to wearing clothes less bizarre, but even those served her poorly: her taste, being untutored, ran to balloon sleeves, pelisses of Persian lamb, and hats that fluttered like winged things. Quietly she dropped the nominal William.

Her campus days over, she removed from Lincoln to Pittsburgh, where for a number of years she taught classes at Central High, devoting her spare time to writing poetry and stories. Teaching was a chore she performed for a living, but writing was rapture, and it led to new and exciting relationships, not only with other writers, but also with composers, singers, people of the stage. It was in the dressing room of an actress that she was introduced to Isabelle McClung, a woman close to her in age and soon to be closer in more significant ways. In that dressing room of Lizzie Collier's began the fervent friendship, the ruling passion, and it would last until Isabelle died long later—beyond that, even, until Willa herself died in nine more years, surely with Isabelle uppermost in mind. But death was unforethought-of in that dressing room: before them spread the dazzle of never-ending life.

Isabelle came from a family among the least likely to accept an irregular connection. She was a daughter of Samuel McClung, the judge who'd presided over the trial of Alexander Berkman, the anarchist accused of attempting to assassinate the plutocrat Henry Frick. A plute himself, McClung was gratified when Berkman was found guilty of the crime and even more so by the stiff sentence it was his duty to impose.

The judge had a hard face. The brow, the mouth, the chin and cheeks, these and every other feature seemed made of material more durable than flesh—plaster, possibly, or possibly stone. Its expression, being fixed, couldn't be left in his chambers and hung with his robe; it was brought home to the other realm he thought he ruled over. To daughter Isabelle, he was a father, not a master, and she lived her life on a long tether. She was drawn from his grim world to a kind more benign, one that pleased the senses and the mind: she dwelt among the rich in the family mansion on Murray Hill, but her real home was in Bohemia

What vistas she opened to the dowdy woman from Red Cloud, Nebraska! In matters of dress, she became a mentor, and for the first time Willa appeared in clothes that became her. Doubtless she was also made aware of foods more exquisite than chicken and dumplings and of rarer wines than muscatel. And what shall be said of Isabelle's constellation of painters, pianists, divas, and ballerinas, what of their ease, their talk, their stimulant ways? And what of this, that she was one of them now, a member of their world . . . ?

But it was Isabelle, not her world, Isabelle herself that Willa cared for: alongside Isabelle, all else dwindled. Many must've thought that Willa's desire had bemused her, that in reaching for the unattainable, she was doomed to be disgraced. What could have addled her, cumbersome Willa, that she yearned for well-turned Isabelle? But so far from being refused, scolded for her gall, and dismissed with disdain, she was received with a fervor that equaled her own. The union, merely fancied in a player's dressing room, was due to be realized in a bon ton bedroom.

When Isabelle proposed to the judge that Willa become a part of his household, there must've been a scene unlike any in the annals of Pittsburgh. What! he must've said, an outlandish scrivener, a person of no standing, no style of her own, a nobody with strange speech and a heavy foot—what call had she on him, on his home, on his daughter's room? She'd be an interloper, an outsider somehow inside, and he'd be joked about everywhere between the Allegheny and the Monongahela. The proposal was out of the question, he must've said, and not to be spoken of again. But it was spoken of, more than once and by both with heat—and in the end, Isabelle had her way, and Willa, already admitted to her heart, bedded down in her room as well.

That room was her home for five years, and through windows on the Hill, she was seen coming and going from the house in all seasons and at various times of the day—one of the McClungs, she might've been thought by those who knew no better. The many, though—what did they think of the arrangement, the attachment, the unmentionable affinity? Were they held in appall, did they scorn the two women, cut them dead as being no women at all? Did they warn their own away, did they withdraw from clubs, did they change physicians and couturiers— or did they moon over the doings in a certain upstairs room?

And what *were* the doings in that certain room? What went on there between two women, one of whom once had dressed as a man? What was she *un*dressed? Was she really a man and Isabelle's lover, or was she, as the McClungs may have prayed, simply their daughter's ungainly friend? None can say now, for both are dead, their murmurings stilled, their letters burned or thrown away. All the same and even so, only children were unaware of the curious affair in a room on Murray Hill. Fancy fed all others, and the unnatural pair were seen lying face to face in a naked embrace, undulating slowly and kissing long. And presently, as if in the room, those others imagined hands and mouths straying, moving to places more esoteric, places moist and warm, places that invited exploration of their dark. A few of the fanciful may have played man and woman both and, so far as they were able, done the dreamt-of doings with themselves . . .

In time, the McClungs grew more receptive to Willa's presence, and if never quite a daughter, she stood much higher than a guest. She was still teaching and still writing, but what time she could find was spent with Isabelle. They went everywhere together, to concerts, exhibitions, and the theater; they read in each other's company, they rode and saw the sights and walked in Schenley Park; and now and then they traveled to a distance from the people and the poplars of Murray Hill. One such sojourn was to England and the Continent, just the twain, alone in cabins, compartments, and pensions, alone for days on end, just the two of them alone. Never would Willa forget their stay at Le Lavandou *fine sandy beach, lawn tennis, view of Île Levant;* all her life, she'd summon, along with the smell of drying lavender, the scent of Isabelle's hair.

Willa's writing won her an offer from New York, and she accepted it despite anguish over an end to her life with Isabelle in their private upstairs room. It would be hard to bear the separation, hard to enter other rooms, knowing that her lover was somewhere else, not to be enjoyed at will, not even to be in the air. She knew there'd be visits, but visits ended, leaving intervals of longing that neither had known before. And worse, she thought—the intervals would be filled with new rounds, new diversions, new friends . . . new friends for *her* friend! Unable to face that probability, she asked Isabelle to make a home with her in New York. This time, the judge would have none of it, and when he forbade his daughter to make the move, she obeyed him. For both her and Willa, that battle was a decisive one: in losing it, though neither then knew it, they lost each other.

Those visits that Isabelle made—they must've been all the headier for their rarity. Awaited on occasion for weeks—for months, even—they must've had to restrain themselves when they met, suppress the desire to do, there on a station platform, what they'd been longing to do in a bed. *A friendship so fervent!* In private at last, how ravenous they must've been, how their mouths must've sought to devour, how grasping their hands for the ever-fresh familiar! And yet even as they conjoined, they must've known that nothing they did would recover the days and nights of the room on Murray Hill, when each had been certain of a constant presence, an endless font of delight. They were gone, those days and nights.

Had they remained as once they were, within reach of each other, disaster might not have intervened. But Willa was in the high world now, and with five books in circulation, she was rising even higher, toward a place among the best of her time. Isabelle, though, had only her usual amusements to sustain her—the local stock company, the second-string opera troupe, the upcountry performer. Among the latter, a sometime caller at her home, was Jan Hambourg, a Russian violinist of thirty-four, six years her junior. In the absence of Willa, no one was privy to the workings of her mind, and therefore no one can say why she forsook her way of living, forsook Willa, and became engaged to marry a Russian Jew. It may be that not even she could've said why after so many years in thrall to a woman she felt free to turn to a man. When the news reached Willa, it affected her like a beating, and the beating was so severe that the pain would stay with her all through the thirty years left of her life.

The wedding took place at the Church of the Messiah in midtown New York, and it was attended by Isabelle's family and friends, many of them in from Pittsburgh. Also present was Willa (how could she not have been?), and in making her way from her Bank Street flat to 34th and Park, she must've found the going as dolorous as the Way of the Cross. The church was a correct one and the clergyman in vogue, but she gave no thought to fashion, nor was her mind on the floral profusion around the altar, the ritual responses, the dry-leaf sound of rustled silk. It was on Isabelle in redingote and skirt, supported, it seemed by a buttress of sunlight. Forgetting that she was in a sacred place, she may have thought herself still in the house on the Hill; thought through the clothes that Isabelle wore to the dales and swells she knew so well; thought of areolas and buttoning nipples and thighs about to part; thought of sensational Isabelle, of the taste of her mouth, her palms, her armpits, of the feel and fragrance of her hair.

From that day forth, she thought, all that solace would belong to a foreign-born fiddler. Her Isabelle would bare herself for a Jew, a Jew would tongue her, handle her, invade her—a Jew would use her Isabelle! Unendurable, her imaginings—a Jew where only she had been before! She tried to still the fantasy, but it was undeniable, and she found herself witnessing the trespasses of a Jew on a body that once had belonged to her. And because she knew it was hers no longer, she could only mourn in silence, sorrow unseen, and weep without tears. A friendship so fervent had ended, but while she lived, it would be the ruling passion of her mind.

With the Instinct of My Race

... Commander Peary's sole companion from the realm
of civilization when he stood at the North Pole was a
colored man. ...
— Matthew Henson autobiography

He was Peary's servant on several expeditions—nigger-servant,
some might've said, though the Freedom War was over by the time he
saw light. If he knew his father's name, he suppressed it, and he did
the same with his mother's. For all he wrote of the event, he could've
been born of immaterial air, and airily too he dwelt on his schooling—
six years in all—and then off he went to sea and the sea's distant places.
Japan was mentioned, and what he called the norhtern shore of Africa,
and Manila (with two l's), and of his past he told no more.

> ... It was in 1886 that I first attracted the attention of Commander
> Peary, and with the instinct of my race, I recognized in him qualities
> that made me willing to engage myself in his service. ...

It was a long engagement, a twenty-year stretch of fetching for a
man possessed by a craving for acclaim. *I want fame!* cried Peary, and
he sought it where a meridian intersected 90° of latitude—at the Pole!
There, at that Holy Cross of imaginary lines, lay the glory he yearned
for, and he meant to have it, whatever the cost. He wasn't the kind to
share it, though, and he must've been frost-bit in the brain when he
photographed his five companions at the top of the world. What if he
chose to deny that they were there?

Henson wrote of him with little warmth. A man six feet tall, he
said, with sharpshooter eyes and hair that was turning gray—and that
was nearly all. Of the Eskimos—of Ooqueah and Ootah, of Egingwah
and Seegloo—he had other things to say:

> ... Many and many a time, I have been to all intents an Eskimo, speak-
> ing their language, dressing in the same kind of clothes, living in the
> same kind of dens, eating the same food, enjoying their pleasures and
> sharing their griefs. I love these people. ...

He could do anything, that black man, and anything is just about
what he did. On each of the many expeditions, meat was indispensable,

and he was the one who was sent out to get it—musk-ox, seal, bear—and then drag it back to camp, where he skinned it for its pelt and slivered it for pemmican. In his spare time, he built new sledges and redesigned the old, and in his sleep (when else?), he barbered and tailored and otherwise chored, and when he wasn't drilling the fiddle-fit dogs, he was doctoring the poorly. The dogs! the dogs! He loved them all, they altogether won him, and he wrote that

> ... they never bark. They fight and fight, and once they have decided, the king is king. A growl, and all obey—except the females, and the females have their way. More wolf than dog, they disdain comfort: indeed, when life is made pleasant for them, they get sick and die. ...

Peary did not disdain comfort. Of his quarters on the *Roosevelt*,[*] Henson wrote

> ... The Commander's stateroom is a *state room*. He has a piano in there and a private bath with a bath-tub and every morning he has his plunge if there is enough hot water. ...

but unlike the dogs, the Commander did not sicken and die.

The party wintered on Ellesmere. Wintered, Henson wrote, but it was all and always winter there, and he had no word for it but *terrible*, by which he must've meant to convey a sense of fright—*terrare*—and well might those storms of wind have stunned the mind. They bore off rocks that weighed as much as he did, took them away on some polar dash of their own. The winds made a wall against all other motion; they almost put a stop to time.

> ... There were thirty-nine men, women, and children, for the Eskimo travels heavy. The best-natured people on earth, they seldom quarrel and never hold spite or animosity. Children are never scolded or punished. An Eskimo washes her baby the way a cat washes her kittens. ...

Along with these uncivilized people, the *Roosevelt* brought north 246 dogs, and in an on-board photo, most of them were shown on the half-deck, together with furled sail, spars, and rigging. They were squatting, standing, lying curled, and one, in the foreground, was star-

[*]The schooner-rigged steamshp that carried the polar party to the jump-off point on Ellesmere Island, 82° N.

ing at whatever it is that dogs stare at. The breed had no enemies, Henson wrote, none but the disease *piblokto*, a kind of madness that many would die of on the way to the Pole, and it would be good-bye then to their wide heads and sharp muzzles, to their cocked ears hearkening to what only dogs can hear. How Henson loved them!

> . . . When on the march, with no food for days, skeletons of their former selves, they will drag at the traces of the sledges and by their uncomplaining conduct inspire their human companions to keep on. . . .

From Cape Sheridan on Ellesmere, where the icebound *Roosevelt* rode like a toy on a war-games table, it was ninety-three miles to Cape Columbia on the seventieth meridian, the line that would be taken to the Pole. On a day in February 1909, several parties set out from the ship, each with three Eskimos, four sledges, and twenty-four dogs. Weather clear, Henson wrote, temperature 28° below. It soon grew colder in the night of polar noon.

> . . . The thermometers are all out of commission due to bubbles. A bottle of brandy froze. . . .

Also one of Ootah's toes, which was thawed, Henson recorded, in the usual way—by taking off the Eskimo's *kamik** and putting his foot inside the black man's shirt.

A three-day march and the parties reached Cape Columbia on the southern edge of the Arctic Ocean. The region, called Grant Land, fascinated Henson. He had no poetry in his soul, he said, no way of conveying the splendor that lay all around him, and therefore he was unaware of conveying it with

> . . . gorgeous bleakness. It never seems broad, bright day: the sky has the differing effects of the varying hours of morning and evening. In the mountains and the clefts of the ice, cold blues and grays brown the bare land, and the whiteness of the snow is dazzling. Above, mare's-tail clouds and cumulus. . . .

From there, he wrote, it was 413 miles to the Pole.

> . . . February 26: Clear, no wind, temperature 57° below zero. I have seen it lower, but after 40°, the difference is negligible. . . .

*A boot made of sealskin.

. . . March 1: [Our] party consisted of Commander Peary, MacMillan, Goodsell, Marvin, myself, fourteen Eskimos, and ninety-six dogs. By six A.M., we were at the upstanders of our sledges, awaiting the command *Forward!* and at half past six we were off. . . .

Off, he might've added, in more ways than one: they were off terra firma on the ice roof of a polar ocean, and when they tried to sound its floor, they failed to find it at 1,260 fathoms.

The going was rough. After a few miles of it along a route hacked out with axes, some of the sledges split, whereupon, wrote Henson, the party had to undo the lashings, unload the loads (550 pounds per sledge), drill new holes for the thongs with a burning-cold brace and bit, and then reload the loads (550 pounds per sledge). His breath froze to the fur of his hood.

And then they were on the move again and a long while covering the next seven miles, their way lying over raftered ice, a formation of slabs like a huge deck of half-shuffled cards. Afterward, for days sometimes, they were stopped by leads, lanes of open water in the ice, and when young ice formed that might bear the sledges, they crossed with care, for it rippled beneath them, crossed to still more of those riffled and frozen decks of cards.

. . . March 5: A bright clear morning, 20° below zero, quite comfortable. First view of the sun today for a few minutes at noon. It was a crimson sphere, just balanced on the brink of the world. . . .

They were halted by open water again, the Big Lead that had held up the expedition of 1906, and there they found MacMillan's frostbitten heel to be in bad shape. It kept on freezing, his *kamik* sticking to the loose flesh so that new skin could not form, but still, Henson wrote, the man woke up smiling, with jokes about being "the life of the funeral." They were seven days at that place, lying in the lee of a floeberg while waiting for the lead to close, waiting for three miles of new ice (new skin) to form—and finally it did. Ahead, they saw dense fog, a sure sign of more open water, but the decision was made to cross, though the floes were hardly thick enough to support a dog.

Beyond, they had 40° below of cold, with gale-force winds that discovered every opening in their bodies and speared them through their clothes. Their pemmican was frozen as stiff and hard as tin, and it tore their mouths when they chewed it, but they ate it all the same. They let the dogs look on, Henson said, for they worked better for a future reward than for a reward for future work. It was so cold now that breath froze into beards of ice, and again there was pickax swink as they chopped their way up sixty-foot pressure ridges, and then down they tumbled, the dogs wild to avoid the sliding sledges.

. . . March 25: Steadily falling snow, the sledges sinking to their platforms, the dogs to their bellies. Some have to be carried. . . .

. . . March 26: At noon, Professor Marvin, soon to turn back, takes his final sighting. We are at 86° 38′ N. . . .

. . . March 27: I go to Marvin's igloo to say goodbye till we meet back at the ship. . . .

But they would not meet at the ship or anywhere else: in trying to re-cross the Big Lead, Marvin would drown.

Snow again, Henson wrote, and ice so thin that it broke under the sledge-runners, and a dog fell in. It was a hard rescue, but he was gotten out and given a thorough beating, not as punishment, but to free his coat of icicles, but it was all to no avail, for he had the dread *piblokto*, and an Eskimo put him down. Snow, deep soft snow, sugar-white granules that frosted the cake of the world. Beautiful to look at, Henson wrote, but it would be death to eat it, for it would lower the body's heat.

. . . March 30: Open water all around us, and we're marooned till it closes. Temperature 35° below, but weather calm, and we spend the day mending gear and unsnarling the dog-traces, sealskin lines twisted and frozen to the stiffness of cable. Later in the day, we're able to make headway, but the ice is so thin it undulates under the sledges. . . .

. . . April 1: At 87°47′, the farthest north ever reached by man, Captain Bartlett turns back. There are only six of us now—the Commander, four Eskimos, and myself. . . .

They were now only five marches from the Pole.

The Pole—goal of many for two millennia, and of many another seeking only what might lie beyond sight. The Greeks were such seekers, and the monks of Ireland, and Eric the Red, and it's said of the Norseman Harald that he did reach the polar seas. Always some ship was making for the freeze, a shallop out of Bristol, a galleon laden with Portuguese. The deeps are strewn with the bones of those on their one-way voyage to the north, whalers, traders, men of science, sailors of this king or that queen, bold men all, bold fools. And now, in 1909, Ultima

Thule was very near for a white named Peary—and quite as near for five persons of color, among them his servant for twenty-one years.

And now the six were there!

Henson's chapter called "The Pole!" is only a dozen pages long, a short shrift for that final sprint to the meeting point of meridians, the ultimate unknown of the earth. Odd enough the brevity, but even odder the tone. It loses lift here, the paeans dying down to prose as barren as the ice: *Peary is in a daze*, the black man writes of that final dash, *and onward we force our weary way*. It's as though they were merely trudging home from work at the close of a tiring day. What took place there at 90° of latitude? What diminished the man who loved dogs and Eskimos? What made him emit such flatulent rot as *Our glorious banner was unfurled to the breeze*? It must've been the instinct of his race.

During the return to the *Roosevelt*, Peary pondered much and said little. Even the orders he gave to Henson were spoken in *the most ordinary, matter-of-fact way*.

> . . . Not a word about the North Pole or anything connected with it. Simply, "There is enough wood left. Make a couple of sledges. . . ."

He should've danced his way back to Ellesmere, strutted arm-in-arm with his five companions, babbled nonsense to the dogs. Instead, he was subdued and brooding, and the reason may have lain in something he'd rashly said: *I do not suppose that we can swear we are exactly at the Pole*. The words might be remembered, he may have thought—but he meant to swear all the same.

At Cape Sheridan, there was a long wait for the ice to open and free the *Roosevelt*. It was a period, Henson wrote, when soundings were taken, when the tides were read and forays made for game, but little was written of celebration and less of Peary and his piano and bath— and then the ice broke, and the ship was under way for home. The Commander stayed with it only as far as Nova Scotia. There, dispensing with his piano and bathtub, he took the train to reach home a little faster. *I want fame!* he'd said, and in a day or two, he got it.

On Henson's return aboard the *Roosevelt*, he was tendered a dinner by the blacks of New York, and Peary, promoted to flag rank, was invited to be present. He responded to the committee's invitation by telegram:

I congratulate you and your race upon Matthew Henson. He has added to the moral stature of every intelligent man among you. He deserves every attention you can show him. I regret that it is impossible for me to attend your dinner.

It was the kind of bibble-babble that the dogs might've enjoyed. The blacks dined without him.

When he died full of honors, the admiral was honored still further in death by burial in Arlington. His servant tarried for thirty years and more. He did grunt work at the navy yard, he became a Pullman porter, a janitor, a custom house messenger (messenger-*boy*, that is)—and at last he too went, winding up under a stone at Woodlawn. It took a grateful nation only another thirty-three years to dig him up and put him where he should've been all along—right next to the admiral. Had he been asked, though, the instinct of his race might've made him refuse.

THE ARMORY SHOW, FEBRUARY 17, 1913

Modern Art on Lexington Avenue

What do you see in that nutty stuff?
— New York cab driver

The Navajo rug in my bathroom displays more talent.
— Theodore Roosevelt

Lack of prescience is a normal human condition.
— Milton W. Brown*

The show was held at the armory of the 69th Infantry Regiment, a brick and granite stronghold a block or so from Madison Square, and it ran for a month in the eighteen galleries into which the vast drill-floor had been partitioned. You were rising nine at the time, and never a word of the event reached your ear, or none that you heard, and you were numb to the occurrence from its beginning to its end. Only after another fifteen years would you learn of the storm that had befallen the stone and canvas world.

Throngs had been borne to the embrasured fortress in Panhards

*Author of *The Story of the Armory Show*.

and Renaults, and some, no few, had walked, but all, paying the small admission fee, had gone inside to see the revolution, the nutty stuff on pedestal and wall. Many came out quite as they'd gone in—the same cab driver, the same ex-president—but some there were who knew that they'd beheld the old order going and the new one coming on.

You had your first sight of a Cézanne in 1929 (was it that late?), and of a Van Gogh, a Seurat, and a Gauguin as well,* but not on the instant were you aglow with light, not at once did the sun begin to shine—how could it have pierced the whirling dust of Remington and the marble clouds of Maxfield Parrish? Only time would disclose the metamorphoses of Arles and Estaque, of the Grande-Jatte and a South Pacific isle—not all of these, though, for your visual acuity did not go deep. It failed to sound the mind of the makers, it did not find, as Joyce had put it, the smithy of their souls. In days to come, you'd feel more at ease before the Yellow Christ and the violence of irises and even the Sunday stillness in the park, but never wholly, and not at all facing the slanting facets of Provence.

The dome of the armory was festooned, making a great Maypole for the eighteen divisions below, and with but a glance at the sixteen hundred works of art, the fancy danced for thirty days. Most of them had come for the dance alone, and flowing from room to room, they took with them only what they'd brought along: for all the show's effect, they might've been a crowd at a game, neither the better nor the worse for the score. Others, and no large number, had not come merely to add to the din and drone of speech, laughter, cries of recognition, and the soft-shoe asper of shuffling feet: they were there to stare at views they'd never yet been shown, at strange forms, at hues in rare combination, at the passing forever of the past. And for a handful (like whom?), it was the quest of a novice, sent by his mentor to see what he could see.

Who had taught the teacher? you'd one day wonder. Had lack of prescience been his once condition? Had he (like you) confronted the new unknowing? Had he too wandered unskilled in the dark until someone lit his lamp? Had there been mysteries solved for him by others—a Blue Landscape, a Boy by the Brook, a Study of a Nude in Oceania? Or had he been one of the few who knew, a soothsayer, a diviner of Truth, and coming upon the incomprehensible, had he promptly understood?

All kinds came to those eighteen shares of the armory floor. In furs they came, and in finery, flash, and run-down shoes; the high world came and the low; the fashion came and the hopelessly passé;

*At the Museum of Modern Art, Heckscher Building, 5th Avenue at 57th Street.

the rich came loud and aglitter and suffered the circumjacence of the crowd. There was a month-long hullabaloo under the swag of streamers from the armory roof, a blend of disdain and praise, of query and awe and innocence, of friendly greetings, of merriment and boredom, of meetings being arranged for tea at the Waldorf. All kinds came to the armory show.

Suppose you'd been there. Suppose, instead of going on nine, you'd been older, old enough to be aware of being unaware. Suppose yourself one of the thousands exposed to writhing landscapes and hallucination, suppose precision abandoned before your eyes and draughtsmanship in a novel dimension—suppose all that, and suppose also assaults of color, green skin, blue hair, a war of color on the several walls. Suppose even more . . .

Alfred Stieglitz bought an Arkipenko for $135. A Brancusi bronze brought $540, and a Cézanne went for $6,700. The Marins did not sell, and of the sixteen listings for Matisse, only one found a buyer—for $67.50. Eakins and Homer hadn't been invited to exhibit, and as for Blakelock—who didn't know he was loco?

"I'll never forget a certain performance at Carnegie Hall," you said. "George Antheil was conducting his own Ballet Mécanique, *a composition scored for twelve pianos."*
"Why will you never forget?" she said.
"I was one of the greenhorns. I threw pennies at the stage."
"You ought to put that in your piece about the armory show."
And you said, "I will."

JOHN REED, 1887 1920

A Land to Love

It was a desolate land, without trees. You expected minarets.
    —John Reed

He saw it for the first time from the roof of an adobe on the Texas side of the river. A mile or so away, across sand, scrub, and a russet stream, it began in the town of Ojinaga. By day, vines of smoke climbed the air, and the sun broke on gunmetal, and pigmy figures crawled, men in white cotton, women in black, and dogs, and when the last light bloodied the sky, toy sentries rode in toward the fires.

97

A land to love, he called it, and it drew him as the pickets were drawn to warmth. Its colors stunned him like a disembowelment—the yellow water and the tangerine clouds, the red and lilac mountains, the flame-blue membrane all around and overhead. The heat stunned him too: a fanatical sun seemed more to rear than rise, and from ninety-three million miles off, it so enraged the earth that it shook, as if about to explode.

A land to love, it was, and he went there, and in its squares he found strewn straw, and in its streets women wended with water-jars among the droppings of burro, dog, and man. The stink of piss made a new element, thick in the sun and lank in the shade, and saddles stank of sweat top and bottom, and somewhere a game was seen, one that was played with a ball, and somewhere else a nameless grief was sung, and from under vast sombreros, small lives spat at death.

It was a land to love, but the minarets would be in another part of the world, and he would go there too, and die, and lie at last at their feet.

FRANCISCO (PANCHO) VILLA, 1872–1923

A Gringo: Do You Speak English?

Si. American Smelting y son-of-a-bitch.
—Pancho Villa

His blood ran hot, just this side of steam, and he'd kill sometimes just to cool it off, to suit, as they say, his trigger-finger, and tales are told of prisoners shot in enfilade to save lead, of a woman made to pick her husband's brains from pocks in a wall, and *corridas* are sung of his blown-up trains, of his rapes and ravaging, of the Chinks he hung by the hair, of how he'd fall asleep after love, after eating, after burning an old sweetheart alive, just close his eyes and doze, a child worn out by a game . . . But such things were very long ago, and he's dead himself now of sixteen bullets he stopped in an ambush, four through the head, though he didn't die, the songs will tell you, till he'd said, "What I do wrong, Johnny? What I do wrong . . . ?"

In the land of brown hills and too much sand, the *péones* sing of him still, and you will learn if you listen that it thundered the night he was born, that bright stars, quite suns in size, faltered in their courses, changed their color, dimmed, and so he was called Doroteo, meaning *gift of God*, for clear it was the part God played in his coming here. The

98

other half of him was Indian, and at sixteen (dark number!), he shot his *hacendado* dead for breaking his sister's cherry, after which he fled a world that Castilian gentlemen owned but never made, where piss-poor lives were short and the shit-rich had it sweet.

He fell in with bad company, one song goes, but in those days there was nothing good on the road, and when he met the bandit Parra, he took a dead bandit's name and became a bandit too. He never denied it: there was only one other thing to be in that day and age: a puller of weeds for some *gachupin* landlord. Death to that! he must've said, and he began to please his trigger finger—fingers, for he had two, one on his gun hand and one between his thighs. They sing, the poor, of those digits yet. They fly their little verses, less songs than sighs, soft, un-rhymed, and mourning, and the air seems filled with love and murder.

He was a bandit. To those who'd eaten today and knew they'd eat tomorrow, he was a bandit, and he was a bandit to a thousand generals and a million priests. To jailers and moneylenders, men with many keys, to savers, owners, counters of things, to buyers and sellers, to legatees, to the careful, the overweening, and the clean, to all who said to the hungry *God will provide*—verily, to these he was a bandit. But to the shoeless, the landless, the simples who had no use for pockets—to them he was not a bandit, he was the Giver, the Defender.

He crossed the Rio Grande once, and by the time he crossed back again, we needed seventeen boxes to bury our dead in. We sent twelve thousand soldiers down there to bring him in—alive if possible, a corpse if not—and we were a year trying to flush him from the brown hills and the sand, with the Mexes all the while giving us false leads and laughing in the shade. We never did catch him: it simply wasn't in the cards, it wasn't in those stars he was born under in zags of fire and claps of thunder, and before we came home, we had to call for more boxes, and when we got them, they were a little out of true—that no-good Chihuahua wood! Down that way, they still sing about such things, softly, sadly, and at the end they spit.

In the songs, they tell of a seller of pumpkin seeds (beware of those that buy and sell!), and they say that one day when Doroteo drove past him at the roadside, he rose from his tray and cried, "Viva! Viva Villa!" —and at once, as if *Live!* meant *Die!* the shots came. Sixteen found his body, four of that number his head. "What I do wrong, Johnny . . . ?" he said.

To the poor, he still lives, and at night in many windows, candles are burned to light his way.

The Uncommon Commoner

> At college, he was skilled in the sport of jumping
> backward.
> —local knowledge

By the time he got squared away, the age he was best fitted for had vanished under a hundred thousand miles of railroad track and a billion tons of brick. Long gone the day of the Soil as the mother of all purity and power, and in its place he found the Machine; but his mind dwelt in the century behind him, and he seemed not to know how quaint was his belief in Justice, Self-reliance, and the Dignity of Labor. They were right things, those, but it was the wrong time for right things, and even the Tom Fools he fought for thought him a fat fanatic with a palm-leaf fan and a Panama hat. They accounted him simple for championing the many against the changers of money in The Street: that only got him beat twice by McKinley and once—for God's sake!—by Taft. He'd flounder thereafter, preaching peace amid a people hell-bent for war; and later, campaigning now against Darwin, he'd die in the summer heat of Tennessee. He'd be sent to meet his Maker with small fanfare and scant praise, but he'd deserve better, because however blind to the new way of the world, he was nobler than the kind that licked the spit of the rich.

Viva la Vida

> Only a mountain knows the insides of another mountain.
> —Frida Kahlo

Long live life—that was the title she gave to her final painting, a study of the watermelon, the *sandía*, a fruit much relished in Mexico. She presented it both in the round and sliced, as if she meant it as a symbol for herself when whole and also what was left of her after thirty-two surgical invasions. *Long live life*, she cried toward the close of her short one, marveling, it may have been, that she'd lasted through so many assaults on her body.

At the age of six, she was afflicted with polio, and its spinal-cord inflammation resulted in partial paralysis that kept her confined for almost a year. Her travail, though, was not yet over: God had something more extravagant in store for her than a withered leg, a fate that He chose to withhold for another dozen years. He arranged for it to befall her while she was riding on a bus in Mexico City. As it crossed a public square, it was rammed by a two-car trolley-train and smashed to flinders — and Frida was smashed with it. So grievously was she injured, so very nearly destroyed, that it must've been hard to distinguish her from the wreckage of the bus.

Carried to a hospital, she was thought to have no chance to live. How could she, with a triple fracture of the spinal column, how with a cracked collarbone and smithered ribs, and what of her pelvis, broken in three places, and her leg, broken in three (Her leg! He still wasn't done with her leg!)? And if she survived all that damage, the *pobrecita*, would she not surely die of this — a steel tube, a handrail, that speared her abdomen and came out through her vagina? How could she live, how, after such massive ruination?

All the same, she did live, but of the thirty years that remained to her, never a day did she know that was free of pain. Still, they were her great years, years of love, causes, fame; years of anguish over amours with men, women, and her self-abusive self; years of drugs, brandy, fury, and Tehuana garb to hide her wasted leg; years of pain (never forget the pain!); years of further punishment that God thought were due her — syphilis, gangrene, abortions, and crucificial contraptions to straighten her crooked spine. *She lived dying*, a friend exactly said.

She was twenty-odd when she married Diego, who was twice her age and thrice her weight — *panzón*, she called him, fat-belly, for he scaled at or near three hundred pounds. Along with the bulk came a monumental rut that he gratified whenever he smelled oestrus, which was almost as often as he pissed — in fact, he likened his urge to pissing, and he couldn't fathom why to some it seemed amiss. Frida was one such, and though she herself took many a lover, she agonized over Diego's, thus adding heart's pain to her never-ending other. Compelled to express it, she found language too drab and turned to the vividry of color — and, Mother of God, what a painter she became!

Her career comprised a scant two hundred paintings, most of them small and many of them laid on sheets of metal, but in all, whether her likeness appeared or not, she painted the subject she claimed to know best — Frida. Only the mountain knew what the mountain contained, she'd said, and when she displayed it for the world, even more could be seen than her torment: what she showed as well was the sorrow of Mexico.

Striking rather than beautiful, hers was the quality that in any company held the eye. Her father was a Hungarian Jew, and her mother was descended of a Spanish general, but she favored neither of them. More did she resemble her wet nurse, a big-tittied Indian with dark skin, dark eyes, and a sheen of tar-black hair—in mind and spirit, she was an Indian too. From all her self-portraits, she gazes out from under heavy brows that meet in the middle, and in every pose, she boldly shows a faint mustache. Unwomanly, some might say, but none more womanly would they ever behold, none with her appetite and reception, none with the depth of her underlying grief.

With those brushes of sable fur that she used, she opened herself as if flesh were only a garment, exposing her organs, her ill-repaired spine, and a bloodstream that sometimes branched from her body to nourish other selves—plants that then entered her to feed her in return. Often there were pets roundabout—cats, dogs, parrots, spider monkeys, a speckled fawn—and there were outrageous flowers, disembodied fetuses, grim landscapes, barren as she was barren, broken as she was broken; and there were skulls and skeletons in her dire array; and there were murders, butterflies, doves, and dead children; and there were phallic and vulviform flora, and there were tears, precisely painted tears, and somewhere almost always there was blood, blood in droplets and blood in pools, bloody roots, bloody skirts and beds and often bloody floors—and the fawn, grown into a deer and wearing Frida's head instead of its own, bled from the nine arrows that skewered it on the run. All the things she painted were Mexico, all the blood was hers.

She loved her people, her race, *la raza,* and like them, she lived a lifelong crucifixion.

Viva la vida.

ALICIA ALONSO, 1921–

Dancer in the Dark

Did they ever meet? you wonder. Frida Kahlo, the Mexican painter, and Alicia, the ballerina from Cubanacán—did their roads ever cross, at a performance of something, say, at a showing, a rally, a soirée, and if not, why were two such put in the same world and kept in separate rooms? They had much to impart, that black-haired pair: they'd've carbonated space with it, charged the roundabout air. They were born to come together one day—Frida, mangled in a streetcar crash and bleeding her pain in paint; and Alicia, her retinas torn loose in some *fouetté* and rendered nearly blind, a Cubana dancing to a flashlight in the wings and the brightness in her mind. Surely a time must've come when they stood in each other's presence, and surely they then embraced—sisters in all but blood, how could they not have embraced?

Just as the one had no inkling that she was riding toward disaster, that she was about to be spitted on a steel rod through her vagina, the other was unaware that her sense of sight was failing. She took it to be a mere lapse that had made her collide with her partner, a matter of timing that had brought her too near the decor, and not even when her balance became uncertain and the stage seemed to spin underfoot did she learn that the source of the trouble was her eyes. Not error, not some mild indisposition, not the heat, the tempo of the music, or the blisters on her feet—none of those transient things. Alack the day, it was a detachment of the lining at the back of her eyes. She'd need surgery at once, her doctor said, and then months of absolute inactivity lest she lose what vision was left—a sudden turning of the head, she was warned, the slightest jarring . . . For a dancer, that was doom—to lie still was to dry up and wither away.

In the accident, all my clothes came off, and I lay naked in the wreckage, skewered and bloody. You won't believe this, but from somewhere—Heaven, maybe—a spangle of gold flakes fell on me, and taking me for a dancer, people cried La bailerina! La bailerina! . . . *Don't ask me to explain. I only know what I was told.*

She lay in bed and motionless for many a month, all light excluded by her bandages and the curtained windows. But however still she was made to stay, there were demands of the body that could not be denied: she had to eat and drink and rid herself of residue; she had to be washed and groomed and more intimately tended at certain phases of the moon; and because dancing too was an imperative, she had to dance—which she did with her fingers, miming on the counterpane the roles she'd performed onstage. It was the better part of a year, in fact, before she was allowed to dance, but the world would ever after be dimmer for her, distance would be harder to gauge, and dangers would wait in her way. Always there'd be spots in her line of sight, and due to a constricted visual field, she'd be able to see to her right and left only by

103

turning her head. But she danced, the blinkered Cubana, she danced in daylong gloom!

When they pulled me out of the ruins, I didn't look like an eighteen-year-old girl; I didn't even look human. I was a sackful of crockery, nearly all of it cracked or smashed—my spine, my ribs, my feet, my pelvis. Oh, and I mustn't forget how I lost my cherry—to a steel rod, for God's sake, a steel rod rammed into my abdomen and out between my legs!

She was still at risk, she was told, and she'd always be at risk if she danced: her eyes had merely been repaired, she was reminded, and if the reparation came undone, she'd be blinded for life. No more straining, they told her, no more bends and leaps and pirouettes, no more trying to kick the moon—but what she heard was *No more living.* That being so, why not die in toe-shoes instead of bedroom slippers? After a year of disuse, though, she was an instrument out of tone, and before she could dance, she had to restore it, tune herself, bring her body back to pitch—and the work was agony. She was limber no more, inaction having cost her muscle its tension, and following exertion, long was she in pain that seemed to pulse in time with her heart. There were many who urged her to leave off, to stop her self-torture, but it was as if the punishment were being inflicted by someone else, someone implacable, and she was unable to escape it. Slowly, though, so slowly as to go almost unnoticed, the pain began to lessen and, as her body gained strength, to last less long. She was at the barre daily now, and she could do with her feet what she'd done with her fingers, and sometimes she did a pas de deux with a partner from the corps.

My pain never went away; it was with me night and day till I died. I longed to complain, but to whom—to God? Cristo, it was God who gave me the pain! All I could do was express myself to little pieces of tin and canvas, and two hundred times I told them what it was like inside my skin.

In time, she danced again before a public, but how different a raked stage from a studio floor, how different a spotlight from an all-around brightness, how different life as a sylph or a swan! She danced with skirted apparitions, with partners she could barely see, shapes that loomed out of nowhere, and she had to count beats and steps, maneuver by guess, throw herself into the air at what she hoped would be there to receive her. But she was dancing, she was dancing!

In those paintings of mine, I complained, but only to myself. I'd been put back together more or less, and when I appeared among people again, I looked very much as they did—human. In my head, though, I wasn't the girl of eighteen, not yet deflowered by a handrail. They'd fixed my body after a fashion, but they couldn't fix my mind—and it bled, and the blood ran out over tin and canvas.

The less she could see, the more her art flourished; vespertine, she blossomed in an evening of her own. All her elegance returned, and with it her timing, her balance, her awareness of place, and she was extolled for quickness, for poise on pointe, for high extension and precision—precision in one who saw mainly with her memory! For all these attainments, and for her versatility, she was sought after by choreographers of distinction, and she danced their roles in kind, danced them with the Bolshoi and the Kirov and Monte Carlo's Ballet Russe. She was a prima ballerina now, but she never forsook her people, and year after year she journeyed to Cuba to perform for them. One such tour, made after the advent of Fidel, was one too many, and it queered her in the Land of the Free: thought to be a Communist, she was kept in exile for fifteen years. Everywhere else—in Canada, in Europe and South America, and even in Japan—she was welcomed warmly, but for fifteen years, she was non grata in the States, Mother of Exiles! At length, though, and with bad grace, the ban was lifted, and she was allowed to dance a *Giselle* at the Met. Fifty-four years of age at the time, she took twenty-three curtain calls during a half-hour standing ovation. Able to see only pinpoints of light, she had to be led on and off the stage and guided through a profusion of flowers, a garden that seemed to grow from the boards.

In my mind, I'd never been reassembled; I was something that God had stepped on and ruined. My back would always be broken, my legs twisted, and my maidenhead smeared on a nickel-plated rod. La bailerina, *they'd called me,* la bailerina!

Did they ever meet, the shattered painter and the dancer in the dark . . . ?

THEODORE ROOSEVELT, 1858-1919

Mt. Rushmore

I'm not up front with George and Abe; I appear at the rear, behind Tom's shoulder, and I seem to be forcing my way past him. Actually, it's the other way 'round: I'm trying my best to back out. I have no call to be grouped with those three, and no one knows it better than I, because I'm the one inside my skin. Many were daunted by my gale-force manner, but I gave pause only to those I knew I could bully. I went far and fast with such gifts as I had, and they won me this sixty-foot face of Black Hills granite and a place just back of the great. Being sheltered, you might say, by my more exposed companions, I'll doubtless outlast them, and I'll still be whole when they've flaked and crumbled—but even as rubble, they'll still be of finer stuff than I.

At the start, I was a spindling sort, with sticklike arms and limber legs, and stifled by asthma, I was given small chance to live long enough to walk. I had to fight for breath, I was later told, and when doctors said the city air would be the death of me, I was taken to the mountains and the seaside and even to foreign shores. The asthma never left me; I still had it when I died of something else. I didn't die puny, though.

I made myself strong with Indian clubs and weights. I rode, I ran, I took up the study of nature, and to learn the ways of beast and bird, I clambered trees and precipitous slopes, after which I'd write of the wolf (*canis accidentalis*) and the bald-headed eagle. In addition, I boxed. No one, I resolved, no one would ever again hold me at arm's length and beat the stuffing out of me (Lat. *faeces*).

I'd always been belligerent, and as president, I grew even more so. I called the Morgans and the Fricks *malefactors of great wealth*, a phrase the populace found so congenial that they thought me the latter-day scourge of the money changers. I liked the moniker. I'd pound a palm with my fist, and I'd foam and faunch about the need of the many and the greed of the rich, and I'd even rant about busting their trusts one and all.

I didn't mean a word of it, but what I did bust was the price of stocks, which sent the interest rate to 100%. I was away at the time, off in Louisiana hunting bear (*ursus Americanus*), and I rushed home scared. The rich awed me always; I should've sent the bear. I wouldn't've had to soothe the plutes before returning to Louisiana to shoot something that couldn't shoot back.

After all I've done, what am I but a figure of fun, an asthmatic geezer, a chunk of granite with a sixty-foot face? From down below, I sometimes hear laughter, but it's never at George or Tom or Abe—it's only and always at me.

With the Voice of Many Waters

I have a right to speak: I'm one of the 1,201 who lost their lives when the ship was torpedoed some forty miles eastward of Fastnet Rock. My name would mean nothing to you, not at this late stage of the game, nor would my sex, my age, or my occupation. Think of me as merely one of the number who drowned on a long-gone day in May; I'm the 1, you might say, over and above the round 1,200. Take me to be a member of the crew, if you like, a stoker, a steward, an ordinary seaman; or let your fancy expand to make me a woman, a lady's maid, perhaps, a governess, a masseuse. However you choose, it'll be all the same to me: I'll still be dead in or near a blown-out hull somewhere off the Head of Old Kinsale.

On that crossing, the ship's last, all those aboard were little more than live bait—all, from the deck swabs and the busboys on up to Captain Turner. We were sitting ducks (down here, we know such things), and what we sat on was a cargo of ammunition and high explosive destined for the British army. The ship's manifest had been falsified by Cunard (we know that now). We were supposedly laden with 696 tubs of butter, 329 cases of lard, 205 barrels of oysters, 500 cartons of candy, 325 bales of raw furs, and 4,000 packages of cheese. In fact, though, each of those containers held contraband: furs did not mean furs, and cheese did not mean cheese. We weren't told, and to this day Cunard denies it, that the hold held six million rounds of .303 rifle cartridges and six hundred tons of pyroxyline, a highly unstable type of guncotton. We know these things now; down here in the dark, we know them in our bones.

There have been reports that we were sunk by a second torpedo, but no second was ever fired by the U-20: the first was enough. It struck us just there where the contraband was stowed, and when the seawater soaked the guncotton, it blew the forward part of the ship inside out. In short, we sank ourselves. If butter had been butter and candy candy, we might've made it to port.

My name? My name doesn't matter anymore.

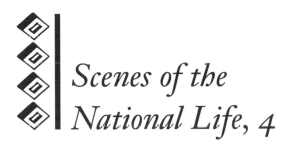

Scenes of the National Life, 4

Mobile Home

It was a shopping cart, a wire basket mounted on castered wheels, and smoothly once had it passed before formations of merchandise, aisles of boxes and cans arrayed in close order, files of cartons standing at attention. Once, in another day, it had gone silently and gleaming as it reviewed the regimental display, but out in the street now, rusted and sprung and guided by a withered woman, it went where it willed, as though on tender feet. Not now was it filled with glinting glassware, with pristine tins and a cardboard dazzle of colors and brands: what it held as it whined along the sidewalk was a pile of old clothing, run-down shoes, and stuffed paper bags—a freight of rubbish making for a station that did not exist.

Maggie said, "Give her something, Johnny."

What else was in the cart? you wondered. What lay deep beneath its heap of rags and tags and trash? Were there odds and ends of brighter times, were there invitations, letters (and from whom?), were there dance favors, menus, a foxed and faded photo of a bride and groom, were there mementos of a trip to the Falls?

"Johnny, give her something."

Was there a dried flower (and from what occasion?), was there a toy (a girl's, was it, or one for a boy?), was there a Book of Prayer . . .

or was nothing under that miscellany but more of the same? Was there really nothing at all?

"Johnny," Maggie said . . .

Gross National Product

Not the goods of glass and steel, and not the woodstuffs nor those of silk and dotted swiss, not the hides, the drink, and the paperwork, not the clocks and crockery, not the units of power nor the hourly yield of the assembly line, not the fees and dividends, not the grains grown and the meat packed and the gains thrown off by money lent, nor the coal nor the oil nor the fragrant weed, not the paint, the dyes, the nails, the wire and the wired words, the sales, the dues, the freight, and not the rent-rolls, the fares and tolls, the revenues—none of those things or groups of things, none of those wares, hard, soft, and in between, no such trades, no such kinds of merchandise, nay, only our six-foot people and their three-foot minds.

Knights-Errant and Errant Knights

All week long the Galahads and Simple Simons appear, six times in black and white and in polychrome on Sunday, the same ill-drawn figures, the same Mutts and Jeffs, the same Happy Hooligans and Captains Easy, and through a series of antic panels, they float balloons of speech for brainless goons: *Zowie! Va-room! This must be the Planet "P" that Professor William H. Pickering predicted! Shaz-am!* There are inorganic objects with superhuman wills; there are dreams and jokes and circumvented scolds; there are schemes that fail and crests that fall, and a cat's eyes cross when it's hit by its daily brick. *Midnight, and into the bedchamber of Morgan Le Fay crawl creatures from the half-world of Whoppo! and Whomp! and Pow! and Blooey!* A hero is trapped by a horde of screaming headhunters brandishing blow-guns and crying *Wogga Zazula!* and *Bogda Maru!*

Ah, for the days of Buster and Tige, for Happy and his tin-can hat!

Remember that I am not without medical knowledge, and if you attempt to drug him Splinch! and Splat! and Bar-oom!

The Flight from Now

They flee it in droves. Through the needle and the nose they flee it, and there are those who, without chemicals, flee it in their minds, each seeking a better time or, better still, no time at all. From this pretty place, this God-thrown ball, this elemental round in space, this kingdom come already here, they fly to the yesterdays of other Edens . . . What is there about this one that they're unable to endure?

What drives them from fact to hallucination? What has made life unlivable? Why has this garden gone to seed? What befell it, what act of nature, what unnatural acts of man? Weren't the bread and the games good enough, weren't the speed and skills of the machine? Were privileges withdrawn, did the fawning of toadies cease, had all things been seen and all joys known, had women palled and the thrill of killing waned . . . ?

But if the salt has lost its savor, shall it be salted with a bitter crystalline alkaloid pumped through a needle or sucked through a nose?

And the Lord Spake

In olden times, He'd speak to anyone He happened to meet, to kings and other sinners, to toilers and spinners and tillers of the soil, and to sellers and buyers in the street. During the Creation, of course, He was forced to talk to Himself, but once His world was whirling, He spoke to Adam and Eve and even to the Serpent. He laid a curse on Cain dire enough to jinx his begats, none of whom ever amounted to much, and He spoke to Noah both before and after the Flood. With Hagar the Egyptian He conversed in the wilderness, and Elijah heard tell of the ravens that would feed him at the brook. To sundry did He speak in those distant days, to Moses from out the burning bush, and to Job as well, and, aye, to Satan . . .

But why in hell would He chew the fat with the Aimee Semples, with Oral and Pat and a slew of Bobs and Billies? With Abraham and Aaron, yes, and with Jeremiah, as when the almond tree was seen, but wherefore would He have chosen to jaw with those in robes, rouged and beaming? Ezekiel and Isaiah knew His voice, and so did Daniel and Amos and Obadiah—but whyfor a blondined soothsayer with a cold-tooth grin?

All along the midway of the world, barkers cry up their sideshows of the Lord, and the air is dense with the din of their nonstop spiel. To and fro they stride, a Bible splayed like the open hand of God, and at times it's proffered as though their hand were His. They're the prophets and apostles of the age, they appear before myriads barbered and aglitter, and they rave to the spellbound of the raptures of the saved and the torment of the damned. Strange, that none of these ranting mongers is seedy or gant. Rather full do they fill their tailored shirts, and never having touched pitch, they're quite undefiled—and those godly beings are ungodly rich!

How intense, these manicured and well-fed gents, how sonorous their sale of salvation! Whence do they come, these monogrammed peddlers, from what high or low level of life? Which of them has thirsted? Which, if ever poor, gave to the poorer? Whose withers were wrung by the anguish of others? What visions did they see or say they saw, what omens did they read in fire, what warning was writ on a wall? Were they told, and by whom, to lay hands on the halt and lead the blind, and this above all—how did they come by their gall?

> The laborer is worthy of his hire.
> —Luke 10:7

That's all they took from the book of *the beloved physician*, and it's all they need to feed their sole desire—gain. Nothing is nearer to the meditation of their hearts, not the Commandments, surely, for they covet and kill and bear false witness, and not the evergreen Sermon on the Plain, nay, nor even the fourteen Stations of the Cross. *The laborer is worthy of his hire*, they say, but the one they have in mind is they, not him who delves all day in the sun.

Beware, babes and sucklings, beware of the preacher, for if the lamb lie down with the leopard, the leopard alone will rise. Beware of the rich that sing the praises of the Lord.

Heavy-Heart Blues

On waves and wire, microphonic grief is sped to bar-rooms, cars, and half-warm beds, and mourning is heard for trust betrayed, for love lost or strayed, for the twain that once was one. The tunes are tinkletankle, and the lyrics loosely rhyme, but a voice manages to mimic sadness for a certain number of measures, at the end of which a line of coke awaits.

They Which Do Hunger and Thirst

Neither for food do they hunger, nor for drink do they thirst. It's Paradise they raven for, and there at the studio gate, as before one of the pearled twelve of Revelation, they stand and wait to be invited in. Day after day they exhibit themselves, the invisible trying to be seen, the forlorn yearning to be found. Hope burns low, but they come early and go away late, they waste and weather, they grow gray at the work of waiting, they age like flowers in a sped-up film, they wilt and daily die. None will ever enter the Eden beyond the gate, but nothing can dissuade them, no rebuff, no slight, no one can douse the glim of hope, the sun that lights their lives.

Latter-Day Jesus

He's bullnecked and huge, and prophets scriven of His speed and power, His stunts of skill, His will to win. Charts are given and diagrams drawn, and times and distances are listed and compared, and numbers measure height and form and final score. No swing, no dash or throw or kick goes unrecorded by the chroniclers of marvel, and their findings, like the Decalogue of old, pass from mouth to mouth with reverential awe. The new Word, the Way of the Latter Day, is expounded in fractions of an inch, in decimal parts of a second, and He is supreme who, with His physical feats, stuns the yardstick and beats the clock.

And yet, what has He done? Has He accounted for His origin, has He abolished Death, has He revealed Truth and made men wise? Alas, nay. He has merely run a mile in nothing flat.

Money Is the Root of All Eval, He Wrote

Henry Ford turned back to the Government every cent of
profit made from war contracts.
— Publicity Department, Ford Motor Company

It was New York that wanted the war, he said, and by New York he
meant Wall Street, and by Wall Street he meant the Jews. Jew York, he
might've put it, and the chances are he did: that was his speed. Granted,
he was good at spewing out those all-alike tin contraptions, but take the
geezer out of his plant, and what little he knew he'd lose. The outside
world would addle him, and he'd see people less as people than as buyers
of his cars — and they were buying fewer these days, due of course to
the war that was due of course to the Jews. That was his speed.

In laying the war at the door of the Jews, he exposed the skin-deep
depth of his mind. Away from his lathes, his punch presses, his moving
lines of flivvers in the making, all he had was a flivver's wit. It never occurred to him that *he* was one of the causes of the war. He didn't seem
to grasp what he'd done to the earth with those black jigamarees he'd let
loose in such swarms: he'd changed it forever, and yet to him it was still
the same. That little dingfod was man's Wheeled Horse, and it gave him
back the freedom he'd lost, allowed him to return to the field and the
wildwood, as in the time before the coming of The Crowd. He didn't
know, he couldn't even sense, that where some went, soon all would go,
and then — presto! — cities would rise where plains had been, and there'd
be pavement and bloodstains on the prairie, and the freedom hard-won
would be lost. With their things! — their things! — he and his kind had
made the war, but he was blind to that, and he laid it to the Jews.

It was a capitalists' war, he said, a war of moneylending Jews, and
those who were dying for them ought to be buying his cars. And he said
this too, *I'll get the boys out of the trenches by Christmas*, and boarding
a chartered ship, he headed for Scandinavia, a nine-day voyage during
which, presumably, he'd be served the foods of his choice — celery, car-
rots, stale bread, and meat, the last taken separately from the rest lest it
putrefy in the bowel. Once in Norway, he'd open his mouth, and — lo! —
out would gush a spate of words, and the words would stop the war.
He'd bring Peace, and even as it was writ, blessed were the peacemakers.

He, the ignatz to whom all history was bunk, he'd be the one to
soothe the ill will of ages, to dim the memory of defeats and humilia-

tions. He was the Stiller of Strife, and he'd quiet fears, he'd make Might mild, and, best of all, he'd bring to light diplomacy's deceits. He, the dizzard, the know-nothing, the tangle-tongued illiterate, he would spiel away slaughter at places he couldn't even spell—along the Somme and the Sambre, the Oise and the Aisne, in the Pripet marshes and the Carpathians, and at the mouth of the Dardanelles. Already there were dead beyond counting, already had a vast of gold been squandered and new hatreds added to old, but this skewgeed greenhorn had the answer to all questions with a question of his own: *Boys, why lose your lives for the Jews?*

Who can say now what took place at sea, what lay in store in the Channel and the Skagerrak, or what befell ashore? *Something* must've putrefied, but all that's known is the way the Man of Peace snuck out of Christiania in the dead of night and lit a shuck for home and Mother, which was what he called his wife. The boys? The boys would have to stay in the trenches yet awhile, some of them, alas, for life.

The Treasury Dept. has no record of any refund from the
Ford Motor Co.
　　—Andrew Mellon, Secretary

ELLA MAY WIGGINS, CA. 1900–1929

The Gastonia Strike

The mill owners here have been mighty good to
their folks.
　　—North Carolina preacher

It wasn't much of a strike. It only took a couple of days before the flush wore off, and the rush of blood became a walk, only two-three days till the millhands tired of Commonist talk and honed for the sound of spindles, the pound of the power looms. A day or two in the open air, and back they tracked, and they didn't seem to care that the strike had been lost—what did it matter? For awhile, they'd made a noise out there in the road, and they'd heard some jaw about a union, but never having seen one in the Smokies, where they came from, they took it to be a Bullshevik word with no ptickler meaning. All they could swear to was that they drew no pay on the picket lines. There was no cash-money in carrying signs, or making a fist, or singing such things as

The boss man sleeps in a big fine bed
And dreams of his silver and gold.
The worker sleeps in an old straw bed
And shivers from the cold.

It was true enough, God knew, but it didn't quit the rent, so back they went for their two bits an hour—the men, that is; the women and children got somewhat less. A day or two or maybe three and there wasn't much left of the strike—a tore-up sign, a picket line pore as a snake, mostly Yankee Jews, and there was your strike, lost in the whirring of the spindles, the stomping of the looms.

Not for Ella May, though. She was still outside the fence, still churning away with a stick and a square of cardboard, still shaking a fist at the windows of the mill, still singing about the boss man and the bossed, as if she hadn't yet heard that the strike was lost. Ella May— who the hell was Ella May? A nobody, you'd have to say, a scrub come down from some farm in the hills, her past left behind with the trash of the seasons, blackened stubble and the dust of leaves, rags, tins, flakes of paper ash. No great shakes was Ella May, a chunked little woman of nine-and-twenty with one fine feature—eyes. Apart from such, she wasn't much to behold; in fact, after nine babies without a breather, she looked a little shrunk and not a little old. There's no telling what her tits must've been with all that sucking—like pockets, maybe, pockets pulled inside out—but her face was plain to see, and there were shrivels in it, as though she'd left her teeth at home. *I'm the mother of nine*, she said, *but four of them died with the whooping cough. All four at once*, she said, and in a few more weeks she was dead herself. For Ella May, only then was the mill strike over—over, yes, but never lost.

She hadn't ever made more than nine dollars a week, she said, and with a family of nine, that came to about a dollar a kid, goddamn it!— one goddamn dollar to do for a kid!—and when those four came down with the cough, she asked the super to let her off nights and put her on days, but he wouldn't switch her, the son of a bitch—*a sorry man*, she called him, *the sorriest man alive*—and four children coughed till they coughed themselves away.

Ella May! When others cast their signs aside, she was an army vast with banners, and where she marched she was many. She never gave up. *We all got to stand for the union*, she said, *so's we can do better for our children, and they won't have lives like we got. Ella May! She was on her way to a meeting when five company gunmen shot her. Fifty people saw it, swore to it with a Bible oath, but a jury found the guilty innocent, let the guilty go.

> If the mill officials get it in for you, they will get rid
> of you.
> —Gastonia minister

Well, they got rid of Ella May, but when they go through the gates of the mill, there are some who say they can still hear her singing, *Let's stand together, workers, and have a union here.*

AUGUSTO CESAR SANDINO, 1895–1934

The Poor Get Screwed, He Said

And he said, because he was given to saying such things, *In order to destroy injustice, it is necessary to attack it;* and he said this too, *Unless we start, we shall never arrive.*

He started, therefore—he started as soon as he was born. In Niquinohomo, that was, a village of corrugated iron and broken plaster that was hard to tell from roadside trash. Even the *campesinos* held their noses as they hurried past a row of shacks in one of which, on a black day for the rich, a few pounds of nay-say slid through a crack between a pair of thighs. He started there and then, the minute he opened his eyes—how could he miss the torn ticking, the pail of piss on the worn floor; how could he fail to see the paper panes where glass should've been, the coffee-sack curtains, the tableware of tin? Had he been able to speak, he'd've said, *Why is God the way He is? Why doesn't He favor the poor?* So he waited till later and said it then, because that was the kind of thing he said.

He was the bastard of an Indian woman who labored as a field hand for his father, the owner of a *finca* in the federal district of Managua. And now ten years go by before the next fact in his history comes to light, and the fact is this: his mother suffered a miscarriage in a prison cell and nearly bled to death. How she got there and whose get she was bearing are not revealed; save for what her son had to say of it, the fact is unadorned. *God and life are pure shit!* he said, because he said that sort of thing.

He didn't learn much from books. He had to quit school at fifteen to earn his bread—or corn, or whatever it was he lived on—but that Indian half of him didn't have to pore over the story of his country and his race. It knew, and it told the other half that, by the grace of God, a people and a place had been plundered, first by the Spaniards and then by the *yanqui* bankers, of all conquistadors the worst. He didn't have to be shown the ruins they made: they were the sagging mansions of the poor; they were the spavined scrags, the barren yards, the outburst sofas, the stove-in chairs; they were the poor themselves, spitting at the dust or staring from a doorway with a *niño* at the tit. He could read the faces; he had no need of books.

The rich had faces too, and what he read in each was this:

It grieves us that you have little
while we have much.
We're saddened by your sadness,
and we ache with your pain.
We deplore your tubercle bacilli,
the banana-bellies of your children,
and your soon-spent and toothless wives.
We're moved by your despair,
by your brief and bestial lives,
by the way you doff your hats to us
and the way you tug your hair.
Aie, Dios, but you touch us,
you clutch at our hearts!
     And yet, *compañeros mios*,
what is man that he should be so bold
as to change the arrangement
of the world?
Must he not do as bidden,
as He above has ordained?
Por cierto,
wherefore the rich must ride
and the poor be ridden.
     No es verdad, Augusto Cesar . . . ?

Not while he breathed. He became the General of Free Men, as his guerrillas were called, and from the Montañas de Colon to the Rio San Juan, he turned the country into fifty thousand square miles of warfare—their kind, fluid and irregular, never standing still and rarely being seen. If caught, and, *mala suerte*, now and then they were, they'd be put against a wall, whereon a few more pits would appear in the plaster, some of them filled with bits of brain.

But where these fell, others rose, and then they too, hitting and running, were hunted by the Auxiliares, by the Guardia Nacional, by the marines, the marines, the *maldito* U.S. Marines! High in the Cordilleras they were sought and low along both coasts, and when found they fought bravely, and sometimes they even won, though they paid for it in blood. *It is better to be killed as a rebel than to live as a slave*, said Augusto Cesar, for he said such things.

In the end, he was taken and killed as a rebel, he who would not live as a slave. Strange, then, that his killers are dead, and he lives yet. *No es verdad, soldados de marinos y* United Fruit?

FIDEL CASTRO RUZ, 1926–

Traitor to His Class

'To read is to walk.
— José Martí

His meaning, assuredly, was a walk in the mind, but with all respect, you will not find there the reason for the *hidalgo* Fidel, no, nor will you find it though you walk in the usual way. Walk this isle from Oriente to Pinar del Río, walk whither and as far as you please, and still you will fail to learn what moved him from his beginnings and sent him to where he went. Walk the high road and the roadless hills, walk the cane fields and the *caminos*, and still there will be none to say, *Oigame, y entiendeme lo que te digo de Fidel.**

From Oriente to Pinar — but you will not have to walk those seven hundred miles before you find the trodden-down and the ill used. They will be in plain sight, and you will see them wherever you look, on your right and your left and straight ahead. Regard the *bohios* they dwell in, habitations so mean, so bare of sustenance that the very cockroaches shun them — do not they explain why the shoeless turn *guerrillero*? Do they not say, as clearly as speech, that a man cannot suffer his woman to sicken and his children to die for a dollar a day in a sugar mill — even so, only for a harvest season that lasts for but a third of the year? Use them, and your eyes will spell out the put-upon, the beggarly, the men

*Listen, and I will tell you of Fidel.

without shoes, and you will comprehend why they rebel and kill. . . . But this Fidel, this Fidel, what will explain the *hidalgo* Fidel?

His father, an *español* rather than a *cubano*, was of the landed gentry, outright owner of three square miles and renter of forty more, wherefore Fidel was born not to the privation of the poor but the privilege of the rich. So vast were the master's holdings that three hundred families were quartered on the *finca* to cut his cane: he was their *patrón*, and they blessed his name when he paid their paltry wage. Being near at hand, their children became Fidel's playmates, he shod and they barefoot, and over the ranch they ranged, he full-fed and they half-famished, and he may not have known who fell by the wayside and who kept pace.

Ah, but he was living the good life, that well-dined and fine-dressed Fidel, and the rest of it promised to be even better. Awaiting him were the best schools and the best girls, and there'd be new games to play, there'd be rare wines, and there'd be pleasures that had no names as yet. He had only to let time pass, and that he did in the company of his dogs, a pack of four over which he shot whatever moved and often what did not. He rode the don's horses, and he swam and fished his streams, and when he wished to see his future, he climbed the don's hills and surveyed the don's domain, twenty-six thousand acres all to be his one coming day.

It would take a bold man to say that he knows why Fidel took the path of rebellion: he was not the kind to wind up in the dock or against a wall. The rich will fight, of a certainty, but they will do so to keep what they have, not to give it away, least of all to the poor. And yet, that is what Fidel did when, with 123 rude fellows, he led an assault on the Moncada Barracks and thus against his class—for the barracks stood for the *hacendados* and the generals and the United Goddamn Fruit. Bold is he who says, *Listen to me, Oigame.* . . . Only God, if there be one, knows the meditations and the wandering ways of the heart. Only He can explain Fidel; only He can tell us why.

On completing a piece of writing, it was your custom to seek out Maggie and read it to her, and you'd just now done so with the one on Fidel. "Well," you said, "what do you think?"

"You know how long you've been doing this?" she said. "Forty years."

"And for forty years, you've listened."

"If I didn't like what I was hearing, I'd've stopped you a long way

back. *This time, though, I want to talk about more than the piece. I want to talk about you too."*

"Me? Why?"

"I don't think you realize that the piece isn't only about Castro; it's just as much about you."

"Where do I fit in?"

"It seems to escape you that you and Castro are alike."

You laughed.

"Don't laugh," she said. "Both of you were privileged, he more than you, of course, but privilege is privilege, and both of you were born to be for the rich. Instead, both of you are for the poor—and when you wonder about Castro, you're actually wondering about yourself."

"I was trying to account for him, and I can't."

"Account for yourself, and you'll have it."

"I can't do that, either."

"I can—and it's why we're still together after fifty years."

EUGENE VICTOR DEBS, 1855-1926

For Gene, in Homage

The master-class has always
      declared the wars;
the subject-class has always
      fought the battles.

That's what he said, being one of the few who'd say that sort of thing, and that's what he meant, being one of the fewer who meant what he said. Lank as a ladder, the man was, all skin and slats and weathered dry, but when he opened his mouth to speak, out came a pour of plain American as pure as a fall of rain. It fell only on those he loved best, the subject class, for who else would've been there to hear the old baldpate spout from a wagon-tail or a flatcar in the railroad yards? The trouble was, that's about all they did—hear him speak and turn away. Most of them reckoned him a crank at best and at worst a layabout with nothing in mind but stirring up strife, a mischief-maker whose joy in life was the discord of others. Subject class! Where was the subjection in giving an honest day's work for a fair day's pay? In all times and all places, that's the way it was, and anything different, anything new, was wrong. Subject class! Master class! The man's only aim was to set one against the other and wait for the fur to fly. That's the sum of what they drew from his proffer of truth—the notion that he was bent on leading them astray. They were his kind, he tried to tell them, they were his kin, but they denied him, they said him nay.

To the last of his days, he hoped to make them see that they were in bondage, but they'd die with the fancy that they were free—and wherefore not, when to them it was plain to see? They toiled from whistle to whistle, true enough, but when the second one sounded, the world was theirs to use as they pleased. They could walk in the park, if they chose; they could sit in the sun or sprawl on the grass; they could watch the river run, watch a tugboat pass upstream. What did they lack? They could idle at a corner or knock back a glass; they could eat, smoke, play catch with the kids, or listen to the news; they could enjoy another walk, another shot, another fiction with a neighbor's wife. They were free, free as the clouds in the sky.

To Gene's way of thinking, they had all the freedom of a catalog in a privy. Free to do what? To lean against a wall? to swill a beer and fault a ballgame? to choose between standing up and lying down? to stare at the eddies in a running stream and day-dream of someone else's wife? Free! If they were free, so were the machines at their place of work—the mill, the foundry, the speed-up line—and so was a mule in a mine. The poor self-deluded stiffs—did they really think they were free to come and go? Didn't they know they were property, affixed to their machines quite as firmly as the machines were affixed to the floor? Only the master class was free, only the owners of All—the earth, the minerals and gases and fluids it contained, and the forests and fruits of the soil, and of course they owned the subject class.

No man more loving ever lived than that gant old innocent with a head like a skull in skin. When he spoke to a mass of upturned faces from a stack of ties or the back of a truck, when he bent toward them, his lean hands extended in an embrace, it was as though he were pleading with a field of flowers to heed his words. They heard his heart in those words; they heard his devotion to their class, of which he was one; they heard their own plight; they were shown their own lives—and while they applauded him and cheered and sometimes drowned him out, while many were even swayed by his passion, in the end they stayed as they were, merely flowers awave in the wind.

While there is a lower class, I am of it, he said; and he said, *I am a Bolshevik from the crown of my head to the soles of my feet;* and he said a good deal more, much of it against the master-class war. That last wasn't lost on Wall Street, and off he went to the penitentiary to serve a ten-year sentence: sixty-some on going in, he'd be seventy-some on coming out, if, indeed, he didn't die in between. Nary a friend did he have among the money-spinners and the merchant princes, the plutes of the world, but he found 2,300 among his fellows in Atlanta. In every cell a rogue, on every tier assassins, counterfeiters, perjurers, deserters, givers and takers of bribes—lowlives all, and all without exception came under the spell of Gene. It was the lowest level of the lower class, and willy-nilly he was of it.

He didn't flourish in confinement, which the master class had expected, but it failed to kill him, which dashed their hopes. Certainly he faded under the deprivations—the solace of family, the censorship of mail, the savorless food, the stale and worn-out air—but he didn't die. He tired easily, he was diminished by the restraint, he gazed often at things that were far away, but Death wasn't one of them, and he didn't die. Indeed, when assigned to work in the prison hospital, he helped many another to live. He must've been a Jesus kind of man.

In the pen, they wouldn't've given the time of day to the Good-Book Jesus, but Gene came without divinity and a crown of light, with straight talk instead of parable—and they took to the man as to the father of them all. During outdoor hours in the yard, they sat at his feet, they listened to his twang and his everyday words, they served him, touched him in passing, revered him because he was only their equal.

He refused to ask for clemency, and he refused a pardon in return for a promise to quit his political activity: *I either go out as I came in,* he said, *or I serve my term to the last day.* He didn't have to. In the White House there dwelt at the time a most disreputable man—a boozer, a poker player, a womanizer, an impious fraud with a blind eye to the knavery rampant right under his nose. In short, he was riffraff, like the roughscuff in the prison yard, and he, like they, had a soft spot for Gene. He signed a pardon, the same to take effect in forty-eight hours, which would make Gene free on Christmas Day. Strange to say, he didn't rejoice. On the contrary, he was saddened by the prospect of leaving his friends—his 2,300 felonious friends, for, as he once had said, *While there is a soul in jail, I am not free.* And being the kind who said only what he meant, he'd still be in jail when outside the walls; he'd still be in a cell or at the core of a crowd in the prison yard; he'd still be sought after, still be touched for luck, still be thought first among equals.

He knew that they'd been wrongdoers and that their wrongs had often been violent, but just as well did he know that there were blackguards in the world who'd never see a cell—the bankers, the proprietors, the public servants who served themselves, the landlords, and the lords of all else. They were not his friends, that kind. Nowhere would they have rallied round him, heeded his persuasions, palmed his sleeve as they wandered away: they were not his friends.

This kind was, though—the hooligans and hotspurs, the forgers, the anarchists, the rumrunners and mutineers—sinners, yes, but no more so (and maybe less) than the bigwigs in their treasuries and their yachts and private cars. Thus, he grieved when the gates began to open for him on the day commemorating the birth of Christ. What rapture, then, when from behind him he heard the voices of 2,300 friends! It was a humming at first, as from a gigantic hive, and ever-growing, it grew until it became a roar. Turning, he saw a mass of faces, for the kindly warden had ordered the cells to be opened and the prisoners to throng the walls and windows so that they might say their good-bye and watch him go, dwindle in the distance, darkening still more their benighted lives. Three times as he went, he paused to reach out to them, as though to clasp one and all and take them along—and then he was gone.

He had five years left to live, and it may be that, as he lay dying, he seemed to hear once again the roar of that convict chorus. If so, he died attended by a multitude of friends.

MICKEY MOUSE, 1928–

What Hath This Rodent Wrought!

The creature was begotten by Walter Elias Disney, a man twenty-eight years of age at the time of its advent—a man to all seeming, that is, for he was man-size, of course, and of manly bearing. But how deceptive the guise of manhood! His mind had remained in the Land of Cockaigne, aswirl with the fable and fantasy of the fairy tale, and never would he leave his nursery mansion. Never would he see beyond the vividness of legend, more real for him than reality, never would he be free of magic wands and soaring castles, of trees that spoke, poisoned spindles, metamorphoses. He'd dwell in enchantment among dwarfs and ogres; he'd be one of the children lured by the Piper into Koppelburg hill; he'd be Old King Cole calling for his fiddlers three; he'd wake a sleeping beauty with a kiss. Somewhere in his lobal serpentine—the Aqueduct of Silvius, was it, or the foramen of Monro?—frogs became princely, and the witchery laid by Evil was ever lifted by Good, and it was just there, in that spellbound realm, that the little mouse came into being, four-fingered, bat-eared, slapshod, and all.

It was the Kingdom of the Kindergarten that his begetter lived in. There only were feet to be found for the slippers of glass; there only did elves delve in forbidding forests; and only there wound the road that led to the City of Delight, red with its rivers of wine and redolent of the pastries with which its streets were paved. All was joy in his toy-store world: wishes were granted there, and dreams came true, and save over the monster and the wicked crone, Death did not prevail. In his cranial domain, want was unknown, and there was no pain, no longing for a heart's desire.

He put that world of his on the screen, where it was seen by children of every age, some of them six and many of them seventy, and one and all they were beguiled by the music of Walt the Piper, and with him they vanished into a hole in a hill, children then and children still.

In Much Wisdom Is Much Grief

The high tide of prosperity will continue.
    —Andrew Mellon

Stock prices have reached a permanently high plateau.
    —Professor I. Fisher, Yale

A severe depression is outside the range of probability.
    —Harvard Economic Society

Stocks are cheap at current prices.
    —Calvin Coolidge

The country is on a sound and prosperous basis.
    —Herbert Hoover

Everybody can and ought to be rich.
    —John Raskob

Bankers, financiers, economists, professors, politicos, and presidents incumbent and ex- —we were dead wrong, every damn one of us, but there's no record of our having lost by making the most monumental blunder in fiscal history. We survived—we always survive—but the small fry lost their all. Few of them flew from high windows, true enough, and fewer the shots that went in one ear and out the other: among the nobodies, sudden death was not the rule. They died slowly, of hope denied, of fear and shame and boundless regret.

They'd come to The Street as to the Horn of Plenty, from which, though all might feast, more could still be had. They went shorn of their savings, their rent money, their carfare, and even the chicken feed in their children's banks; they went in a daze of shattered dreams. The poor bastards—some of us almost felt sorry for them. What gulls they'd been, what Simple Simons! They'd clamored for whatever we had to sell—they'd've bought bridges and ferry-boats, hell, they'd've bought shares in Bedloe's Isle.

Who and what were they, that slew of greenhorns, that swarm of April Fools? Where had they come from, what were their names, and what had they done to put a pittance by? Were they cabbies and fry-cooks; were they busboys and corn-doctors and parish priests; did they dress hair, press pants, and read palms; were they glassblowers, faith healers, ballplayers; were bartenders among them and how many; were there steeplejacks, flunkies, floozies, pimps; were all the -wrights there and the -smiths; were cops, soda jerks and housewives from Washington Heights?

But, shoot, their identities didn't matter; with us, all that counted was that they came to buy—and buy, great God, they did! They slavered for Radio and J. I. Case and Montgomery Ward, for Steel and Westinghouse and White (for Christ's sake!) Sewing Machine, and they couldn't get enough of American Can and Seaboard Air and Otis Elevator—which, along with every other, went up and then came down.

The jaybirds! They snapped up General Motors at 73 only to see it drop to 8; they bought Monkey Ward at 138, and down it slid to 4; and they thought Steel was a steal at 262, and pity 'tis, it sank to 23. The rubes! The boobs! The chuckleheads! We sold them out after bleeding them of all they could beg or borrow or swipe from a blind man's cup. And to whom did we sell their forfeited shares? Who wound up with their Westinghouse and Seaboard Air?

Guess.

The God with the Glass Head

The New York Stock Exchange is often the scene of
gigantic speculative investment, and enormous sums are
won and lost from time to time.
—*Encyclopedia Britannica*

The Exchange, designed by George Post and built in 1903, stands diagonally across from the Sub-Treasury near the corner of Broad and Wall. The Corinthian façade is of white marble, its six fluted columns crowned with acanthus leaves, and in the triangle of the pediment, a group of classic statuary sprawls. The effect is rather like that of a temple, the habitation of a deity—but no true god, were he ever so minor, would've deigned to enter it, and none, however avid for veneration, would've dwelt there.

The marble front is a false one for a false god, and behind it rites most un-Christian are performed from Monday morning through Saturday afternoon. It's the mummery of heathens, and far from seemly are they at their spurious devotions. Their jigging and gesturing, their outcry, their spastic frenzy and disarray, their invocation with smoke—it's simply diablerie for a Presence that responds in logograms and numbers, a stream that flows unstemmed until Saturday at noon.

Passersby rarely heed the tumult inside, if indeed they hear it at all. They take it to be the usual order of the usual day; nor are they aware on such a day of anything uncommon in the street. The hurry of crowds is there, of course, voices mingling with the sounds of traffic and the friction of shuffling feet; the comings and goings at Morgan's are normal; and no signs of concern can be seen on those who stop for a handshake or a shoeshine or to scan a headline while lighting a cigarette. On the ordinary day, there are only the ordinary things, and few so little as dream of the one in the making behind the grooved columns and the frieze of the Exchange.

But a few there are, and now and again, even on an unremarkable day, they feel a chill when others feel only the sun, and no more do they pass below the seven balconies of the Exchange heedless of the much-ado inside. They're alert to the flowing numbers of the only river that runs uphill, and they dread the day, the day of doom, when it begins to run the other way, as they know it will.

The day is Tuesday, the 29th of October.

Birds of ill omen had been seen in the weeks and months before, and storms of fear had swept the temple floor. A great shuddering was felt, as of walls coming down, and columns as well, and the figures beneath the eaves. For the idolaters, it was as if, with their incantations, they'd caused a convulsion of the earth, and they paused in panic until the spasm ended—and when it did, they glorified their ticking god all the more.

In the Exchange, the 29th of October did not come to a close at three in the afternoon; at that hour, the glass-headed god was nearly five hours late with the news of its fall in appalling disaster. Numbers were rippling from it that belonged to the past, for the stream had turned to seek its proper level, which, as the hours went by, seemed to be in the realm where minus quantities dwelt.

Within, there was delirium.

Three thousand image worshipers wandered as if stricken by the God of all gods, waded deep in a daze through a brash of castaway paper, discarded clothes, and smoldering cigarettes, all the while bawling to those who were bawling back—and neither heard the other, nor even heard themselves. The golden times were over, the balmy weather, the palmy days—all days were over, for the end of the world had come to The Street.

Without, there was despair.

The day was a fair one, though a coolness in the air could be felt in the shade, and a gust now and then swirled skirts and spun up gyres of dust. Many, from windows looking down on the Exchange, watched the throngs passing to and fro below them, and some may have noted that they went without haste, as if there were no place to go where they'd be free of their folly, their greed, their irreparable ruin; as if there were no haven for them, no hope of heaven. Of those watching from above, though, a few found a way out of their sinful skins: they flew from the windows and broke themselves open on the street.

The god with the glass head? It still ticks away, it still spits out numbers and symbols, but now it quits at three-thirty on Friday afternoon.

The King of Louisiana

There are a lot of dumb people in the world.
—Huey Long

He was no worse than any other politico, but he sure to God was no better. He ran those parishes of his like a set of toy trains, and when he sent himself to the Senate, he meant to run the country too—and but for a nobody name of Weiss, Carl Weiss, who shot a hole in his kidney, he just might've made it to the Mansion. That's where he was headed, and he'd said so from the start. He'd even spelled out the steps he'd take to get there, and he took them one by one till, in the act of reaching for the doorknob, he heard a pistol shot—and after a day of dying, he was dead.

He got a big funeral, and from far away and farther, a lot of those dumb people blew in to see him laid under. They couldn't hate a man who hated Standard Oil—or *said* he did, which came to the same, because, one or the other, he fought the monster like he was Jack the Giant Killer. For true, nobody got much out of the fight but Huey, who rose high—a champion of the people, the dumb people thought—and he was on his way to ruling forty-five thousand square miles.

Born in Winn Parish, one of the sixty-four in that fief of his, he strode across life dragging a whole croker sack of adjectives behind him. Bold, he was called, and crass and crude and bumpkin flashy—sticks and stones, all such, but they broke no bones in Huey. Truth to tell, he welcomed the slurs: they fixed him in the popular mind, made him out to be a sure-enough one-gallus boy, the kind that had the mostest votes.

Whyfor he pleasured when the blue bloods snobbed him for being lowbred and loud, and it suited him fine to be scorned as a foulmouth and a boor and a braggart and a boss, all of which he purely was, especially the last, it being commonly said that *If Huey couldn't pitch, he wouldn't play*. Ah, that Huey—he wore hard names shamelessly, like the orange ties he flaunted with his purple shirts.

He had a passion for power, a craze, really, and the more he got, the more he longed for, but power in Winn Parish was, after all, parochial, a weaker grade than his nature needed. For which reason he climbed aboard that Standard Oil steed and flayed it across Louisiana from Shreveport to the Delta—and in time he had more than Winn Parish kissing his ass. He had all sixty-four, each of them swole up with his

129

henchmen, his fixers and cashiers, and of course a slew of peapickers and sapsuckers, some of whom thought he was a come-again Jesus. Nobody seemed to notice that his horse was still alive and pissing.

That is, nobody but Huey. He'd ridden the horse hard, true as true, but the last thing he wanted was for the animal to die: it still had to carry him to where he aimed to go, a river of waters called the Potomac. That took skill and guile, and he had a store of both, being peculiar for more dark ways and vain tricks than the heathen Chinee. He played dirty, and so did his enemies, but he played dirtier: where they planned, he schemed; and when they used argument, he used force; and if they were less than candid, he simply lied. And he could lie with the best of liars, because for all his pigsty stories and dunghill wit, he could talk slick and elegant when he chose to. He wasn't limited to folksay and Cajun, not him: he could speak in any way that served his end, and his end was always and only Huey Long.

Well, he got to the Capital, all right, but his mount would never do on the Hill, and he had to find another, which he straightway did. Share Our Wealth is what he called it, a piebald jade that drew the eye of a motley crew, all of whom trailed it, hopeful of droppings. Alas, there were none, nor could there have been: nothing had gone into the front, and nothing could fall from the back.

But Huey was troubled not at all; he knew he was on the way to his sixty-fifth parish, the eighteen acres of the White House grounds. Power had gone to his head, and he'd forgotten what he once had said to a delegation from the oil-and-gas parish of Caddo: *I will teach you to get off the sidewalk, take off your hat, and bow down low when Huey Long comes to town.* Forgotten too was the hope he'd given his jugheads and weed-benders that every man Jack could be a king. It was power now for power alone, and most fatally forgotten was his own predicted doom: *I'm a cinch to get shot.*

And he was, but even had he recalled his prophecy, he'd not have dreamed of an end at the hand of a doctor holding a Belgian .32. Bodyguards put a few dozen holes in the doctor, who'd put only one in Huey, but through that one poured all his bluff and bluster, all his carbonated notions, all his japery, his rudeness, his taste for orange ties, all his power hunger, and finally the power itself. Nevermore, as he'd done when first presented, would he enter the Senate chamber flicking a lighted cigar. He was dead.

Zelda Reconsidered

I am as I am because of my wife.
  —F. Scott Fitzgerald

There was a time when you thought as he did, when you too laid the blame on Zelda for his decline and early fall. She was a caution, that one, a small-town belle, willful, bold, and capricious, the kind who'd say, *Let's do something for the hell of it*—and then, shucking her bathing suit, she'd dive into the pool. A real devil-may-care, she was, fast enough in the open and maybe even faster with some halfback in the dark. Little wonder, then, that she was run after, that she danced every dance at the country club, that she drank drink-for-drink with the stags—and with that blue-eyed blond boy from St. Paul.

I am as I am because of my wife, he'd said, and you agreed. Who but she could've made him squander his talent, drained him dry, and sent him, still young in years, to die spent and sad at forty-four? Strangely, though, lying in his coffin at a mortuary, he didn't seem to be the bled and used-up man only lately seen alive. Strangely, he was again the handsome soldier of a long-gone day, the one on the way across a ballroom to begin a twenty-year dance with Daisy, Gloria, Nicole Diver. Strangely, death had repaired the damage done by time, by himself, by his several fictions, all of them Zelda, and once more and now forever he was the spruce lieutenant she'd whirl with until the music stopped, and the world waltzed away.

The age they gave a name to was very much your own, and it was while you were at college that first you heard of the dazzling pair and read of their heady doings—ah, those rides atop a taxicab, those dips in the fountain at Union Square, and how thrilling, you thought, their round-and-round in revolving doors! They held you in a spell with their novel and daring didoes—turning in false alarms, arriving late and loud everywhere, showing a bare ass at a theatrical. Not as yet by all was their ad lib drinking known, their ceaseless strife, the skimble-skamble manner of their lives. Not yet had it been noised about that they were rude, slovenly, and disruptive, and that wheresoever they'd been they left wreckage in their wake—broken glass, scarred furniture, stains, cracks, burn-holes, stuffed toilets, and overflowing tubs, and amidst all such lay their scatteration of offcast, their empty bottles and spoiled food, his dirty laundry and her menstrual rags. Few, though, were aware of the waste they laid in private—they were so sparkling in public, so fair and golden and gay.

But it was beginning to be noticed that they were always in motion, always on the way from where they'd just been to where they hoped to stay. And this too was noticed, that once there, they kept on moving—or were they fleeing, like the wicked of the proverb, in flight from themselves? If so, they never got away from their pursuers, or from their thirst, their perpetual civil war, their deleterious ways.

The prize they were ever contending for was Zelda, she striving to retain herself and he to acquire her by eminent domain. His was the superior right, he insisted, and it was a right that embraced even more than the person present: it took in as well both her future and her past. Her powers and preferences and tricks of speech, her habits and desires, her fancies and daft doings, her family, friends, and privacies— all that belonged to him. She was his mine of material, and though he mined every vein he could find, he fought her whenever she tried to do the same.

They fought for her all over the western world. Drunk, half-drunk, liverish, or sober and shaking, they fought at this Ritz or that, in bars and cabs and trains and even in the streets, and they fought too on plages, slopes, dancefloors, and in the presence of their guests. It was out in the open now—their infidelities (what, the darlings of the Age!), their antics, their spending sprees, as when, deep in debt, they hired four in help and drove a Rolls Royce. It was common knowledge at last, their all-night parties, their three-day binges, their suicidal bent.

No one stopped them—no one could've. Their friends—Ernest, Max, the Murphys, Ober—could only watch them chute the chutes. Unremarkable, then, that after a decade of drinking, warfare, and wandering foreign strands, Zelda showed wear and tear. *All I want is to be very young always*, she'd said, but instead she'd lost her figure and her looks (was she really only thirty?), and she'd lost her mind as well, winding up a schizophrenic in a Switzerland clinic.

It was then that the range of her husband's claim became clear. Due him as a matter of course, he'd felt, were Zelda's Dixie setting, her young-girl escapades, and her views in all their curious shades, and his too were her secrets, her talents, and her unpredictable stunts. But now, having so much, he wanted more, wanted all—and for his sole and exclusive use, he took possession of her illness: it was his material, grist for his particular mill.

Her delusions and hallucinations were for his use only, and so was

132

whatever she wrote or said during the course of her disorder. Be they long-winded or laconic, her letters, her diaries, her questions and answers, her idle talk, all of it was his property, not hers, and his too were the charts that recorded her intimate numbers—her pulse, her temperature, her respiration. All, all belonged to her anguished, her heart-wrung husband.

Save for brief excursions when apparently sound, she'd be in sanitaria for the rest of her days, and he'd be off on his killing round of earning enough to cover her keep and also the cost of his booze. In addition to the trash he wrote, he was years at the work of telling the tale of their roman-candle lives, of the shower of sparks, the brightness they'd given off, and of their fizzle and fade to a remembrance of the light they once had shed.

In her more balanced intervals, she tried to set down her version of their pell-mell history, of the promise they'd given and broken. After all, it was her history as well as his, and she sought to tell it as she saw it in the cloister of her mind, a dark region seldom open to him. She cared little about the anecdotes she'd told and even less about her explanation of the customs and jargon of Alabama, and he was free to assign what he pleased to his numerous Zeldas of fancy. But title to the actual Zelda was held by her, and she meant to keep it. Her husband objected hotly, as if she were a squatter asserting a fictitious right, a wrongful right. She could not, he insisted, she could not treat as hers what he regarded as his, and he railed at her for the arrogation. *You're a third-rate writer,* he said in the hearing of others, *and you're encroaching on my literary territory.*

She was unwell when he scolded her—unwell in body and incurably so in mind—and he must've known that his cruelty was bringing her lower. Almost, it seems, she was prey, and his onslaught was the breakneck pounce of an animal. How, you wonder, could he have been so unfeeling toward his partner in a hundred fabled frolics, his slapdash girl who loved to dance on tables and flash her rosy thighs? Why could he not have seen that he was assailing the nearly dead? She was hardly now in life, having lived it away in a dozen years, left pieces of it in cabarets, in railway cars, in transatlantic suites, strewn it in hotel lobbies and at parties in private rooms. All that remained were her instrumental numbers, her readings, her semblance of being quick.

Far down, she went even farther when her once-radiant soldier called her a third-rate writer and blamed her for his reduction: *I am what I am because of my wife.* In so saying, he was wrong twice: she had enough ability to make him fear it, and she was not the cause of his ruin. He'd been a drinker, a drunk, even, before he ever met her, and he drowned his nonesuch talent in a nonstop pour of beer, brandywine, and gin rickeys. In time, he went from trim to slack, and his fine face sagged, as though the flesh had come loose from the bone, but his expression alone would've been enough to betray him. Where once it had shown him as vital and zestful, it spoke now of hopes fading and a dread of defeat. The fineness had gone, and the luster.

In his casket, though, he didn't seem the sodden and jazzed-out man of story, the belligerent, the disrupter, the noisy nuisance. Instead, he was again the radiant soldier, the Golden Boy of the Age, and in a moment, you fancied, he'd wake and rise and wander away to find Zelda, and perhaps when found she'd tell him that she'd been dreaming of a place where it was forever warm, where it was midsummer forever . . .

Scenes of the National Life, 5

The Safe Rebellion

They wear their caps ass-end-to and think they're bringing down the world, but the rich are delighted by such stupidity. They have no fear of sham buccaneers in bandanna bandeaux, of those who flaunt nullified flags and uniforms with spangled epaulettes. Nothing is endangered by the ciphers they scrawl on walls, by the squalls of sound they send through the air; nothing is won them by their pigtails, their jewelry, their tribal loyalties; nothing is gained by their thievery, for they steal from their own. They're tough, true, and they're deadly, but rarely do they fight their enemy, who laugh as they watch them fight themselves. They corrupt their noses and scar their arms, they shoot unknowns from passing cars, but nothing is overthrown thereby, nothing descends to them from those who own the world, and they go young to their doom, never knowing why they lost, or even to whom.

Whatsoever Ye Shall Ask

> information: (sense 2c) facts, etc., ready for
> communication or use, as distinguished esp. from those
> incorporated in a body of thought.
> —*Webster's International*

Not to think—what a joy! Like children on the floor with a set of trains, they sit before their latest toy, a somnolent machine, and rousing it with a question, they scan its reply on a screen. Let the query be a poser, let it call for a secret shared by few, let it call for a variable—prices, vogues, the weather in Peru—and lo! a string of words comes into view. Call for numbers—the rainfall in Singapore, the distance to Dublin, Caracas, the Pleiades. Call for the atomic weight of manganese, the suicide rate in Mozambique, for dates, danger zones, or the national debt of Greece. Call, and from some measureless store (the mind of God?) comes an answer accurate to the fraction of an inch, an ounce, a cent, a second—and thus informed, the grownup children may turn from their toy to . . . to what, for Christ's sake, to what?

They've merely been equipped to get the jump on the slow, to buy low and sell high, to grow strong on the weak, to acquire more, more, as though infinitely more made for infinite life. They've been given useful data, but none of it is knowledge, none is wisdom, none a movable heart or a sense of honor. Such things are not to be gotten from a machine.

Women Seeking Men

> abbreviations: (A) Asian, (B) African-American,
> (c) Christian, (D) Divorced, (F) Female, (G) Gay,
> (H) Hispanic, (J) Jewish, (L) Lesbian, (M) Male,
> (s) Single, (w) White, (ISO) In Search Of.

How lonely they must be to advertise their loneliness; how desperate to confess their desperation! Their vines languish, but no man has come to pick their fruit and try its savor before savor goes, wherefore they display themselves as in a doorway or at the crossing of two streets. *Strikingly elegant, fun-loving, amorous, well-educ.,* they proclaim in little boxes of newsprint, each akin to every other in its plea for a partner, a squire, or, please God, a cavalier. *Vivacious, sexy, str8forwd lady ISO honest romantic M to love and be loved.*

What do they do while awaiting a voice from the vastness of space?

How do they beguile the time—do they read, do they listen to music, or do they weep in the taciturn dark? *Smart, curvaceous redhead, very funny, loves life, ISO a WM for whatever happens*—and if her call comes, will it be the right call, from the WM she pined for, or will some other be on the line? *Cath high sch tchr seeks cult WCM for trust, convers, love, marr.* In agate-line shorthand, they specify the qualities they desire in an A, B, H, or whatever: sincerity, humor, warmth, financial security, good looks, refinement—all that for *lovely, enchanting, slender SF 5'9" 120lbs. of passion.* A rare bird seeking its heart's desire, a lament from the unchosen to the unwilling, a sad sound in the daylong night.

Do they sit still till the call comes for *embraceable brunette, Caribbean beauty, shapely DJF, playful Sagittarius, experimental blonde,* or do they kill time at Solitaire, do they mend a split seam, do they pluck gray hair and mutely scream? What, when no call comes for *SBF affect indep cuddly trim likes animals wants gentman 4 frndshp love marr?* How then do the hopeless behave? Do they stop pleading with the void for the unattainable—the handsome, witty, athletic, soft-spoken, experienced charmer precisely thirty-five years of age—and offer to settle for a nondescript, a clerk of forty, a mechanic of fifty, anyone of even more?

Do they come clean for once, and so that only they can hear, do they allow that they're plain and past their prime, that their intelligence is average and their figure less so, that they tend to talk too much and say too little, that they're not at all amusing, sweet, trim, cute, sensual, spirited, romantic, or inflammatory, and that they have no particular liking for photography, children, or walks on the beach? Or, in the pierglass of their minds, do they still see baby dolls, Latin jewels, women of valor, wise, daring, true blue, and classy—only in the end to beseech the world's empty room, saying, *Please, in the name of God, please . . . !*

At the Speed of Light

electricity: one of the fundamental quantities of nature, characterized especially by the fact that, when moving in a stream, it gives rise to a magnetic field of force.
    —*Webster's International*

Its name is new, but its property was anciently known. Six hundred years before the coming of Christ, Thales of Miletus noted the attractive power in jet and amber, and so too Theophrastus in his treatise on stones; nor may Pliny the Elder be overlooked, he who studied all day long save only when in his bath. The force so observed, the phenome- non of an invisible affinity between particles of matter, was thereafter dwelt on by many another, most of them unsung and, worse, anony- mous—until, in the reign of Elizabeth, one Gilbert (or Gylberde, as some have it) made the heady claim that the very earth was a magnetic force, and now the aim of all was to persuade it to run in a steady stream.

How they labored through the ages, those who'd never die and those who'd never live! They built crude and unsightly devices of lead and zinc, things of glass and foil and copper wire, and in thunderstorms they flew kites with silken wings—and in the end, the force had a name, and a few would be remembered for inducing it to flow as one and all had dreamed.

These days, it lights and heats and informs the world, uses that both the deathless and the dead might survey with pride. But what of the use called news and amusement? Would they laugh at the relentless quips and japery; would they cheer the all-important outcome of all- important games; would they care about crimes, disasters, war, and the weather in Alabama; would they stare in wonder at the ruin wrought by man? What would Maxwell say of such entertainments? What would Ampère, Volta, Faraday . . . ?

They Still Walk, They Still Speak

It was reported in the Boston *Traveller* that 154 men and women had been arrested in Charlestown, cited for sauntering and loitering, a misdemeanor, and fined the sum of $5 each. The lawbreakers had comprised a Death Watch outside the walls of the state prison while, within, a shoemaker and a fish peddler were being taken from their cells and led to the electric chair. Six years earlier, the pair had been found guilty of murdering the payroll guards Parmenter and Berardelli—and never through those years had they ceased to proclaim their innocence. From the judgment of the lower court, they'd appealed to a higher, and on being denied, they'd gone to the very highest—all to no avail. Numberless the names on petitions that came from far and wide, and numberless too the masses that met in streets and squares; speeches had been made, songs had been sung and prayers prayed, volumes had been written, and tears had been shed, many and many a tear—all to no avail.

At or near midnight of August 22, 1927, the two Italians were given an electrical charge that briefly dimmed the lights of Charlestown and forever extinguished their own. Their skin blistered, their temperature elevated to 128°, and their hearts tetanized in permanent systole; they were dead on the instant—painlessly, it was said—and soon thereafter the unwrung remains were sent on their final journey, to the Forest Hills crematory, eight miles away through Boston and beyond Jamaica Plain.

Two hundred thousand faces walled the way, all but a few of them grieving. Here and there hatred was seen and revilement heard, and in places the police interfered with the procession and diverted it into a bypath or a dead-end road; but finding its proper channel again, it flowed slowly on to the graveyard. There the bodies were reduced to a pound or two of ash, but before the urns could be placed in the earth, part of the crowd turned violent. It was as though random and separate hostilities had been passed along the line, and joining forces, they'd exploded at last. Bystanders and marchers were assailed alike by the jingoes and the constabulary, noses were broken and crowns clubbed, clothing was torn, and blood was let—and when the fracas died down, six years of agony were over for a shoemaker from Torremaggiore and a seller of cod and eels. Their shades, though, their shades still walked the world. . . .

"Don't misunderstand me, John—I approve," Maggie said. "But is there any aspect of the case that you haven't dealt with? You've been at it for more than forty years, and you've covered the two Italians from the night of their arrest to the day of their exoneration. The Bridgewater trial, the Dedham trial, Judge Thayer, the jury, the D.A., Sacco's wife, Vanzetti's sister, Governor Fuller, the Italians themselves, and now their funeral . . ."

"I wonder why it took me so long to get around to the funeral."

"They haunt you, those two," she said.

Yes, but did they haunt Beacon Street and Louisburg Square? Did they haunt the statehouse steps where two women once pleaded for the lives of an edger of shoes and a fishmonger, only to hear the governor refuse? Two men had died when he moved away downhill toward his club, his bar, his sporting house, but did he feel a sudden chill and fear to turn lest he find, along with those of the Italians, his own shade close behind? He did not. He felt nothing, nothing at all, and on he went to the Algonquin or the Union Boat or possibly to Estelle's.

JUDGE WEBSTER THAYER, ?–1933

Speaking Off-the-Record

Their trial was unfair, you say, because I was prejudiced? Of course it was unfair, and of course I was prejudiced. I *wanted* a guilty verdict, and that's what I got—and never once did I think the two ginnies shot the paymaster Parmenter and his guard Berardelli. I didn't care a rap for the guard—he was only another ginney—but Parmenter was a white man, and somebody had to die for killing him. Who better than those anarchists—Sacco and Vanzelli, or whatever the hell the dago name was. Anarchists had no particular right to a fair trial, and I made sure they didn't get one.

Between you, me, and Bunker Hill, the commonwealth had a half-assed case. A decent defense lawyer could've beat the whey out of the D.A., a pettifogger name of Katzmann, who had only half an ass himself, but, hell, the lawyers for the ginnies had no asses at all! It was

140

pure sinful, the trimming they took, hardly knowing I was breaking their bones.

I gave Katzmann all the leeway in the world and then some. I let him ask questions that even a law student would've known were improper; I let him badger witnesses, especially Sacco, who didn't seem to realize he was digging his own grave; I let the D.A. introduce hearsay; I let him playact scorn, anger, and disbelief for the jury; I let him be the Avenging Angel—and all the while, the lawyers for the ginnies sat there looking stupid, or, when they opened their mouths, I shut them.

The case was circumstantial, every last bit of it. Nary a witness had gotten a real good fix on the killers; the best that anyone could attest to was a couple of dark-complected men wearing dark-colored clothes. Some swore that they were tall, some that they were medium, and others that they were foreign-looking—sweet Jesus, one of them claimed that they ran like Italians! *Ran like Italians*—not even Italians run like Italians! But I let it all go into the record, the loony along with the sane, any damn thing that would inflame the jury against the ginnies, including evidence of their draft dodging, which had nothing to do with the murders—material, in other words, that was *im*material.

But, knowing that the ginnies' lawyers were chowderheads, I got in my best lick by saying nothing when the Commonwealth put Captain Proctor on the stand to testify about the bullet removed from the body of Berardelli. Proctor didn't state that it *was* fired from Sacco's pistol; he only said that it was *consistent with having been* so fired. There's a whale of a difference, but the lawyers for the ginnies made little of it, and I sure God didn't help to make it much. Shoot, I'd've knocked hell out of the Commonwealth's case.

Well, the trial ended the way I meant it to end—with the ginnies going to the Chair—and I'm proud to say they went there because of me. Time and again, had I been so minded, I could've horned in and helped them, but I *wasn't* so minded, and with me on the bench, they were goners from the word go. We're *all* of us dead now, everyone who figured in the case—me, the jury, Sacco and Vanzetto, the lawyers, the D.A. that some thought to be a Jew. Seventy years have passed, and we're all as dead as Parmenter and Berardelli—we're equals at last, you might say. But I say no: the ginnies have been exonerated, and people come to piss on my grave.

SS St. Louis

The ship, displacing 17,000 tons, flew the house-flag of
the Hamburg-Amerika Line. Built for the transatlantic
passenger service and manned by a crew of more than two
hundred, she made her maiden voyage in 1929.

Ten years later, at mid-May of 1939, she sailed from Hamburg
under the command of Captain Gustav Schroeder, her new master,
and headed for Havana with a company of 937 Jews, all of whom had
beggared themselves to purchase permission to leave the Third Reich.
Some few among these may have believed that they had also bought
permission to enter Cuba. If so, they were in error. The Jews, all of
them, had parted with their money for a mere round-trip to the New
World, which they would see only from the decks of the *St. Louis*, for
nowhere in that world would they be allowed to land. In truth, they
hadn't even left Germany: on a buoyant part of it, they could go ever
so far without having started.

Most of the passengers hadn't been beguiled by expectation or
by the pleasures of the voyage—the dancing, the games, the picture
shows, the inconstant colors of the sea and sky. Ever within them
stirred the dread that they might not yet be free: despite the bright
prospect offered by motion and distance, they were still subject to the
will of those who thus far had shown them only ill. Scarcely six months
had passed since the *Kristallnacht*, the Night of Broken Glass—but
say, rather, of broken hearts, for with their pissed-on Torahs and shit-
on graves, they knew they were no longer Germans; they were only
dirty Jews.

Unknown to Captain Schroeder, his ship was deeply engaged in es-
pionage. Certain members of his crew were also members of the German Intelligence, and regularly were they ferried across the ocean on
their secret missions. But whatever their character aboard the *St. Louis*
—whether deckhand, machinist, table steward, or stoker—each of the
crew was a Nazi, meaning every man Jack was an enemy of the Jew. Not
so Captain Schroeder, though. He scorned the Party, and he loathed
its ruthless puppets, the bullyboys, and while the burden of his passengers was heavy enough, it would've been unbearable had Schroeder let
the ruffians have their way. He was regarded as a compassionate man,
even by one of his Nazi firemen (*He's a fool over the Jews*, he said), but

all the same, it was beyond his powers to cure the sickness already at work in some of his passengers: grieving for his homeland, one of them died; another opened his veins; and a third threw himself overboard and drowned.

Among the remainder, there was no real gaiety: smiles were masks, and half-wit laughter was heard, and talk for fear of silence. Fear—it was ever-present, as inevitable as a shadow, and it dogged their days and dreams. But it was more than a shadow: it had weight and mass, and it bore down on the spirit, compressed the air, drained the senses of sight and sound. None was easy in the mind. Behind the thoughts of all was memory of the Night of Broken Glass, when twenty thousand Jews had simply disappeared, a fate in store for those on the *St. Louis* should she ever be ordered back to Germany. Only too likely did that become when, clearance to dock being denied her, she was compelled to ride at anchor in Havana harbor, where she became a floating oven in the tropical heat. A week of parleying effected no change, and hopes guttered as the ship weighed, steamed past the castle, and made for the Florida Straits. There, barely a mile off the port rail, Miami was a throng of hotels and mansions, and a blaze of bright umbrellas could be seen on the beach. But for the weary Jews, the homeless and hounded Jews, no welcome awaited in the Land of the Free, and the *St. Louis* turned away from the Golden Door and headed for Hamburg, four thousand miles to the north and east.

"When I began to write the piece," you said, "that's where I meant to end it. But it can't end there."

"I don't see why not," she said. "It says all it needs to say."

"But not all I need to say . . . Did I ever tell you that I went to Europe on the St. Louis?"

She let a moment pass as though, not expected to speak, she were awaiting more from you; but you were awaiting her, and when she said nothing, you repeated yourself.

"I went to Europe on the St. Louis."

"I know you went, but I don't recall that you mentioned the ship."

"Back in 1930, it was—nine years before she made that trip with all those Jews. They walked the same decks that I did. They ate in

the same dining saloon. And one of them slept in my cabin, in my bunk! But there was a terrible difference between my trip and theirs: I was going to Europe for a good time; they were going there to die."

Again an intermission, but this time there was no doubt about whose turn it was to speak; it was hers, and she spoke, saying,

"There's more to this, isn't there?"

"Much more," you said, "and it's been on my mind for years and years. Most of the time, it's inactive, but every now and then it comes awake and plagues me. My guess is that I want it to, that I stir it up."

"Why?"

"To punish myself."

"For something you did?"

"It's more like something I didn't *do . . . I met a girl in the south of France, a Jewish girl from Paris. We were staying at the same pension, and after dinner we'd talk for awhile, and pretty soon we were friends. Friends is all, but it turned out to be a lasting friendship, and later, after I came home, we exchanged letters several times a year. The war was still a long way off then, but in 1939 — the year of the* St. Louis . . ."

For you and the Jews, you thought, the selfsame ship and the selfsame ocean sea, but the lone Jew had been on one of his harebrained excursions, and the many in despair on their way to the grave. To them, nothing could've been as it was to you, nothing safe, nothing free from care — and how otherwise, when for you the future was boundless, and they knew where it ended?

". . . but in 1939, the year of the St. Louis, *the girl wrote to say that she'd be in danger if the Germans took Paris, and she asked me to sponsor her for a stay in the States."*

"Don't tell me you refused!"

"Almost as bad. I did nothing."

"My God, John!"

"I mean, I did nothing for a couple or three weeks. I don't know why. I didn't want the responsibility, I guess."

"But the girl was a friend, John!"

"Yes, and one that I had high regard for. One I'd've hated to lose."

"And yet you did nothing for awhile. I simply don't understand that."

"I don't understand it myself."

"What was the upshot?"

"I got around to moving, finally, and found out what I'd have to do."

"And did you?"

"By the time I filled out all the forms, I heard from the girl again, urgently now and through a third party. I was told to drop whatever I was doing and forget the whole thing. I gathered that she was secure and didn't want to risk being traced. Her luck was good, and she lived through the Occupation."

"That being so, you did her no harm."

"No," you said. *"But think of the harm I did to myself."*

You remember, when first you read of the futile voyage of the *St. Louis*, that you'd taken her to be a different ship, a replacement for the one you'd known, sunk somewhere or sold for scrap. But once her photo was shown, you realized that what you'd tried to do was sink or scrap your memory: the new ship was the old ship, slow and ungainly, and she'd borne 937 Jews toward the sung-of lamp-lit Door, just as she'd borne you away.

"There's a saying," you said, *"that goes like this:* Who gives quickly, gives twice. But I didn't give at all."

"In the end, you were going to. That ought to count for something."

"I should've acted at once—you know it, and I know it. But I waited (for what? for what?), and after that, nothing counted. I've tried to forget the delay, justify it, explain it away; but the fact is, I failed a friend, and it weighs on me now as it did fiftysome years ago. I can't forgive myself."

"Suppose someone had failed you," she said. *"Would you be just as unforgiving?"*

"Do you know what I've asked myself? What if I'd been called on to help the Jews on the St. Louis*? Would I have dawdled while they were on the way to the camps?"*

"And how do you answer?"

"I'm afraid to answer!"

ail once, and you fail always. Is that it?"

hat else can it be?"

u did wrong, and you've punished yourself for it. It's a good
to be troubled by a bad thing, but fifty years of regret is
enough."

"Why do I have the feeling that a hundred won't be enough?"

There was a pause, as though she were wondering whether to say
what at length she said: "Probably because you've never told the girl
what you did—or what it took you three weeks to do."

You looked at her, and you looked at her long.

"The girl," she said. "She's the one you ought to tell."

The *St. Louis* did not return the Jews to Hamburg. Their plight,
when put before the governments of England, France, Belgium, and
the Netherlands, excited so much sympathy that each agreed to receive
a share of the passengers. All were debarked at Antwerp, where they
were apportioned to the several receptive countries. Only those sent to
England survived—some 240 of the original number. The others were
gathered in during the German invasion and exterminated.

At war's end, Captain Schroeder was accused of having had Nazi
sympathies, and he was brought before a tribunal for interrogation.
Among the witnesses in his behalf were many of those he'd carried from
the Old World to the New and then back to the Old. All these testified
that he'd befriended them, and he was exonerated.

The Royal Air Force bombed the *St. Louis* to junk in Hamburg
harbor—and she *was* sold for scrap.

NATHANIEL WEINSTEIN, 1903-40

Nathanael "Pep" West

"I was hunting for something in the Concordance the other day,"
you said, "and I happened on a reference to Nathanael, a disciple
who's mentioned only in St. John. In Hebrew, the name means
God's gift."

"Pep was no gift of God," she said. "Not to me."

"You never liked him. Why?"

"He had a bad effect on you."

"Because of his example, I became a writer, and through my writing, I met you. I call that a good effect."

"You became a writer because writing is your lick. All Pep did was make you aware of it. He sure as life didn't intend to encourage you."

"Why do you say that, Mag?"

And she said, "Ah, Johnny, Johnny."

"That sounded like a sigh of despair."

"You're a melonhead about people, and most of all about Pep. You were friends for a good part of his life, and I met him only once—but I know him a sight better than you do."

"What did I miss?"

"This: that he didn't welcome your writing."

"Maybe he didn't like it."

"Did he ever say so?"

"He never spoke to me of my writing. Nor to anyone else, so far as I know."

"Would you call that a welcome?"

"I don't call it anything. He wasn't bound to receive me at the door."

"Yes, he was, Johnny. But you defend him every time his name comes up."

"That's because I owe him. Whether he meant to or not, he put me on the road to you—and without you, darkness."

"I like that," she said, "but when will the debt be paid off?"

"Never," you said, and your mind rewound to the past. "Never," you said, "and that's odd, because I didn't really like the guy myself."

She said nothing, as though waiting for you to explain, but how could you explain to her what wasn't clear to you . . . ?

You'd seen him first in your Harlem days. You were playing some kid's game on the sidewalk in front of an apartment house called the DePeyster—shooting marbles, pitching campaign buttons, tossing Sweet Cap cards—but he wasn't playing, not Nate Weinstein, or Natchie, as you later heard his mother say. He was just standing on the stoop and watching others play. You were no champ at any of those games, but you tried your best against your betters, and now and then you came away with a pocketful of winnings—chromos of lighthouses and clipper ships and flying machines—and your hands were seldom clean and your stockings often torn. Natchie, though, Nate Weinstein, he never played.

From those hazed-over days, only two scenes with him come into view. One of them took place on a traffic island, where you and Nate were vying in a game that he *did* play—naming the make of cars coming up or down Seventh Avenue—and he was good at it. He could tick them off from a block or more away: *The red one's a Stanley Steamer,* he'd say, *and the green one's a Winton, a Lozier, a Chalmers, an Apperson Jack-rabbit.* You wondered how he knew so much about such meaningful things, not then realizing that the solution could be found in the second scene, wherein he said, *I read all of Tolstoy by the time I was nine.* Though you'd never heard of Tolstoy, you marveled—all of Tolstoy by the time he was nine!—but later, when you were not quite so benighted, marvel changed to doubt and, later still, to disbelief. By then, the Harlem years were over.

"I wonder," she said. "I wonder how much more you could've done for someone you did *like. For Pep, you've done all that was ever asked of you and a lot on your own. You've given material to everyone who sought you out—nobody got turned down. I remember the letters you wrote to Jim Light for his book on Pep. One of them must've been a dozen pages long. And for his biography of Pep, you spent two whole days talking to Jay Martin. You wrote a review of* Balso *for a Paris magazine and a memoir for the Screenwriter. And after he died, you dedicated a book to him."*

"So . . . ?" you said.

"Do you think he'd've done as much for you?"

"No."

"You've known that?"

"All along."

"Most people would call you foolish."

"He'd've done nothing for me," you said. "If anyone had ever come to him for information, I know just what he'd've said: 'We were both from Harlem, but we never got to be friends. He was married to a screenwriter, I think, and she'd be the one to help you. Trouble is, I forget her name.' "

"And in spite of that," she said, "you kept on honoring his *name."*

148

"I had to. It would've been wrong to hold back what I knew."
"I admire that. I don't call it foolish . . ."

Ten or a dozen years passed before you saw him again. It was during the summer of 1925, and, unaccompanied, you were playing a round of golf on a course near Asbury Park. Some way ahead of you, a tall fellow was doing the same. On overtaking him at one of the tees, you found him to be Nate Weinstein, the Natchie who once had watched childish games from the stoop of the DePeyster.

"I see you've given up marbles," he said.

"And you, you're actually fumbling with a bat and ball."

"Julie Shapiro, isn't it? What're you up to these days?"

"I'm in my second year at Fordham Law," you said. "And you?"

"I'm writing a book."

ImwritingabookImwritingabookImwritingabook. You seemed to have heard the reverberations of an explosion. A four-word bomb had gone off in your mind—Imwritingabook, you thought—and the bomb seemed to go off again. You've never been able to recall the rest of the round, the rest of the day, or even the rest of the summer. All that comes back is ImwritingabookImwritingabook, and it comes with its original force, eruptive and cataclysmic. Still, you did not resolve then and there that you too would one day write a book: the pursuit was in another range of experience, a realm so strange that as yet you could only gaze at it in wonder from afar. But this much you sensed at once: a dwindling pride in your own profession.

By summer's end, you and he had become friends—a better word might be *friendly*—and on returning to New York, you saw a good deal of each other, spending many an evening walking about the city, usually after your classes at law school. And on those walks, through the dark Village or along incandescent Broadway or up the Avenue to the park, the talk was almost always of literature; and his knowledge of the field was so vast that, for the most part, you listened as to a sage. What had you been doing, you'd wonder, while he was growing wise? What trash had beguiled you, dimmed your mind, made you blind to Joyce and Eliot, to Perse and Pound and Stein? Ah, the names he launched on the nighttime air—Pater and Yeats and Radiguet—the appraisals he made, the anecdotes he told, the tales of high living and of wild and wasted lives! You heard too of aberration, of failure and madness and suicide, of who was serious and who was killing time.

149

With the months, more and more did the law lose its hold on you, and more and more did writing draw you—and on momentum alone, it seemed, you passed the bar and were admitted to practice. By then, though, you'd already taken your first unsteady steps in the new world: some of your pieces had been printed in a small magazine!

On that Asbury tee or green or fairway, West had said the witching words, Imwritingabook, and he'd spoken the truth. Called *The Dream Life of Balso Snell*, it was accepted by Contact Editions, and in his one-room Bank Street flat, you read proof with him through four or five sets of corrections, becoming so familiar with it in the end that you could recite whole paragraphs by heart.

"When I was a kid," Maggie said, "we used to joke about running away to join the gypsies. You guys actually did it."

"He was managing the Kenmore, a cheap hotel on 23rd Street, and I was in my office, helping one son-of-a-bitch sue another, and very little writing was getting done. He was the one who proposed that we shake our jobs and go off somewhere—anywhere, so long as it was good for the work we liked. I said, 'You're on,' and as it happened, I turned up the perfect place."

"I remember the way you wrote about it," she said. "You made me want to see it."

"Jay Martin did see it, but it was too late. It had to be seen as West and I saw it sixtysome years ago, and what we saw is gone."

"What you wrote isn't gone."

"I didn't do it justice—but how could I? I was trying to describe a twelve-hundred-acre paradise that came with a cabin and a spring-fed pond. The forest began at the water's edge, and it was dense, dim, and deep in brash, as it must've been when the Algonquins roamed it, and for all we knew, it was still alive with their shades, hunting, feasting, dancing, doing what they did before they died. Apart from the cabin, we were five miles from the nearest house."

"The woods, the pond, the cabin—why do you say they're gone?"

"What I mean, I suppose, is that we saw the place first with younger eyes, saw it the way you see only once. After that, it's there only in your mind. If we'd gone back, we'd've seen something different, something less. But that first time, that first time . . . !"

The cabin consisted of six or seven rooms, depending on whether the kitchen was reckoned in the count. The living space could be closed off into a pair of suites, one of which was taken by West and the other by you. As it happened, your work-tables stood against the opposite sides of a wall, and as you well remember, it was a thin wall through which, hardly muted by the papered plaster, the tap dance of typing passed. Always along with West's, though, came the tones of his voice, for he was unable to compose without reading the words aloud. It was as if he could measure their worth only by their sound.

"Guys as different as you two," she said. "How did you manage to get along, being so close-herded?"

"Writing had brought us there, and I guess it was writing that kept us from getting shirty. Neither of us expected the other to hew all the wood and draw all the water, so we simply split the chores and got them out of the way. The only one we didn't split was the driving; he was so terrible at it that I always took the wheel. We'd write every morning, or nearly, and afterwards we'd swim, explore, or shoot at paper targets, and sometimes we'd fish Brant Lake for pickerel or the Hudson for small-mouth bass. The evenings were cool—cold as the season wore on—and we'd sit close to the stove and talk, mostly about books . . ."

When you paused, she said, "About your own *books?"*

"No."

"Why was that?"

"How could I talk about my book when he wasn't talking about his?"

"Ceremony. You should've told him."

"I felt he should've asked."

"And did he never . . . ?"

"Once," you said, "and I almost wish he hadn't . . ."

The Water Wheel must've been closer to completion than you knew when you came away with it from New York: after several weeks of steady work, you were able to go back over the pages and fix such flaws as you were then equipped to find. You were in the midst of making those changes when, one evening late in the summer, West asked if you'd let him read the manuscript. Greatly surprised and, at the time, greatly pleased, you gave it to him, and he took it to his room when you parted for the night.

One of the books on your bedside table was Fowler's *Modern English Usage*, and as usual you read through a few headings (Fused Participle, Needless Variants, Pedantic Humor) before turning down the wick of your coal-oil lamp. West's was still burning, and through your window, you could see the flying jib of light that came from his and faded among the trees. For awhile, you lay listening to sounds from the darkness, an animal raking the trash pile, a loon plying the pond, an owl asking its one and only question.

Why had West asked for the manuscript, you wondered, and why had he waited so long—and you were still wondering when you fell asleep. In the morning . . .

"We'd done the chores," you said, "and I was about to get at my typewriter when he gave back the manuscript. This, or something very like it, is what he said: 'You can't reveal the girl's identity like that. It simply isn't done.' "

"What else did he say?" Maggie said.

"That's it. That's all."

"Nothing about the story? Nothing about the style? Nothing about what he thought of you as a writer?"

"Not a mumbling word."

"Well, then, what did you *say?"*

"I was so floored that I couldn't say anything. I could only watch him close the door. I tried to work, but working was impossible, so I went outside and sat on the dock, or maybe I took a swim, or maybe I drove to the village and bought something—or maybe I just stayed where I was and listened to West through the wall."

"Don't tell me you let it go at that! Why didn't you let him have a piece of your mind?"

"Meanness gags me, and he had a mean streak. He wasn't bound to like my book, but once he'd asked to read it, he was *bound to say more than he did. Instead, he hung me out to dry. What could I have said about that? Nothing."*

"He was worse than mean, Johnny. He was cruel . . ."

Whatever he'd been, naturally mean or unnaturally cruel, you were too benumbed at the time to take your cause further—nor did you at a later time. He talked much of Letters, as he called it, ranging its vastness and variety from Wyndham Lewis to Williams, and Hemingway to Apollinaire—but never again did he speak of your writing, not even to slight it, and for all you know, he did not read either of your two other books published during his lifetime.

The summer was winding down. Trees had begun to shed red and yellow leaves, covering the forest floor with small imploring hands. Now and then, a trout would break the surface of the pond, briefly rippling the reflected sky, but for the most part, the water seemed to have been stilled by the approach of fall. Always now a fire burned in the stove, and the windows, closed against the outdoor chill, wore veils of vapor that blurred the view. The pond, even at the height of day, was too cold for prolonged swimming, and the two of you spent your spare hours in the woods, an out-of-the-way hill and dale, as wild as in a bygone day.

To all appearance, no change had taken place in your relationship with West. The odd jobs were shared as usual, each of you still respected the other's silences and privacy, and in the evenings, as before, cigarette smoke surged above your lamplit talks. All the same, there *had* been a change, and both of you knew it: it was submerged, a reef to steer clear of, but it was there. You'd stopped being friends and become merely friendly.

"You were always quick to resent a slight," Maggie said, "sometimes too quick. What I don't understand is why you let that one pass."

"I didn't know what he meant by it. And I don't to this day."

"Suppose I tell you: your book took him by surprise."

"You'll have to explain that."

"When I first met you, I thought you were a decent sort—intelligent, courteous, pleasant to be with, and that's about all. But then you let me read The Water Wheel. *It opened my eyes, Johnny, and I saw what I'd missed—that you were a talented guy."*

"And that's what West missed?"

"By a mile," she said. "Up to the time he'd read the book, you were simply good enough company for a summer in the woods. After reading it, he knew there was a writer on the other side of the wall."

"Well, what if there was?" you said. "How does that account for the way he acted?"

"I love you, Johnny, but you never knew the difference between a crow and a crane. When West saw what you'd done in The Water Wheel, *he knew he was in for a race."*

"And I love you, my loyal little dame, but that book wouldn't've scared anybody, least of all West."

*"*The Water Wheel *had its faults. It wasn't the greatest novel since* Moby-Dick. *But it was a long way better than* Balso Snell, *which was all West had to show at the time. Later, both of you would do better, much better, but up there at Viele Pond, I say you got his attention."*

"If so, why didn't he give me a slap on the back, a nod, a wink, a word?"

"Some teachers resent a bright pupil. They feel they've given part of themselves away . . ."

And now the Adirondack summer was over, and save for *The Water Wheel* episode, it had been one you'd remember with pleasure for the rest of your days. It would prove to be imperishable, for whenever you were so inclined, you could bring it to mind and know it anew—taste the water of the pond, as fresh and sweet as rain, breathe the unused air, hear the outdoor sound of stealthy lives, and you'd feel as you'd felt long before, when you were twenty-seven years of age.

On the road back to New York, West took the wheel out of Albany while you read him the book reviews in the Sunday *Times*. Once across the Hudson, he made a wrong turn, and, absorbed, you failed to notice the mistake until you were well on the way to Pittsfield, Massachusetts.

Maggie said, "How could you stand the guy after The Water Wheel *thing?"*

"At the time, all I felt was disappointment. He was better informed than anyone I knew, and his opinion counted. When he said nothing, I gathered that he had nothing to say—nothing good, that is. It was a letdown, but I didn't get my tail over a line about it. But the next time—"

In the fall of that year, West became the manager of the Sutton, a residential hotel on East 56th Street, and soon after being installed, he invited you to live there, rent free—a handsome offer, you thought, and of course you accepted. At the Sutton, while *The Water Wheel* was being shown to publishers, you tried your hand at the short story, and you wrote four or five of them, each based on a real or fancied episode of your stay at Viele Pond.

West occupied a suite on the topmost floor of the hotel, and your single room was several stories below, so encounters were infrequent. Only on one occasion did you go to his quarters, and that was when he telephoned to say that he had a visitor who'd asked to meet you. The visitor proved to be William Carlos Williams, and admittedly you were so awed by his presence that afterward you were unable to recall what either of you had said during the only meeting you were ever to have.

Later, West told you that he and Williams were editing *Contact*, a magazine founded in Paris by Robert McAlmon and preparing now for its appearance here. The periodical had been highly regarded abroad, and knowing that its first American number would receive wide critical attention, you were eager to be among its contributors. You were overjoyed, therefore, when Williams invited you to submit a story for approval. Through West, you offered him one called "Once in a Sedan and Twice Standing Up," and all the greater was your joy when he informed you that Williams had accepted it.

The ribaldry of the title, if ribaldry it was, originated elsewhere. During the previous year, you'd boarded for a few weeks at the Adirondack farm of a man named Shaw, and it was there that you met the game-warden Beakbane. Both men, knowing you to be an attorney, had urged you to represent the complainant in a local case: a young servant-girl had brought bastardy proceedings against the Long Lake parson. You'd agreed, and at the hearing, she testified that she'd been seduced *once in a sedan and twice standing up*. You wrote the story with little adornment, and it seemed fitting to give it a title inspired by the girl herself.

Again, as at Viele Pond, you and West were under the same roof, making it simple for evening rambles through the streets, and again, as before the cabin stove, names would charge the air, carbonate your blood, and make you unaware that your feet touched the ground. And how you longed to be one of those names (Dos and Scott and Joyce and James), how you soared at the thought of that transcendent day! The story, would not the story light the way? At times, you scarcely knew where you were or what West was saying. You saw window displays, and cars and people passed, and music could be heard, but all sound seemed filtered and all motion screened, and it was almost as if you were flying without wings.

It was on one such flight that you came to grief. You and West had just finished dining at a Broadway restaurant, and preceding you toward the cashier's booth, he half-turned his head to speak over his shoulder, and he said, *Williams thinks we have too much sex in the first issue. Your story's out . . .*

"*What a way to tell you!*" she said. "*What did you do, Johnny? What did you say?*"

"*Nothing.*"

"*You just paid the cashier and walked away—is that it?*"

"*Up at Viele Pond, disappointment kept me quiet. This time, it was as if I'd lost the power of speech.*"

"*You could still think, though! What did you think of a stunt like that?*"

"*Oddly enough, I didn't think about it at all. I thought about something else, something from one of those tours of the city in the dark.*" *You paused, and the past replayed itself for you.* "*It was late,*" *you said,* "*and we were heading back toward the Sutton across 57th Street—why do I remember that we were between 5th Avenue and 6th?—when a woman came from a doorway and made a play for West. He stopped, and I went on for a few paces, waiting for him to thank her and say, 'Not tonight.' But he stood there listening to her as if they were settling on a price and place. In the end, this is what I heard from him, and I can hear it yet: 'What's that on your lip—a chancre?'*"

"*I told you he was a cruel guy . . .*"

Imwritingabook, he'd said, Imwritingabook, and the four words as always returned as one. Because of them, you too had written a book, and the book had brought you to Maggie. But you and West weren't friends; you weren't even friendly.

156

The Businessman

Business was his whole life.
—Paul Mellon

Carnegie ran up steel in sheets and steel in bars, Frick's lick was cooking coke, and cars one-a-minute were born of Ford, but all Mellon ever made was money. A mortal slew of it, true enough, numbers that grew greater by the year, and before long, it was wrong to call him a man of money merely, for clearly he was a financier. *They that will be rich*, said a different Paul, *fall into temptation and a snare*, but the apostle notwithstanding, Mellon fell into nothing of the kind: he simply kept on making money.

Grant him this, that he had the nose for it: no matter where it lay or how well hidden, its whiff wound up in his smeller. Let it be in a sock or a pocket or buried in a cellar floor, let it be a store of the stuff or a fistful of change, let it be only the vaporous prospect of money— whither or whatever, it was found by the Mellon nose. He'd come into this life with a single sense, it seemed, but time would show that he had no need for the rest. That sensitive snout of his could snuff a seam of coal half a mile beneath him; nor did it miss the nether world of crude. It could even scent the future, the event about to happen, thus giving him the opportunity to be a buyer at the bottom dollar and a seller at the top. Pittsburgh was stiff with his sort, but he ended up with most of the nickels, and it was his dowser of a nose that did the trick.

What field had it not gotten into, what lode, what stash, what El Dorado had it failed to smell out? It was everywhere, and with the Mellon flair, it always led to another something that added to the Mellon mound of cash. Coal and gas and Carborundum were some of those somethings, and so were lumber and glass, and so too trolley lines and real estate and rails, and not to be ignored were shipyards and power and Pullman, and mention must be made of aluminum and a bounding main of oil that went by the name of Gulf. *He that would be rich*, said Paul to his colleague Timothy, *he that would be rich* . . .

Why, having sucked up so much, was he compelled to tuck in still more? No animal fed beyond satiety, and Mellon, sated, tried to stop, but money had grown independent of his will, and though he'd had his fill of it, he wasn't suffered to stop. Already there were billions—billions!—in the Mellon treasury: there were shares of stock and stacks of gold; there were securities, patents, titles, and rights-of-way; there were Raphaels and Titians and, rarer than these, van Eycks; there were strings of horses and strings of homes and an oceangoing yacht manned by a crew of thirty-two. Early had he sought to get rid of his hoard. Vast sums were passed along to universities, to institutes for research, to charities by the score, and he funded this and that foundation, and he built a national gallery for others' art and his. But, alas, the more he gave, the less he paid in taxes, and he found himself the richer for trying to give riches away. At a stage he'd scarcely been aware of, his money had acquired a life of its own, along with the power to reproduce, and its golden eggs of income, unwanted and beyond enumeration, were laid at his door. It was oviparous, and he could not shut it off.

His photographs reveal a lonely man, one of the loneliest and, for all his chattels, a sad one too, repressed — *com*pressed, rather, by the weight of what he owned. He spoke little, it's said, and that little softly, as though subdued by his heavy estate — his banks, his bonds, his rolling stock and locomotives — by the things that now owned their possessor. Wherever found, he seems to be there for but a while, ill at ease and awaiting the shutter's blink. Only when he's smoking one of those slender twists of tobacco that he orders by the thousand, only then does he seem free of his burden, at home for once and there to stay.

He'll not stay forever, though, for the pitfall bespoken by the apostle — Death — is real after all.

Business was his whole life.

DAVID GREENGLASS, 1922–

aka Little Doovey

I was the dunce of the family, everyone said, a blockhead at school and a fool at everything else. I was no good with numbers and worse with machines, and when jobs came my way, they were lowly, menial, only a step above mopping floors and rubbing brass. But whether it was demeaning or not, I couldn't even do the donkey work I got, and I took to shirking, calling in sick, or just plain quitting. Having no money, I'd kill time roaming the streets or sitting on the docks, staring at the tugs and ferries, at a river that looked like sewage, at nothing—goddamn it, sometimes I'd stare at nothing!

Only one person was ever good to me—my sister, Ethel. She was seven years old when I was born, and she looked after me like I was a special kind of doll, a doll that had to be fed real food, bathed, played with, put to bed—and I soon knew her voice better than I knew my mother's. It was musical enough when she was only talking to me or telling me stories, but when she sang—*Shema Yisroel*, I was hearing an angel, and I loved her, I loved her! In time, I came to know that I was hearing arias from operas, and the one that I'll remember till I die was Cho-Cho-San's from *Madame Butterfly*.

When my schooldays began, Ethel helped me with my homework (it was always over my head), and later on, after I'd flunked every course at Polytech and gone to work, she coached me on how to behave, on what to wear, on what to say and what not to. None of it did much good, though: I was still the family bonehead. Then, *schlecht*, Ethel met and married an electrical engineer named Julius Rosenberg, and things got worse for me at once. He was a college man, and he made no bones about looking down on me like I was something he'd stepped in by accident—dog shit. He never tried to hide what he thought of me, and Ethel, being caught in the middle, tried to keep things smooth, even going so far as to get Julius to take me into his company. Me being a bungler, it didn't pan out, especially when he shamed me by putting a supervisor over my work. I hated the sight of him, the snotty son-of-a-bitch.

Along came the war, and the next thing I knew I was in the army, and account of me once being around electrical stuff, I was sent out west to a place near Santa Fe called Los Alamos. It was up around seven thousand feet, and at that altitude I must've gotten even dumber than usual, because when I laid hold of some secret information, I passed it along to Julius—or maybe, knowing him to be a Commie, I meant to get him in Dutch.

Which I sure did, but I got in just as deep, and we were both arrested and charged with treason, and so was Ethel. A conviction would've got me the death penalty, and when the government offered me a deal—a prison term if I testified against the others—I took it. I was a dumb-bell, all right, just like the family said, but I wasn't dumb enough to die for a prideful prick like Julius. Of course, I also had to testify against Ethel, but that was part of the deal, and she went to the electric chair with her electrical engineer. Someone reported that she sang *Un bel di* one day in her cell, and that the jailers applauded. Well, why not? She had a beautiful voice.

Juanito y Evita

We must be tyrants to make the people freer.
— Juan Perón

Without fanaticism, one cannot accomplish anything.
— Eva Perón

It didn't look like she'd ever amount to much or that much would ever come her way. Being the fourth daughter of an unmarried mother in a dirt-street pueblo far out on the pampas, she didn't promise to get where — name of God! — she finally got. Her features were only passable, and her figure was only fair, but what made her quite dreary was a mediocre brain. Sallow, sullen, plain, and cheerless, she seemed headed for *nada* there in the dead-end dust of nowhere. She, rise to the top! She, become First Lady of Argentina! To believe that, one would have to be *loco de remate*.

She wouldn't've believed it herself. Her notion, born of a three-line role in a school play, was an acting career — a slim chance at best — but when she fell in with a touring singer named Magaldi, she took the chance and ran off with him to Buenos Aires. On the way, he taught her to tango — which is to say, she lost her cherry. At the time, she was fifteen years of age.

Countrified, badly dressed, and so lacking in talent that she was laughed at, she had to beg for parts, bits that paid only a pittance. Always short of rent and food-money, she pieced out a living by taking on lovers, one of these a screen actor. Through him, jobs became somewhat easier to find, but while no longer faced with hunger and eviction, she had to face a fact no less painful — that she was not, nor ever would be, a great actress; that in truth she was no actress at all. She didn't know, no one knew, that greatness awaited her on a different kind of stage. Ill-favored and still almost anonymous, she was a driver, that little *muchacha*, and she had a will hard enough to cut marble — but how could she have known what lay in store? How could anyone?

Juan Domingo got off to a better start; it saw him through military college and into the soldiering profession, but by middle age, he'd risen only to the rank of colonel. He was not without ability, though: known in his younger days as a rough-and-tumble fighter and later as a bang-up horseman and a crack shot, he owned a flow of plausible talk, a smile ever at the ready, an eye for the girls, and, most important, the air he seemed to wear—that of being a comer. All the same, he had yet to arrive, and had he not met Evita, he might still have been coming at the age of forty-five.

They were two chemicals, that pair, each inert until exposed to the other, and then—bang! An hour after their meeting, she was under him in bed, she twenty-and-some and he quite twice her years—and for Argentina, there and then began the Perón decade. It's too much, of course, to suppose that they laid out a plan while lying front-to-front that night, but what they were doing was hardly a novelty for either of them, and at moments their minds may have drifted to what they cared for more deeply than working up a sweat face-to-face: *power!* If so, they must've known that power would elude them unless they had a base. Juan could fetch the colonels, true, but colonels without an army were simply custom-made uniforms. The army had to come from the multitudes, from the poor, from the wretched nobodies too untutored to serve themselves—and there, just there, was the base that the coupling couple needed—the poor, too numerous to be numbered!

Juan had been heard to say, and he never denied it, that Mussolini was the greatest man of the century, and what he proposed to Evita (after some grunting junction) was the use of Il Duce's methods while avoiding his mistakes. He'd begin by being a champion of the many against the few, by pretending, as Benito had done, to be a *uomo del popolo*, a righter of wrongs, a lover of the lowly and the least, and to his flag would flock the ragged, the ill-used, the spat-upon—the mighty regiments of the despised. Your masters, he'd tell them, your masters dwell in frescoed halls and you in stalls of cardboard and tin, they underpay you for overwork, and they kick you out when you're old or sick—they kick you out when you *kick!* Death to that! he'd roar at the floor of faces in the public squares. Death to those who would keep all, for they will lose all! And as for Benito, the greatest man of the century, the people would fly to pledge him their souls and lives. *Pey-ron!* they'd cry, *Pey-ron!*—and, enraptured, they'd gladly wear their chains.

But lacking Evita, Juanito would've been gasconade and bombast. Better than he, she knew the futility of a helping hand that held no gift. Rant would fill the plazas, yes, but it was shirts that needed filling—

and for the *muchacha* from the sticks, that was no trick at all. Being the *muchacha* of The Power now, she made the rich pitch in and pay for her bounty, which was measureless—and wherefore not, when what she gave she got from others? She built schools and hospitals for the people; she doubled their wages and halved their hours, she commanded paid vacations for them and built them resorts where they could disport themselves for beans—but best of all, she provided homes for bottom-dog families that had lived their lives thus far in a room!

For her largesse, she asked but little in return—their love, if they would give it . . . oh, and membership in the Confederación General del Trabajos. Their love they gave as they'd've given their blood, and with tears of joy, they rushed to join the union. They couldn't've known it, but save for pissing, that would be their last free act in the Perón decade. Unwittingly, they'd made themselves slaves, and as long as they kept their traps shut and did as told, as long as they saw and heard and spoke no evil—in short, as long as they refrained from thinking, they were allowed to keep on pissing. A strike, and they were dead—worse, alive in some forgotten hole and buried to the neck in lime. *We must be tyrants to make the people freer.*

In the Perón years, only the tyrants were free, and those who thought otherwise disappeared without a trace. Sure as God, the workers weren't free, nor were the members of the Fourth Estate, who, when they printed the truth, ate the type—roman, italic, and bold. And the rich, neither were they free, nor their riches: whatever they owned (roughly, all of Argentina) was subject to repeated assessment, and to cover Evita's giveaways, they smiled with cold teeth and coughed up part of their plunder. Well did they bear in mind what Juan had proclaimed: *He who seeks to keep all . . .*

The people, bemused by their new condition, dazzled by the gilt they took for gold, drowned in Evita's benevolence, cheered her every word and move, even if she'd done no more than belch or blow her nose. They were spellbound by the blonde *chiquita*, quite as if in the presence of a being touched by Heaven—and indeed many were moved to pray that she be sainted while living.

If she merited sainthood, so did every other who painted her face and looked out a window. Behind her show of love for the *descamisados* smoked a hatred for those who'd taken her lightly—the great ladies of the *estancias* and the high-toned snots of the Avenida Alvear. No slight was too small to be resented, no sneer or snub or ridicule, and being vindictive out of all reason, she forgave and forgot never. She used her station to punish—say, rather, persecute—all who'd been rash enough to decry her, omit her from a guest list, deny what she thought her due as the consort of Perón. She bore herself as one already consecrated; in her mind, she *was* Santa Evita.

She was Paris-gowned now, sheened in sables and encrusted with diamonds, but for all her adornment, for all her acclaim and circumstance, she was still at heart what she'd been at the start—the natural child of a come-together out in the Argentine tules. She still had no taste, no good judgment, no understanding of what was seemly and what was not, and therefore she compounded error and made it boundless. When mingling with the shirtless ones, her beloved sons of toil, she always flashed her finery (*They desire to see me so*, she prated), but she was singularly vague about the money (the tribute) she exacted in their name. Some of it went to them, certainly, and certainly some to her and Juan—not much, though, barely a hundred million.

And what of Juanito the while? What was he up to as Evita praised him to the skies? Was he out on some balcony, a Benito sticking his chin into the air, or was he aboard a teen-age *moza* and sticking his you-know-what into you-know-where? But whichever, it would've made no difference: he and Evita were running Argentina like a set of toy trains.

But all reigns end, and after a high-flying decade, so did theirs. Evita's early death may have been one of the causes, for without her to inflate him, he was a dwindling balloon. Another may have been that he ignored the people in his passion for unripe fruit—the *muchachas*. Chided for taking up with a thirteen-year-old soon after Evita was gone, he shrugged and said *I'm not superstitious*. They didn't hang him upside down, as *il popolo* did with Il Duce: they simply drove him out of Argentina.

Long later, he came back to die, a jazzed-out old soldier whose only shots had been fired in bed. Can it be believed that there were still enough half-wits to elect him president? Well, there were, and they did.

The Journey of Death

Batter my heart, three person'd God.
—John Donne

Among the Jews, the saying goes, it's the old men who are beautiful, but this blue-eyed youth put age to shame. How young he was when the photo was taken—twenty at most!—and with that unblown look (girlish, some might call it, virginal), he seems to be sounding the unknown days ahead; and though his longing is for the distant, it's hard to tell whether his gaze is out or in or both ways at once. His features each are fine, and finer still the face that combines them to form an oval of astonishing appeal. Among the Jews, the saying goes.

He was more, though, than pleasing to the eye: he was bright, and more too than bright—he was brilliant. Of late, he'd applied for admission to Cambridge University, and by way of qualification, he'd listed credits for courses in the calculus of probabilities; courses in heat, hydrodynamics, Bessel's function, ellipsoidal harmonics, and Legendre polynomials; courses in statistical mechanics and the quantum theory; courses in linear differential equations and the mathematical theory of relativity. He was admitted.

You and he had been born only months apart and within a mile of each other, but it was a far cry between your minds, farther than time could embrace or space express. Brilliant, you'd said of him, but he was more, even, than brilliant: he was aglow and glittering, like a city seen from the air at night. His readings, his studies and literary taste, his poetic correspondence, and, at twenty, his comprehension!—all such, had you sought to match him . . . but never could you have matched him, not on your best day and not on his worst.

Had he been good at games, you wonder, could he run, could he skate, could he swim the crawl, could he call the make of passing cars? Could he dance, you wonder, could he shoot an agate, name the ballplayers, speak of favorite movie stars? Did he follow the funnies, did he sleigh-ride the hills of Central Park, did he daydream of girls and fiddle with himself in the dark . . . ?

Early, he may not have foreseen where his interests were taking him. He may have supposed them abstract, theoretical, quite apart from useful application. If so, it was one of the few shortsighted moments in his life. From the start, from the rock-collecting years of his childhood, he was being borne toward the Jornada del Muerto, a well-named sink

164

in the gypsum sands of New Mexico—the Journey of Death. There were three hundred square miles of that whiteness, a whiteness worn even by its reptiles and insects; it was an unspoiled place when the pretty boy arrived, a place of immemorial purity. It was not quite so pure when he left it, and he lived to rue the day: he'd known sin, he said, knowledge that could never be lost, and all his life he rued the day. What had happened there at Trinity? What had cost him his pristine look?

What had he done when classes were over and the halls were dimmed; where had he gone when he closed his books and turned off his mind? Had he walked the streets and threaded the crowds; had he shopped the lighted windows, read the signs written on the sky, seen any of the many faces as they were going by? Had he heard chance phrases, laughter, bells, a fire engine siren that made him think of the Doppler effect? Could he turn off his mind . . . ?

From two hundred miles away, from the mountains north of Santa Fe, a device had been brought by men of science who'd sought for years to perfect it—and here in this white wilderness, it was to be put to the test at last. Few were sure that it would pass, fewer still what would happen if it did. Nothing might happen—a small flash or no flash at all, no smell of smoke, no sound save scientific sighing for fruitless years. Or something of unimaginable magnitude might happen, an event so stupendous as to rival the Beginning: the End of the world.

Wherefore had he been the rare one; what had made him take his own tack and wind up on the heights far above a pack composed of such as you? At what age had he begun to quit the paltry entertainments of the common run—the clambakes, the carnivals, the jamborees? When had he parted company with high jinks and practical jokes; when with idling on a beach or at the meeting of a pair of streets? Or is there no way of knowing how or when or why he rose beyond your reach . . . ?

There among the gypsum dunes of New Mexico, the device, the creation of the scientificos, was to be put to the proof. It was a bomb constructed of materials never before used, and a million hours of thought and another million of work and worry would be justified only if it exploded as hoped for by all, among them the fine-featured, the pretty-boy Jew. As the time for the trial drew near, he must've been torn between the fear of failure and the equal fear of success; either, if realized, would result in loss. He'd given a share of his life to the project—given all, indeed, for had he not from the outset been heading for these sands? Success would validate that life; failure would punch it void. Success would make worthwhile the preparatory years, the meditations on the not-yet-dwelt-on, the conjecture about the not-yet-known. Still, in those final moments before Trinity, it must've come to him that success would be the greater failure. He and his fellows would be lauded, garlanded, and recorded in the chronicles of the age, but inscribed there too would be the outcome of their triumph—the killing of a numberless number called The Enemy, anonymous and remote, beaten, it was said, dead on their feet and ready to fall.

Now, with only seconds remaining, he found that he could hardly breathe, hardly support himself, and clutching a post in the bunker that shielded his team, he stared away at no one and nothing, his bloodstream slow, his heart at speed, his brain at a halt. And then the critical instant came, and ten thousand yards away, there was a sky-high flash that could've been seen from the moon, and whyfor not when the generated light equaled that of twenty suns? Heat ionized the air, dyeing blue and orange a cloud that grew to a height of forty thousand feet from a vast crater of fused and sea-green sand. Within its span, all things had died—flora, sidewinders, squirrels, birds, insects of every size and kind. In the bunker, the professionals, behaving like novices, stood stupefied or spastic in the presence of what they, not God, had wrought.

The pretty boy—was he at a standstill yet, or had he joined in the slapping of backs and the mutual praise? Was he, like many, dancing a jig, hugging himself or others, longing for a swig—or, his body still moored to the post, had his mind set sail for Japan . . . ?

He was a onesuch and marvelously gifted (he'd taught himself Sanskrit for his private amusement), but was he visionary enough to think beyond thought and see beyond sight? Could he dream up twenty rising suns and the cinders of three hundred thousand students, nurses, shopkeepers, cab-drivers, children at play in the streets? Even for him, how impossible to imagine charcoal passengers still seated in trolleys that would never arrive! And however oracular, could he have foretold the drowned so numerous as to impede a stream?

And yet, it may have been that he *could* see without beholding; that he perceived himself to be there, standing amid ruination. Given his sensibility, maybe he was able to penetrate the future and witness a woman wandering to nowhere with her headless child; maybe for him a madman sang and danced. And if those things, why not these?—corpses lying with upraised hands, as though pleading, faces with fried-away features, a fetus dangling from a riven mother, skin hanging in strips like loosened wallpaper, a fall of black rain, entrails, skulls, bits of brain. *Everywhere*, Dr. Takashi Nagai would one day write, *everywhere the sweet smell of young bodies burning*—and the pretty boy may have breathed it from afar. An odd conceit—that he, as one of those who'd fashioned the bomb, might be one of those it fell upon; odd that he might so intimately foresee its cataclysmic effect. Odd that in the instant of the Trinity explosion, he might've projected himself into the undoing to come, wandered the scree of brick and bone, smelled the stench of blood, pus, and emptied guts, *of young bodies burning*. And if thus far, why not farther? Why not to the living who'd die of damage to the lymph glands, of skin cancer and malignant tumors, of trauma and malignant grief? And why not to the living who'd live with blindness, low sperm counts, deformed and microcephalic children, with atrophying kidneys, cataracts, dysentery, sterility? Farther, even, to baked arms extended as if to be thrown away, to a man holding an eyeball in the palm of his hand, to a woman carrying a girl's head in a bucket, to a wall scorched with a human shadow, the last trace of him who'd cast it. Farther, then, to a pair of citywide junkyards, where tiles and tools and bent rail rest, and wire too, and wheels, skulls, and horses, and unidentifiable machines; yes, and farther still, to the forecourt of a cathedral, where the head of a beheaded saint lies amid the trash.

In body, of course, he'd never left Trinity, and few knew better than he that fallout had been heavy on much of New Mexico, and he knew, therefore, that the same was due to happen to Japan. Devices, bombs would be dropped over Hiroshima (would it be?) and Nagasaki, and the clouds they formed would be dispersed by the winds and their particles carried far, and children would gather flowers dusted with plutonium and Strontium-90 and inhale their fragrance along with their pollen of death.

In body, he was still in New Mexico. In mind, he may have fared to places where shock had suppressed the power of speech, where multitudes drifted in silence among shreds and fragments, odds and ends that had once been parts of people and things. *The blue mountains are immovable,* Dr. Nagai would one day write, *and the white clouds come and go*—but it would be long before the cicadas sang again in the camphor trees.

When the Ethical Culture boy (and Harvard, Cambridge, and Göttingen too) was shown photos of burns, maggots in festering flesh, a child sucking at a dead mother's tit, of instant mummification (legs caught in the act of running)—when he scanned those indictments, did he too yearn to run, not from manufactured fate, but from himself, from guilt, and did he know he'd never lose it, no matter how fast or far he ran . . . ?

167

bare of Men

... for they will deliver you up to the councils.
  —Matthew 10:17

They were brother Jews, he and Oppenheimer, but even as in the Scriptures, he delivered up his brother to be scourged—for which he was afterward shunned in public places, his hand was refused, and once friendly faces were turned away. The chill went bone-deep within him, and many a bodily ill fed on the anguish he was made to endure. To the eye, though, save for his seat below the salt, he was still what he'd always been—one of the wonders of the age.

Born to accomplished parents, he was thought to be retarded for his failure to speak until he was four, but once he started—oh God!—he was hard to stop—and he spoke, mind, not in monosyllabic simplicity but in sentences grammatical and compound. Very early under the spell of numbers, he did tricks with them in his head, and he was deep in the dazzle of mathematics, toying with its abstractions, while classmates were still baffled by long division. So facile was he at the piano that his family foresaw a life for him on the concert stage, and witness for good measure his mastery of the game of chess. Far from being retarded, then, he was most marvelously advanced.

The young Oppenheimer was quite as brilliant, nor did his lustre diminish with age: he was always a match for the bright Hungarian. Politically, though, the difference between them was vast. Teller had been a boy in the Budapest of Bela Kun, and then and there had Communism become odious to him, and ever further with time did the aversion deepen. In contrast, Oppenheimer was perfectly at ease with the system, and though never a Party member himself, he was constantly in the company of those who were—and wherefore not, when his wife was one of them?

Sooner or later, the two men were bound to collide, and when they did, each would bring about his own kind of ruin.

It was the issue of the H-bomb that found them in open dispute: Teller was on fire for its immediate development, and Oppenheimer was equally ardent against it, positions surely dictated by their antipodal attitudes toward the Soviet Union. Each believed he was in the right on the issue, but one was imbued by hatred and the other by horror: one had recoiled from the part he'd played in the building of the A-bomb;

168

the other, well knowing its catastrophic effect, burned to produce one with a thousand times the power.

The advisory committee, of which Oppenheimer was a member, reported to the secretary of state that *We think it wrong on fundamental ethical principles to initiate the development of such a weapon. No limit exists to its destructiveness.* Teller didn't care spit about how destructive the H-bomb would be; in fact, the more so the better, since it was meant for the Enemy, satanic and abhorrent. Most of the leading physicists felt as Oppenheimer did, that it would provoke the Soviet Union to an effort to surpass it, which in turn would provoke the United States, with never an end to provocation until one used the bomb to prevent its use by the other. Already Oppenheimer had blood on his hands (the ash of blood), and all his life would he think of them as soiled things he was doomed to die with. Before the hawks were through with him, he'd be soiled all over.

In a paper to President Truman, Lewis Strauss, a financier friend of Teller, said that *A government of atheists* (meaning you-know-who) *is not likely to be dissuaded from producing the weapon on moral grounds*— whereupon Truman ordered the God-fearing to proceed. Proceed, he told Teller and his supporters, moralists all—proceed, he said, and to hell with right and wrong. The Hungarian was overjoyed, and so was all of Wall Street, from the churchyard to the river.

Soon thereafter, they were even more so. On Elujelab, an island in the Eniwetok atoll, an H-bomb was tested. The island disappeared.

Oppenheimer, physicist though he notably was, had never confined himself to the study of inanimate matter in motion; he was concerned as well with the peregrination of man. Man was matter too, and man too was in motion, having come from his obscure beginning, when his numbers were few and there was room for all, to a stage where there were many and their share of the planet small, barely enough for their lying down and rising up, for living out their instant and quietly dying.

For the multitudes, peace and plenty had long been rare; until Lenin spoke at Smolny, they'd known little but want and war. But now, in that realm of tyrants, priests, and ignorance, a call had come for a new order, and a new order arose—and to Oppenheimer, it seemed to promise a future far better than the past.

He gave it his endorsement—with a susceptible nature, how could he not?—and he gave it money as well, and he espoused its causes, entertained its members, and openly voiced his sympathetic views. All the while, though, even during his tenure at Los Alamos, he'd been under surveillance by Guardians of Loyalty, but only after a decade of scrutiny was he called before the Security Board of the Atomic Energy Commission and questioned about his conduct. Sad to relate, he made statements at variance with statements made earlier, and when asked why he'd lied, he said, "I was an idiot." Lie he did, and idiot he was, but nothing was shown against him, because nothing *could've* been shown save his vulnerable heart.

And now the Hungarian was summoned as a witness:

Q.: Dr. Teller, do you want to be here?
A.: I would have preferred not to appear.
Q.: Do you intend that your testimony suggests that Dr. Oppenheimer was disloyal to the United States?
A.: I know Oppenheimer as an intellectually alert and complicated person, and it would be presumptuous if I tried to analyze his motives. But I have always assumed that he is loyal to the United States.
Q.: Do you believe Oppenheimer is a security risk?
A.: I have seen Dr. Oppenheimer act in a way which was confused and complicated. I would like to see the vital interests of this country in hands which I understand better and therefore trust more. I would feel more secure if public matters would rest in other hands. . . .

That response led to the revocation of Oppenheimer's security clearance, thereby putting an end to his public career. Verily, even as in the Gospel, the brother shall deliver up the brother to the Councils.

Not even after twenty years did the Hungarian understand that he'd been the deemster of Oppenheimer's doom. Nine out of ten of his colleagues scorned him, exiled him from their good graces, thought him a Judas. But unlike Judas, he'd taken no silver, nor did his bowels gush out on the field of blood. Rejection anguished him, but he didn't understand what he'd done.

And yet, how could he not have understood? Had he become dim-witted and dense, he who spoke so well in tongues and numbers; was he a stranger to the political world and stranger still to the scientific? Was he ill at ease with the cosmology of Einstein, the nature and composition of light, the mechanical effects of radiation? Was he confused by the quantum theory and the laws of thermodynamics; had he grown foreign to differential equations, had he forgotten—had he never known?—the eighty-eight keys of the piano and the sixty-four squares of chess?

Nay. The Hungarian understood right well. He'd done only what he'd intended to do—deliver up his brother—and the damnation that followed lies at his door, and it'll be there still when he dies.

PAUL ROBESON, 1898-1976

The Moor of Princeton

Among white men, I am always lonely.
—Paul Robeson

There were some who may have thought that he'd known bygone times and places and brought traces along in his bone and blood; he lived, they may have fancied, as one who'd lived before, and he'd never be at ease in these subsequent days. How could he have been otherwise than lonely among the whites, they may have asked; how, coming from this myth or that legend, how could he not have been a one-and-only in the sycamored streets of Princeton?

Born there in the parsonage of his father's church on Witherspoon (African Lane, it was called), he'd wander off as soon as he learned to walk, stray across the way to the graveyard where Burr lay and Grover Cleveland, range the fields that saw the bobtails beat the British, ford the dust or slush in the turnpike, and stand there staring at the closed enclosure of Princeton. He'd see the Dean's house and its cast-iron porch, its keyed lintels, its windows of twenty-four lights, and he'd see grass he'd never tread and paths that led to heights for the white-skinned only. How could he not have been lonely there under the catalpas, the chestnut trees of Princeton?

From where he was then, on the outsider's side of Princeton, he'd see his life to come as though it were one that he'd spent before, and having lived it once, he'd wonder why he had to live it again. He'd know that nothing would change; standing on the townie side of the road; he'd know that no pain would be remitted and no spear withheld, nor would the sponge this time be sweet; engraved in snow and grown in ivy, what was on the way could be clearly read—another round of the same.

He'd see his blind mother burn and die when a coal ignited her dress (calico, poplin, gingham, which?), and his father would lose his pulpit (why?) and fall to hauling ashes for the rich—he'd see these things of his coming life as if they'd happened in an earlier life. He'd see the towns he'd one day live in, and he'd see their several byways—Jackson, Quarry, Green—each another African Lane, and therefore, no matter where he was, he'd still be in Princeton, he'd never be quit of Princeton.

He'd be allowed to school at Rutgers, though bright enough for better, and there he'd excel at games as well as studies, but he'd never dwell within the walls, never make a white friend, never dine in the dining halls, never attend a dance: he'd bed and board in Jigtown and jig there with his own. Four years would he spend on the banks of the Raritan, but halfway to the end, when his father died, he'd have to wait on tables to meet his fees; he'd have to tend furnace and rake leaves shed by the campus trees. It all lay ahead because it all lay behind him, and he could see it from where he stood beside the Princeton road.

There in the dust of Princeton, in Princeton snow and rain, he'd see the years of the Great War, and through its smoke, he'd see blacks fight a foreign enemy hard to tell from the enemy at home—there it was, that war, on the gates of Blair, on the blocks of Stuart Hall. And he'd see beyond the war to the summer of 1919, when blacks were killed for swimming in Lake Michigan, for stepping on a white woman's foot, for *looking* at a white woman's foot! From some corner on Nassau Street, one by one he'd see them die, shot for nothing in Knoxville, lynched for less in Tulsa, gelded for fun in Omaha. He'd see it all from a Princeton roadside.

He was only a boy then, tall, skinny, and quiet, a black boy staring, it seemed, at vacant space, but in truth he saw much from his place beside the pike that led to Trenton: he saw the future foretold by the past. Over the rolling hill and dale, over Stony Brook, and farther over Jersey, he saw the come-and-go of his allotted life. He saw days and nights and crowded ways, he an integer in the traffic, and in passing, he'd hear someone say, *That's Paul*, and others, knowing which Paul was meant, would be glad that their skin too was black.

You could've been in one of those crowds, and at some curb or crossing, you and he might've passed within each other's reach; or, stopping to peer at a window display, you might've been near a black giant doing the same; or, in countercurrents along the sidewalk, you and he might've brushed sleeves, two worlds so lightly grazing that neither was aware of the touch—and if you heard someone say, *That's Paul*, you'd not have turned to look, for no Paul you knew was black.

He'd know you, though: he'd seen you and your kind from a road-side in the borough of Princeton. He'd seen the hardened mass that you were part of and lived his lifelong anguish in advance. He'd shake you with his temblor voice; he'd play for you in convict stripes, imperial frogging, and a purple doublet; he'd rumble of a river just rollin' along—and he'd be extolled for his roles but refused for his race. He'd seen it all from Princeton.

Drawn to Spain, he'd entertain a ragtag of noble nobodies come from afar to fight a war to forestall the war in the making. Many would die there, among them a share of blacks, and though he said this to the rest, *The people are a powerful source of power,* he'd know that when they got back to Baton Rouge and Memphis, they'd still be unable to sass a white or piss in the Mississippi.

He'd hear of a country where the power of the people *had* wrought a change, and he'd go to that country, go more than once, and his welcome there would be warmer than any he'd known at home, but it would come long too late to lessen a loneliness imposed now from within. Well received, he'd still be a black among whites, and he'd still be lonely, wherefore back he'd come to the country he still thought of as home, all the while knowing that he was homeless.

All the same, he'd keep insisting on the power of the people, and he'd thus inflame the jingoes, the Klan, the Church, and, sad to say, many and many a black. He'd pay a price for his views. He'd be cried against, vilified, caricatured, hanged in effigy, denied the use of private forums and public air. He'd be suppressed by the press, condemned in sermon and sermonette, and cut by timorous one-time friends. He'd be maligned and misquoted, he'd be scorned and shunned, but being a monumental whipping boy, he'd be denied a passport in order to keep him handy. It would be issued after awhile, but not before breaking a heart that had begun to go at Princeton.

Among white men, I am always lonely.

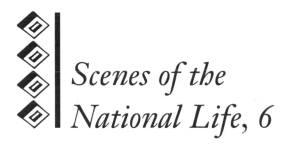

Scenes of the National Life, 6

Roy Cohn

Near the end of a base and impious life, he expressed a desire to see Israel, and in his dying days he went there. This Jew in name only, what did he seek in the Promised Land; what did he hope to find in its rare and sacred air? Did he think the evergreen Promise held good for him, he who'd betrayed the Jews even as Judas had betrayed The Man? Can he have been so fond, so far gone in fancy that he supposed himself one of the Chosen still?

J. Edgar Hoover

He had two faces, one that he wore for the Bureau and one that he sported at home, and never had their places changed. In the office, on Pennsylvania at 10th, he was the scourge of the wrongdoer, the stern and scowling chaser of Dirt, and relentless was he in pursuit. At home, though—ah, there did his other face appear, as when he shed his street-suit and slipped into that love of a frock, an off-white chiffon splashed with chrome yellow and lavender. Rather like the colors of a Japanese iris, he thought, as he sashayed before a glass.

But did he ever frightfully dream of forgetting himself, of turning up at the Bureau clad in silk and shod in shoes to match? Did he ever wake up sweating . . . ?

Lee Harvey Oswald

He did *what?*

His rifle was a bolt-action Mannlicher-Carcano that he'd bought for twenty dollars from a mail-order house in Chicago. Firing a 6.5 mm. cartridge, it was inaccurate against a stationary target at any range. Against an object in motion two hundred yards distant, Deadeye Dick himself would've been hard put to get it off three times in less than six seconds—and score twice. Oswald, a mediocre shot, couldn't've hit a barn with it, not even from inside the barn.

Charles Lindbergh

Seventy-two years old when he died, he seems to have been alive only for a scant thirty-four hours, just long enough for the performance of a dazzling act at the age of twenty-five. It was the one such act in his life. He'd done nothing to foreshadow it; nor later, with chances galore, would he even try to match it. It was as if he knew that in a single spree of brilliance, he'd spent his store of splendor. Thereafter, though always in the air, he never really flew; he merely used up his years and stopped living. He'd had a one-act life.

A Person Named David Lang

When you drew up for a traffic light on Ventura Boulevard, you glanced past Maggie at a car that had stopped alongside her. Its driver was a man you recognized from a newspaper photo printed some months earlier during the hearings of the House Committee. There he'd given testimony as a cooperative witness—in short, as an informer.

Nudging Maggie, you said, "Have you ever seen that guy?"

She turned for a look and then turned back. "No," she said. "Why?"

Instead of replying, you spoke across her to the man in the nearby car, saying, "Hello, Dave."

"Hello yourself," the man said. "Am I supposed to know you?"

"I really do think so, Dave."

"I can't think of a reason."

"I can, you fink son-of-a-bitch! You gave our names to the Committee!"

The man stared, and then he said, "I'm glad I did!"

And now the traffic light changed, and he drove away.

Charlie Company

How come they don't like us?
    —a GI

—You could beat the living shit out of them, and they wouldn't tell you nothing. Only *Me no VC*, and that's all.

—I flang an old man down a well, and then I threw in a M16 grenade.

—A bunch of us caught a woman was out working in a field. We took turns raping her, and then we killed her. Also, we killed her baby.

—Some old women and little children was praying when we come along. We shot them all in the head.

—A troop carrier drove by with maybe twenty human ears tied to the antenna.

—A woman stuck her head out of some brush, and we shot her. You could see her bones flying in the air chip by chip.

—We shot everything in sight.

—I seen a GI chasing a duck with a knife.

—I seen another slaughter a cow with a bayonet.

—Two boys, they was maybe six-seven years old—a GI shot them both.

—A GI fired a rocket launcher at a water buffalo and hit it square in the head. He said, *You don't get to shoot water buffalos with a M79 every day.*

—Then another GI took the launcher and fired it into a bunker full of gooks.

—They wouldn't tell you nothing, those people.

—An officer grabbed a woman by the hair and shot her with a .45.

—A GI said, *Hey, I got me another one.*

—Another GI said, *Chalk one up for me.*

—A girl was laying there with a bullet in her belly. The captain went and emptied a clip into her.

—Loot Calley shot a two-year-old boy.

—We shot a slew of them dinks, and only a small child come out alive. Then somebody carefully shot him too.

—A couple GIs slashed a baby to death with their bayonets.

—Three GIs went at a woman all three at once. You know what I mean? Front, back, and in the mouth.

—By the time we broke for lunch, we must've knocked off maybe four-five hundred. It was a turkey shoot.

—No matter what you done to them, they wouldn't tell you nothing. *Me no VC*, and not another word.

—How come they don't like us?

A Sinner in the Hands of an Angry God

It says here, Jesse, that all your life you were mean for Jesus—which, I take it, is the lingo in Carolina for being an out-and-out Jesus-lover. If so, it's a point in your favor, because I happen to be partial to the boy myself. But, goddamn it, Jesse, it's the *only* point in your favor! I've gone through this resumé of yours twice over, and curse me if there's another decent thing in it to your credit. That's serious, Jesse, and for this reason: being mean for Jesus cuts no ice in this place unless you were also mean for what He stood for—and died for, I might add. He was mean for *people*, Jesse, *all* people, not just those lickpenny banker friends of yours. That's the kind you lackeyed for, and what it got you is enough bad points to wipe out your only good one. You're in big trouble, Jesse.

Like as not, you never heard of a Tarheel name of Jackson, Andy Jackson, who was born over in Waxhaw, only a hop and a skip from Monroe, where you hail from. You might've taken a page from his book to your sure advantage, because he was a different sort of hairpin from what you turned out to be—a kiss-ass for the money-changers. Andy never praised them up the way you did; he kicked the sons-of-bitches out of the temple. Talk about being mean for something! Now, He was purely mean—but you, Jesse, you were only mouth-mean, and it'll cost you dear.

Face it, Jesse, you never cared for people worth a sneeze—and when I say people, I'm speaking of ridge-runners and weed-benders, of rednecks, wool hats, and piss-poor punkin-rollers. For all your gas about being mean for Jesus, you were never mean for that kind—*His* kind. The helpless, the sick, the young and old, the ones that spoke an outlandish tongue—you never even knew they were there, because you have a cold eye, Jesse, and it goes with the cold heart that shows in all you ever said or did on earth. That doesn't recommend you for glory, if you want the god's honest truth.

I note that you were a lifelong member of the Southern Baptist Convention, a Calvinist sect with the curious notion that immersion washes away sin, as if sinners are simply soiled clothes: soak them, black with sin, and back they come, spotless lambs one and all. If that's what you believe, Jesse, you're due for a shock. Go in a sinner, and you come out a sinner, the same sorry snake, only now you're dripping wet.

You Baptists are pretty easy on yourselves—you take a dip in the drink, and—presto!—you're pure from top to toe. Well, it doesn't work like that, Jesse. You can't rinse away sin, you've got to *live* it away, and you were never so imbued by what I sent my Son to teach you. What did you do in your decades of power? Did you save the lost and heal the broken-hearted? Did you aid the weak or brighten the spirits of the meek? Did you make them welcome, warm the room they dwelt in, lighten the gloom?

I'm afraid not, Jesse. On the contrary, you burdened the heavy-laden still further, and you heard their lament faintly, as from afar. How could it have been otherwise? Your mind was on matters more pressing than those of the deprived, the beaten-down, the hopeless who'd hoped for so much from their servant—you! Time and again they sent you forth to bring rain to their withering lives, and time and again you failed them, forgot them in your concern for the pinch-fist peddlers you really serve. You never gave your goods to the poor, Jesse; you took their own away.

That won't pass you through these gates, Jesse, but it'll be more than enough for where I'm shipping you. Down there, you can talk your head off against abortion, labor unions, equal rights, and all the rest of your wrinkles; down there, everyone has wrinkles, and you won't be heard above their rant. It's time to say good-bye, Jesse, and you go with a warning: don't try to wash clean down there; the water's as dirty as you.

JOHN F. KENNEDY, 1917–63

That Old Gang of His

The dread finality of decision that confronts a Senator
facing an important call of the roll . . .
—*Profiles in Courage*

In reading his book, it might be better to forget his father's quarter of a billion bucks, to rid the mind of Harvard, of prep-school days at Choate (riding stables, eighteen tennis courts, and a minimum of Jews), to be blind to his continental tours, his cars and clothes and sailboats, and his sport in private seas. Suppose him a mister merely, someone you'd pass in the street, a common sort, really—in short, a cheaper cut of meat . . .

"Apart from all that big money behind him," Maggie said, "do you think you're any different?"

"F. Scott F. said the rich are different from you and me."

"From me, maybe, but not from you. You never worked for wages, and I did—at a candy counter in Woolworth's. You never walked a picket line, and you never saw the inside of a mill or a mine or a rank hotel. And like Jack, my dear Johnny, you took in the wonders of Paris, Rome, and Madrid. Where's the difference . . . ?"

He deplores the dread finality of casting the die, of voting aye or nay. Bleed, hearts! he seems to say, for eight brave senators who voted right, knowing that right was the wrong way to keep a Senate seat. That was his main gauge of courage, the risk a man ran of looming defeat, in daring the pain of repudiation, in betting the Capital's delights against the dimmer joys of home, fishing, and the writing of memoirs. That's all those paragons had to do to win Jack's praise—dice with their jobs and the honors of office.

What a rimption he made over little or nothing! How unafraid, his eight sayers of yea or nay, how undismayed! Behold the stiff upper lip and the bold gaze; note the air of rectitude, the noble bearing— all this as they kiss good-bye to their senatorial pay, their rights and immunities, their chairmanships, their postal privileges. Sad to say, he knew better. Seen against their fellows—time-servers and party hacks in the main, boozers and blowhards and wearers of someone's collar— of course the chosen eight shone, and how should they not, being bravest of the craven and the owned?

But the truly heroic, and well Jack knew it, had never sat in the Senate chamber: they weren't mean enough to be members of the Club. For his gallant band, he could've picked any Indian, any organizer, any black or Jew, any mick who'd fled the Famine, but instead he drew on what he found within the walls. Settling for the best of a bad lot, he culled the second-rate from the third-rate rest, and then, for nearly three hundred pages, he exalted mediocrity and worse.

The best of the bunch was J. Q. Adams, son of a president and himself a president-to-be, and the worst may have been L. Q. C. Lamar, a Confederate to the core and a believer in the Lost Cause long after the cause was lost. In between were the renegade Daniel Webster, who harangued the Senate in a three-hour speech favoring the return of fugitive slaves; and jack-of-all Sam Houston, clerk, teacher, lawyer, and c.-in-c. of the Texas army; and Thomas Benton, peculiar for decrying slavery while owning slaves; and Edmund Ross, who seems to have spoken but once (*Ross?*); and somewhere close to the top is George Norris; and hovering just above the bottom is Robert Taft.

But top or bottom or buried in the pack, which of the eight would've said, as John Brown did, *Had I so interfered in behalf of the rich?* Which, with Gene Debs, would've *dared* to say, *The master-class declares the wars; the subject-class fights the battles?* There were greats out there in the unforgiving world, but Jack didn't pick them for his pantheon: he let the world hang them or stow them away in jail. *The people are a powerful source of power,* Paul Robeson said, but the people, meaning people like Jack, vilified him and drove him from his own, his native land. And in Jack's backyard, there were two wops, one of whom said, *We no want fight by the gun;* and the other, *You will not fire on your own brothers just because they tell you to fire, no brothers* — for saying which they were shot full of voltage by the Lowells and the Cabots and their Cape Cod god. They failed to make Jack's list, and so did fat little Emma Goldman, who told Union Square crowds that a better life was theirs for the taking: she came too near all those Kennedy bucks, made him fear for his cars and clothes, his junkets and his flunkies, wherefore he didn't care that she was cried against, scorned, spat upon, denied a room to rest in, and slept instead in whorehouses and public toilets. He shunned that kind. He wasn't overcome by Martin Luther King, and how wise he was! He'd've cost himself a Pulitzer Prize . . .

"Why did you compare me with Kennedy?" you said.
"Oh, I just wanted to see what you'd say."

Das Kapital

black hole: an object, created by the implosion of a star, into which anything can fall and out of which nothing can escape.
—Kip Thorne, theoretical physicist

Nothing.

Nothing that enters the gravitational field of a black hole—other stars, spiral galaxies, white dwarfs, gas clouds, particles of dark matter, sound, *light!* even—nothing can free itself from the immeasurable power of a black hole, a power so great that it can bend time and turn space to foam. A human, if ever he were to be sucked in by its attractive force, would not simply sink from sight, as in a quicksand; he'd be expanded sideways and lengthwise until torn to shreds, and then, in a further expansion, the shreds would be further shredded, and then further still, always further, and in the end they'd become as finespun as smoke, and like smoke disappear.

But to find a black hole to fall into, why journey a vigintillion miles through space—why, when a striking likeness exists on Earth? True, it's microscopic by comparison, but having similar properties, it has a similar tendency—to feed on all that comes within its grasp. To the lofty, it's known as commerce, and to the less so, it's supply and demand (meaning they have the supply and others the demand), while to the least, it's merely good old-fashioned horse dealing. Whatever the name, though, it's only an alias for the legal way to steal: The System, the black hole of the world for all and sundry, for Tom, Dick, and Harry, for every man Jack. Drawn in, they're in forever. No one escapes; nothing escapes.

And, *hombres y mujeres*, it'll happen to you, and to you, *Menschen und Frauen*, and also, mister and madame, to you. In the gut of the glutton, you'll diminish day by day, your skills will spend, you'll be drunk dry, you'll age beyond your age, and when you've only your lives left to lose, you'll die as you lived, on the cheap. Doubt it not: once in the digestive system of The System, you'll be digested; you'll have been there only to have gone away.

You'll enjoy few of the pleasures of the few, but you'll bear more than your share of the pain. Theirs is the feast, and yours, more's the pity, is the smell. For paltry pay, you'll sell them your lives by the hour; you'll run their machines and peddle their wares; you'll delve in their ditches and swab their latrines; you'll take in the fumes in their mills and mines; and while you make do in soot-stained rooms, they'll swill wines from crystal flutes.

They'll soak you at the company store, but not a word will you say if you're wise, nor will you squawk when they speed up the line, and your only chance to piss is to piss in your pants. You'll bow to your landlord and scrape for your boss, and since the two are one and the same, you'll be fired for talking union and clubbed for walking picket with a sign, after which you'll be turned out of your dingy castle along with your regal trash—a worn-out wife, a sprung mattress, a pair of baby shoes, a blood-stained Teddy bear, and a chromo of Niagara Falls.

They won't let it go at that, though; you'll be locked out, Black-listed, enjoined, fined, hounded, and ridden out of town. And finally, when you can endure no more, you'll make common cause with fellow helots; you'll pitch into the scabs and goons and railway dicks; you'll be shot in the liver, the lights, and the head—shredded, it might be said— and you'll die as you lived, on the cheap. Dead as a smelt, and dead broke as well, you'll be buried only four feet deep.

Nothing escapes the Black Hole. No one escapes The System.

THE WATERGATE BREAK-IN, 17 JUNE 1972

A Man Named Frank Wills

burglar alarm (n.)—a device for automatically giving an
alarm in case of burglary, as on the opening of a window
— *Webster's International*

In essence, that's what Wills was—a device, a structure of elements so delicately poised as to produce a signal if in any way disturbed. Let a switch be tripped or a circuit broken, let a knob be turned, let a foot fall on a hidden button—and suddenly there's stunning sound and as-tounding light; and if the intruder stands where he is, he'll hear a hue and cry come ever nearer.

On that mid-June night, Wills, a young black employed as a secu-rity guard, was just such a contrivance. True, his nature was corporeal rather than inorganic; still, he would be held worthy of his hire only if flesh and blood performed as well as spring steel and copper wire, only if he became in fact the bell, the button, the spark that set the train afire.

On his two o'clock round of an upper floor, he caught sight of a door on which a strip of adhesive tape had been laid crosswise of the escutcheon, thus sealing the bolt within the lock. Had he been given to metaphor, he might've thought of the door as gagged, but he wasn't known for his flights of fancy, nor would he now be known at all had his response been other than electrical: he made a telephone call to the Washington police.

No one could have conceived that the call would lead to infamy for many; nor could any have deemed, least of all Wills, that for him it would lead to oblivion. Indeed, it would be as though the world had drunk of the Waters of Forgetfulness—not, however, in ignorance of their properties, but all too aware: it would dismiss him by design.

In the writings that touch those days, rare is the mention of his name, and where cited, it's cited but once—*Wills, Frank*, one may read, and history is quit of him. He was only twenty-four years old at the time (a likely sort, as once he'd've been advertised, learns quick, condition prime), yet for all the good he'd get out of life, it could've ended then and there, with that phone call to the police.

No sooner did he make it than he became an abomination—and no less to the righteous than to those about to fall from grace:

> we did not praise or decorate him,
> we did not raise his salary
> or give him a new uniform,
> a new flashlight,
> a gold-filled watch—
> we hated the sight of him,
> and we shunned him,
> hell,
> we expelled him from the human race.

Though his hand had been raised against no man knowingly, the hands of all were raised against him, and none would tell the why and wherefore. It was as if, like the son of Hagar, he'd been born into the world only to be excluded from it, and he spent his days trying to re-enter through doors that wouldn't open, that really weren't there; he wasted himself as in a hindrance-dream, striving ever and ever failing.

And so it might be said that his life *did* end with that phone-call. Once he'd sounded that alarm, he was dead. He'd become an informer, which was thought a virtuous thing against *you-know-who*, but not for Christ's sake *us*! That made him a witch, and he could not be suffered to live.

185

The Other President from Illinois

One eye on Heaven and one on the main chance.
— W. M. Thackeray

He could shade that, and he did: he kept *both* eyes on the main chance, and he succeeded beyond the realm he reached in dreams. He started low, what with a drunk for a father and a psalm-singing mother, but he meant to rise, and with his eyes (the pair) ever where desire drove them, he rose higher than mediocrity usually goes; nor was his repose uneasy for these words of Luke: *Woe unto you that are rich!*

Well built but largely vacant, he was a ten o'clock scholar and a skindeep thinker; his memory was poor and his comprehension slight; and burdened with few ideas, each and all mundane, he was heavier than air, the pundits said, and he'd never get off the ground. They were wrong: he soared. It was a marvel, the way the wingless flew!

But stay—why marvelous? He was altogether of his tinhorn time, an ordinary component of the crowd, and he shared the beliefs of the crowd, the crowd's likes and aversions: he had the crowd mind. When he spoke, and he had a modest gift for speaking, it was with their mouth, they thought, and they heard him as if they were hearing themselves discuss the best things in their benighted world—beer, ball games, and quiff.

Others heard him too, the rulers of the many—the rich, always on the Erie for a member of the crowd who'd screw the crowd for a price. He had to be one who, however base, would sound noble; he'd need a guileless face to hide his guile; he'd have to say the right things while doing the wrong; but above all, he'd have to know who his masters were and who owned the collar he wore.

They found him an ardent flunky, a plausible double-dealer, a righteous squealer, an Alger-boy in reverse (he *derailed* the train!), and for his mean zeal, they rewarded him with two terms in Sacramento and two more in the White House, which, when he left it, was much less white than before. But he was rich now, and he lived well on his mainchance gains.

Abe's dead, but he lived better—and he'll live longer.

A Prudent Wife Is from the Lord

She was never one to disclose her inner feelings.
—a friend

It would be wrong to call her secretive, though; she was simply reserved, the possessor of knowledge that required no display. So reticent was she that even those who knew her best could speak of little more than they were shown—her beauty, her intelligence, her purposeful ways. It was a delight to be in her company, they said, but few ever felt that she was quite in theirs. A part of her was always withheld, a private region that no one was permitted to invade. A prudent wife would Patricia make, a wife from the Lord.

She met Nixon at a reading for roles in an amateur theatrical, and on the instant, he was a goner—struck, as he might've put it, by a shaft from the bow of Amor. Not so she; and when, on that very evening, he declared that he meant to marry her, he must've sounded like the juvenile called for in the play—a blushing youth, eager and faintly collegiate—and she dismissed his avowal as callow trifling. Not so easily, though, was *he* to be dismissed.

His ardor, if something less than incandescent, was at least unquenchable, surviving the drench of indifference and, not seldom, avoidance. The skewered swain was not to be put off by such denials, nor even by her preference for others. Ever before him, whether in her presence or not, was the vision of her *titian-colored hair,* a description he chose over prosaic reddish-brown. He proved to be a veritable gnat of a suitor: he kept on coming, and she'd bat him away. He'd turn up at her flat at odd and inconvenient hours; he'd bring fetching gifts (a carved pumpkin, a miniature evergreen, and once—for God's sake!— a clock), and if refused admittance, he'd slip effusions under her door, inanities about the stars and the moon, about *the restless rustling of the palm trees,* and doubtless about her hair, concluding with *You see, Miss Pat, I like you.* Like, he said, which fell short of explaining the clock.

She kept him at arm's length for quite a spell, for years, in fact, but not at all because she was artful. The reason may have been that she was only mildly impressed by the man and even less by his thirst to *belong.* Early she must have discovered him to be a joiner of whatever there was to join—a club, a class, a committee, a team. The closed door, hers and every other, had to open for him. He *had* to get in!—almost, it seemed, as if only then would he be part of the human race. Later, on a day of candor, he'd say, *I had to win. That's the thing you don't understand.* He'd be talking to someone else, not to her, but long had she known of his compulsion, and being perceptive, she'd known this too—that he'd allow nothing to bar his way, no standard, no scruple, no rule of the game. He had to win!

She herself was resolute, but only to the point where she felt her independence to be secure. His determination was boundless: it drove him to victories that drove him in turn to further conflicts. He had no purpose other than winning. For him, life was a lifelong game and hardly worth living without the momentary satisfaction of coming in first. Ultimately, he wore her down (he won!), and, no doubt with *inner feelings*, she became the wife of winner Dick. But what thoughts did she refrain from revealing; what misgivings did she have about a nature such as his?

After Pearl Harbor (eight months after), he decided to join another clan, clique, circle, frat—the navy—and on receiving a commission, he was assigned to a perilous base in Iowa, where he spent half a year in harm's way before being sent to the South Pacific. There, as a procurement officer, he was again stationed far from shot and shell, so far indeed that he could have been hit only by a meteor. Still, he *was* in uniform, which proved that he was helping his country to win the war (win!), and long after it was over, he kept on wearing it.

It cleared the way, he found, but was his wife on to his aim of using brass and braid to proclaim his bravery? Was she aware that he was even then running for other doors and better junctions? Did she watch his tricks from her cloister, did she hear his smears and slanders, did she deplore his discard of honor; or did she slowly come to know that he had none to throw away? Alone with her covert thoughts, how did she grade him? How did he compare with those over whom he rose by defamation and guile—did she bend with his bent for cunning, or condemn him for his worm, his need to outdo all and leave the world behind?

There's nothing mysterious about Dick. He's merely an Alger-boy gone bad, not the tin Jesus of fiction but the evildoer of fact, a Galahad malign. No, it's Pat who's enigmatic, she who starts the machinery of the mind. She was there for nearly all of his public life. She could not have been unaware of his political shenanigans; she must've seen his face when he lied, when he scandalized an opponent, when he spewed patriotic rant while wearing his favorite suit of clothes—the flag. She watched him soar ever higher until he reached the place where nothing remained to aspire to—and still, she saw, he was striving to win, as though he did not know he already had. It was a sickness in him, she must've thought, that need to inflict defeat, and she dreaded the day when, with no one else left, he had to defeat himself—and the day, though long in coming, came. City attorney, congressman, senator, vice president, and president twice—his day of doom came at last.

How did she feel when it did? Sequestered till then, did she unseal herself and tell him she rued his ruination and his shameful end? Did she say that she pitied him his fall and that, in spite of all, she loved him still, that she'd be at his side come what may. Or, contrary to her show of pride for the camera, did she give him what-for when away from its eye? Did she say, *You poor stick, was I ever the First Lady, or did I always play second fiddle to First and Only Dick?*

ANDY WARHOL, 1930–87

Painter

> a. an artist who represents objects or scenes in color on a
>   surface;
> b. one who covers buildings, ships, ironwork, and the like,
>   with paint.
>   — *Webster's International*

At times, he was quite at home as (a), constructing scenes in color on a surface, and at others, he felt that his métier was (b), painting Pullman cars and red-leading the cables of a bridge. The ambiguity troubled him, and in his art-factory, amid the daily throng of hangers-on, he often found his fancy far from the fanaticos, the coke-sniffers and courtiers, the glorious who'd come to flaunt their glory—habitués and sons of habitués one and all. Where did he truly belong, he'd wonder—alone with his visions under light from the north or swaying on a sling above a stream? Amid the comings and goings, the smoke and the chatter, the never-ending to-do, time and again his gaze would turn inward, away from the self-seekers and the celebrants, away from the wasteful here and now, and enter the privacy of a wide-awake dream. Varying only in detail, it was forever the same dream: he'd been commissioned by the Pope to improve on the art in the Sistine Chapel.

In the fantasy, he was already there, and he saw himself on a scaffold some sixty feet above the tiles in the presbytery floor. He was free, though, of the fear of heights; indeed, feeling lighter than air, he

189

seemed to need no support to remain aloft, just below the central field of the Sistine vault. He studied the string of panels above him, and noting the many cracks in the paint and plaster, he likened them to a meander of varicose veins; and then he surveyed the frieze of prophets and sibyls that curved with the curve of the walls (*Zachariah*, he heard a voice say, and *Delphi* and *Cumae*); and at length his eye fell on the gear he'd brought with him from The Factory—the tubes of pigment, the brushes and palette, the mottled pile of rags.

Where would he start? he wondered, and once more he scanned the surrounding array. Would it be with the panel depicting *The Separation of Light from Darkness*, or would it be *The Expulsion from Eden*, and if either, with what would he replace it? He pondered a few possibilities: soup cans at parade rest bedecked in red and gold; a battlement of bottles; tautological two-dollar bills. He rejected these, and he rejected the panels as well; nor was he drawn to *The Drunkenness of Noah* or *The Flood*, lighting in the end where he'd always known he'd begin—on *The Creation of Adam*, the panel just above him and near enough to touch.

When had he not longed to expunge it with a creation of his own? When had he not envied the hand of God outstretched toward Adam's, His index finger about to impart life to the body newly made? When had it not angered him that no hand had ever reached for his? They were an affront to him, that monumental pair, and monumental they truly were, sculptures in paint—Adam, flawless in form and about to come alive in a flawless world, the first and last who'd ever see it as it was meant to be; and the Lord, clothed in a red mantle and a blue and violet cloak, a mighty presence afloat in space, with all His might in a single finger of His extended right hand.

Staring up at the veined fresco, he was tormented by the notion that it was there only to humble him, that the Florentine had had no intention of pleasing his patron Sixtus IV or even of pleasing himself: *he wanted me to be photographed against the sun*, thought the man from The Factory; *he wanted to black me out and make me disappear.* What sweet revenge, to pay him in the same coin! How fitting, to make *him* disappear! Taking up one of his brushes, he simply fondled it, as if it were a weapon—ah, but it *was* a weapon, and he sought the right way to use it.

There were many possibilities. His old tricks were available—his boxes and bottles and sheets of currency, of course, and, going farther back, his caprices with shoes. None of these seemed suitable, and he weighed the effect of, say, a giant cartoon, or—wait!—a redundancy of lips, lips a hundred times repeated, a thousand, even. But those conceits dwindled too, and he moved to others, to a huge headline, to a car crash, to four blownup images of himself. Yet as before, he felt dissatisfied. He could not have said why—any of his stunts would obliterate the fresco—but he knew that he still hadn't hit on the one that would do it best.

He dove to the dark deeps of memory, stirring up a sediment of whims, all of them indulged in until they'd worn thin: there were eagles and athletes and elephants; there were dollar signs and movie stars en masse; there were skulls, commissars, a revolver, and the ass of a headless nude. They had nothing left to offer: they'd yielded what juice they had, and they were rind now and pulp, they were garbage. . . . And then, through the murk of his mind slithered the elusive serpent: the Idea!

An electric chair!

The brush he was holding seemed to move on its own, as if it had been imbued as well as he, and it seemed too to have taken control of his hand, to be conducting it toward his tubes of umber, sienna, and indigo, of lake, cobalt blue, and vermilion, to be choosing a set of hues for the laying on of an electric chair, for conveying voltage in color, for killing pilgrims come to see their Maker in the act of imparting life. What a way to even the score, what a day of reckoning—to reward the reverent with a vivid shock, to perform a chromatic execution! He could almost see them below him, some fallen anyhow on the tiles, some still on the slant-backed benches, all of them stunned to death, all—the exquisites, the connoisseurs, the lovers of classical art. And more, ever more, were making the journey to look upon the faces of Daniel and Isaiah and to see the Libyan oracle and the Persian, and finally *The Creation*—and looking up in awe, they'd be stricken where they stood, on the bodies of the delicate dead. The scholars! he thought, the arbiters!—and he fell to mixing his paints . . .

At that instant, the wide-eyed dream always ended, and he was back at The Factory, a place he'd never left. Roundabout him were his silk screens of boxers and players, his acrylics of disaster, his mother, and himself—all of them *Kinderspiel*, garish, slapdash, and skin-deep. And constantly in motion was his clamorous throng of smell-feasts, hangers-on, and lickers of spit, his ever-present claque, his retinue of addicts, oddities, and expensive gash. Amid them, though, and hemmed in by his assemblage of trash, he was lonely, a vacancy in a void, and soon, he knew, he'd have to seek escape in the only way open to him, the enclosure of another dream.

191

The Nominee

> There are two Clarence Thomases — one who says nice
> things about civil rights, and the other . . .
> — Althea Simmons, NAACP

She was wrong: there was really only one, a black with small regard for brother blacks, especially if they were as black as he. And black he was; so black, some said, that if he were any blacker, he'd be blue — and in a certain sense, he *was* blue, blue because he wasn't white. That the cards were stacked against his race was true, of course — *had* been true for three centuries — but while, for many, the cold deck had resulted in black solidarity, for Clarence, it had led to a liking only for the light-skinned, the high yellows, who could boast a dash of white.

He was born in Pin Point, Georgia, a right good name for a place that never quite made it to a map. All it had was a store and a dozen shacks belonging to shrimp-catchers and oystermen, a starveling lot of blacks that got by on scant food and tidewater air. In one of those shacks lived Clarence and his mother, and he was six or seven when it burned to a pile of cinders in the marsh grass, forcing her to dump him on his grandpa for support. At six or seven, then, good luck grew from bad: for Clarence, no more pasted-up newspapers to keep out the wind, no more coal-oil lamps and outdoor crappers; and though, in later years, he drew tears with tales of childhood want, never after the fire was he on the outside looking in. Grandpa was no black angel, and often, as Clarence told it, he beat the shit out of him — but if shit was beaten out, it only proved that he'd eaten.

For Grandpa, schooling had ended with the third grade, but he was no man's fool all the same: to save Clarence's tuition at St. Benedict the Moor, he converted to Catholicism. There the boy had pocket money — *He never went without anything*, a classmate said — but even that early in life, he was creating the myth of a slave-driven childhood. In after years, he'd claim that he overcame a poor education, but the truth is that the Franciscans gave him a good one, a damn sight better than anybody got who couldn't come up with the $20 fee. His triumph over ignorance — it made a touching story that fit in nicely with the myth, and he kept on telling it till he believed it himself . . .

"You've written a good deal about blacks," she said, "and you've always given them the best of it. This is the first time you've ever lit into one of them."

"I have no respect for a black who's on the white side."

"Why is that worse than a white who's on the black side?"

"Because whites are the wrongdoers, and blacks are the wronged. I can switch sides and be right, but a black who switches is just another wrongdoer. He's on the Supreme Court bench for one reason only—he's black—but he's voting with the whites and against his own. He's a wrongdoer now, and I'm against him."

It was a nun who steered him to Holy Cross, where he became one of the better students, ranking ninth in his class and graduating with honors, but ever afterward it stung him that he'd gained admission through affirmative action—that color, not excellence, had been the criterion. He smarted all the way through law school (not just *any* law school, mister—*Yale* law school!), for there too his skin had gotten him in, not his merit. *I never felt looked down on*, a black classmate said, but it seems that Thomas did, and having little esteem for himself, he had less for others, and for women none at all. His language in their presence was so crass, so unveiling and invasive, that it stunned them to silence, and the rest of the company as well, even those who knew of his appetite for racy films and risqué magazines. His coarseness would be remembered long, and one day it would come back to haunt him.

He was no shooting star at Yale, finishing near the bottom of his class (average, it was said of him, not particularly bright), and the leading law firms of Georgia turned down his every application for a job. He saved their letters of rejection, using them to nourish his bitterness at being *unable to return to Savannah to right the wrongs of his childhood* but that was simply more of his myth-making blague. The wrong to Clarence Thomas (*what* wrong?) was the only one he meant to right.

And then, once again, his color, the color he despised, served him well. A Yale alumnus named John Danforth had become the attorney general of Missouri, and he returned to New Haven on the hunt for an assistant—in particular a black one—to integrate his staff. He chose Clarence Thomas, who promptly dropped the sham of helping his brethren, still tied to their ill-paid toil in the Georgia canneries, still shucking oysters and shelling crab along the Ogeechee;

and quitting the Democratic party, he joined the Republican, saying *I can go further*—and he did. Instead of helping his brothers, he helped himself.

When Danforth was elected to the United States Senate, he took Thomas along to relieve the glare of his white-skinned aides. After barely a year in Washington, no great shakes there and quite unknown, Thomas announced his heart's desire and his unwavering aim—a seat on the Supreme Court. For that, he'd have to slide still more to the right, and being a smooth slider, he slid into the camp of the champion slider—Ronald Reagan. It was a caution, then, how ardently he supported Reagan's opposition to every progressive measure on the books, among them busing, rent control, affirmative action, and welfare. Each of these was of benefit to his people, but he was out to benefit himself, and if it weren't for his skin, it would've been hard to tell him from the Imperial Wizard.

He made quite a show of wanting no place in government that dealt with racial issues, but whenever he was offered one, however reluctant he pretended to be, he took it, thus becoming a cloak for the Reagan attacks on civil rights. It was while Thomas headed the Equal Employment Opportunity Commission that he came to know a black woman named Anita Hill . . .

She said, "Is he simply an opportunist, do you think?"

"He's that," you said, "but he's a hell of a lot more. Simply— there's nothing simple about him. He's one tangled-up guy, and the more I learn of him, the harder he is to understand. Black skin doesn't get much in this country, but it got Thomas lots more than most, and he got it just because *he was black. Always looking out for Number One, he took it, but he was dead set against handouts for others, holding that it would demean them to be 'house Negros.' That's a little complicated, wouldn't you say?"*

Anita Hill, the last of thirteen children, was born in 1956 in Lone Tree, Oklahoma, a settlement not unlike Pin Point, Georgia. She too went to segregated schools, and being strictly raised, she too worked from "can't see to can't see" in farmyard and field. Unlike Thomas, though, she was reared amid affection and returned what she received. By all accounts of her nature, she was quiet, reserved, given to study, and moral, owing much to the biblical teachings of her mother. It was also well known that she was truthful.

At high school, she was a first-rate student, and graduating as class valedictorian, she won a full scholarship to Oklahoma State University, where, with straight A's she became a National Merit Scholar and a Regents Scholar, and for good measure, she earned a place on the Dean's Honor Roll. For these achievements, she was given another scholarship, this one to Yale Law School. After graduation, her aim having always been Washington, she took and passed the District of Columbia bar examination and was admitted to practice there. Her deportment too remained constant: she was still retiring, still bookish, still of a religious turn of mind. In no long time, she was offered the post of special assistant to Clarence Thomas, head of the civil rights division of the Department of Education. She was well on her way now, she may have thought; she could hardly have known that it would take her back to Oklahoma . . .

"Thomas got his job because he was black," you said. "Some little show was made of his being the man best qualified for it, but only the people were taken in. A quarter of a billion dummies who'd drink piss if you told them it was cider."

"You always had the notion that Americans were rebellious," she said, "but I know them better than you do. They'll stand for just about anything, and your hero was wrong: they can *be fooled all of the time."*

At the outset, Hill and Thomas worked well together, and each stood high in the other's regard, but within a few months, she'd later testify, he sought to expand the working relationship to a personal one by asking her to meet with him socially. She declined, and not wishing to endanger her position, she based her refusal on impropriety. But as she'd one day say, he persisted, using any office encounter to press for a change of mind. Repeatedly denied, he fell to making work situations his chance to dwell on sexual matters, which he did explicitly, she'd claim, and in vivid detail. *He spoke of acts in films involving women having sex with animals, and films showing group sex and rape scenes,* and she'd swear too that he held forth on outsize breasts and penises and ultimately on his unusual sexual prowess . . .

195

"All the same, she agreed to go along with him when he moved on to a more important job. Why? I wonder."

"As she tells it, he'd quit making advances. And there's this—she too would have a better job."

"She had no way of knowing that he wouldn't pick up where he'd left off."

"You don't believe her story, then?"

"Forget me," she said. "When she followed Thomas, she gave others a fact to fault her with."

"I don't see it that way."

"That's because you believe her."

"You're right," you said. "I do."

When Thomas became head of the Equal Employment Opportunity Commission, the EEOC, Hill again served as his special assistant, a position regarded as a plum, but within a few months, he resumed his earlier behavior. This time, though, his remarks narrowed from the random to the particular. Many of them were directed at Hill's personal appearance—through her dress, he said, he could see her slip, and through her slip, he could see her body. At the same time, he continued his efforts to draw her into a more intimate relationship, a campaign that failed, and after a period of torment, she left the EEOC to become a teacher of law in Oklahoma.

Some years later, the White House needed a black to succeed Thurgood Marshall. It nominated Clarence Thomas . . .

"Thurgood Marshall was as fine a jurist as ever graced the bench," you said, "but Clarence Thomas can only do the opposite—disgrace it. We've had some second-raters on the Court, the mean-spirited, the bigoted, the servants of the rich, but Thomas is as bad as the worst. He doesn't even serve his own people."

To inquire into his fitness to serve, the Senate Judiciary Committee held a three-day hearing, and Anita Hill, now a professor of law at Oklahoma State University, was among the witnesses who testified against him.

196

—She said that he repeatedly asked her to go out with him.

—She said that despite her refusals, he persisted.

—She said that it was his habit to turn an ordinary business meeting into an opportunity to speak of sex.

—She said he dwelt on the subject of women with large breasts engaging in sex acts with animals.

—She said he described in great detail the sex films he'd seen and the enjoyment they gave him.

—She said that he urged her to see them too.

—She said that he often referred to the size of his penis.

—She said that he boasted of his sexual prowess and the frequency of his sexual acts.

—She said that when she could endure no more of his gross behavior and was about to leave the EEOC, he told her that if she ever revealed his conduct, she'd ruin his career.

She did reveal it, but the committee confirmed his nomination all the same. *Her* career, though . . .

"She was so soft-spoken at the hearing," you said. "She was so decent, so plausible. What reason would she have had to lie? A college professor—why would she have risked her standing unless she was telling the truth?"

"I don't think she realized what she was up against—not just Thomas, but the whole administration."

"Their mudslingers on the committee—they had one aim only, to make Hill look bad. And that's what they managed to do."

"I'm sorry."

"Why do things always turn out this way?"

"In one of your books, you said the Lincolns never shoot . . ."

Don't get mad. Get confirmed.
—Clarence Thomas

My dad told me way back that there's no difference between a white snake and a black snake. They'll both bite.
—Thurgood Marshall

Kaddish for a Dead Fink

You met him through Ed Rolfe, a member of the Abraham Lincoln Brigade who'd given two hard-lived years of his life to the cause in Spain, surviving the war only to die at forty-five of a worn-out heart. He'd spent himself at Teruel, and along the Ebro, and in the Guadarrama Mountains—died there, really, before coming home to die through the rest of his days. You mourned him, as did all who'd ever been graced by his presence, and among these was his great good friend Ben Maddow, a writer of no little promise.

No quill-driver, Ben; no inkster for the marketplace: his words had cadence and command, and they made limpid pages that opened on a better world than the one roundabout, a visionary world, as he well enough knew; but for him, vision was illumination, and it brought paradise into view. He did not believe, as many another did, that man was a knave by nature, a sinner born and a sinner to the grave; rather was he a ruined innocent, a white soul soiled by the system of the rich.

His early work bespoke where his late would lead him—to the left—and once there, he seemed to have found his home. But he was a writer only for the truly literate, for those to whom books were as the pearls and precious stones of the Revelation, and readers such as they were far too few to pay his way. Compelled to divide his time, he wrote scripts for the screen by day, reserving the night for the production of his rubies and sapphires and ornaments of gold. The going was heavier now and the progress slower, but he was in motion and on the road to recognition and renown.

He dwelt in an unquiet age, though, and travel was hazardous, the more so for those on the left-hand side of the road. A long war had just been fought—the wrong one, some thought—and a hue and cry was being raised against a former ally, the enemy now that peace had come. Loud grew the talk of subversion, and loudest was it heard from the politicos, those ardent public servants of their avid private selves—and Ben Maddow was one of the number summoned before the Congress to confess their sedition and reveal the names of their fellows. He refused, whereupon punishment was imposed, swift to fall and severe; he was placed on the Blacklist of the motion picture industry, and at once his livelihood was cut to nothing.

Five years passed thus for Ben Maddow, and toward the end of 1956, he wrote to you, saying:

Hope to do something drastic this year. It seems absurd to strike a heroic pose for a principle now become meaningless. . . .

You and Maggie, your wife, had appeared before the same committee, and having taken the same stand as Ben, both of you had been on the Blacklist quite as long as he.

> *You said, "Do you realize what he's telling us?"*
> *And she said, "It's clear enough."*
> *"He's getting ready to sing for his supper!"*
> *"Eddie would've tried to stop him."*
> *"Eddie's dead."*
> *"Then you try," she said.*
> *"If a guy's bent on disgracing himself . . ."*
> *"Try, John. You owe it to Eddie."*

You wrote to Ben that very day:

If your letter means nothing in particular, I apologize in advance. If it means what it seems to, you don't really want my opinion; you want Eddie's. Let me give it to you. His whole life was his opinion; he'd've died before doing what you announce. One request: don't name Eddie when you spill. Name me instead and let him dream on about Madrid. Por favor.

> *"That'll never stop him," she said. "It's too contemptuous."*
> *"What's the guy entitled to — my respect?"*
> *"Yes, until he loses his own."*
> *"You're too forgiving," you said.*
> *"So far, there's nothing to forgive. If he ever finks, I'll show you how forgiving I am."*

In reply to your letter, Ben wrote:

I haven't done a damn thing so far except mutter aloud, probably to the wrong people. Regarding your note, I still fail to find any solution to the Blacklist problem. I think it's high time, humbling and painful though it be, to bring a little ice-cold logic to bear. . . .

> *"Well," you said, "how does it look to you now?"*
> *"He's still on the fence, John."*

"Not in his mind, he isn't. In his mind, he's spilled the beans."

"You may be right, but I can't help feeling sorry for him. To cave in after all this time!"

"I've never been close to him. What made him confide in me?"

"Don't you know?" she said. "Wherever he's going, he'd like to have your company."

"Are you serious, Mag?"

"What else would've made him write to you?"

"If you thought my other letter was contemptuous, wait till you see this one."

You wrote:

You say you haven't done a damn thing so far, but that's more of a comfort to you than it is to me, because I think you have done something: you've called for an opinion on the taste of spit. You never asked me for a solution to the Blacklist problem. I'd only have told you what you already know: there isn't any. Finking is a solution to something else altogether—how to get rich . . .

You never heard from him again, nor did you ever see him. Through others, though, you learned that he'd discarded principle (meaningless) and relaxed the heroic pose (absurd), that he'd brought ice-cold logic to bear and done the drastic something he'd had in mind—that, in short, he'd become a fink.

"He was worth saving," Maggie said, "and now he's worthless."

But to all seeming, he prospered. In return for his betrayal, he was restored to good standing, and in the years that followed, a spate of words issued from his hand—a flood of stories, stage plays, and poetry—and you learned that, both at home and abroad, awards had come his way, and prizes, and certificates of merit, and with all these, and many times over, had come his thirty pieces of Judas-pay. But no tidings came that he'd repented, or that he'd cast away the blood-money, nay, nor that he'd ended suspended from a rope.

In his travels, had he, you wondered, had the hardihood to take himself to Spain? Had he gone where Eddie had gone, stood amid the shades of shot brigadiers, dwelt on the stones they'd stained, the starred walls? Had he made long marches in his mind, endured the cold, forced down the food, rued the good lives lost; had he written to wives to say they were widows, had he wept for what dishonor had cost him—his gentle friend Eddie? And what of his words, his jewels of silver and jewels of gold, his topaz and coral, his pleasant stones and amber—were they as rich as the old . . . ?

> *"I'm thinking of Ben Maddow," you said.*
> *And Maggie said, "Why?"*
> *"I don't understand him. I understand other finks, but not Ben."*
> *"Where's the difference?"*
> *"I never thought he was cut out for that sort of work. It was beneath him."*
> *"But when it came along, he did it."*
> *"That's what baffles me. What made him lower himself? What made him take a place below the salt?"*
> *"He was five years finding it out, but that's where he belonged all the time."*
> *"You know what you're saying? That anybody can wake up to the fact that he isn't as noble as he thought."*
> *"Not anybody," she said. "Only those who were no good from the start."*

You'd read of his palm leaves and laurels, his plaques, his citations, his medals and statuettes—honors all, but had they given him an honorable life? The festivals at Edinburgh and Mannheim and Venice, the acclaim, the tokens of his worth, the mentions of his name—had they stilled the voice that told him that he'd sold himself for a song? How had he felt on accepting the wreaths, the ribbons, the literary degrees; what had gone through his mind, what memories had he tried to forget? Had his heart been dry, had it merely ticked away time, each systole remindful of Eddie, somewhere as yet in Spain . . . ?

> *"Are you still thinking of Ben?" she said.*
> *"I'll always think of him."*
> *"He got a lot of jobs after he blew the gaff, and he wrote a lot of screenplays. Did you know that one of them was called* Kiss the Blood Off My Hands?*"*

The Waters of the New World

Nameless once, it was merely many leagues of main strewn with nameless isles; only later would the isles be called the Caribees and the seas, the Caribbean. In the ancient age, the shallows were pure, and so too the steeps of the trenches and the fractured floor. The bottoms were an ooze of clays of several hues, reds and blues and greens, the remains of plankton, algae, molluscan shell, and weed, and of fish and fallen birds as well; and added to these minims was the immemorial runoff from the land, the twigs and logs and leaves, the gravels and the volcanic ash, all such fragments forming a plastic mass bonded by carbonate of lime. Suspended in this submarine slush were traces of lead and zinc, of cobalt, nickel, and manganese, of silver and gold—*oro y plata!*—and these last drew the People from Heaven in their ships!

Seeking such riches only, they bartered for much of it with bone buttons and bits of tinted glass, for to the arcadian creatures blessed with the treasure, it had little value and was best employed as jackstones in a game their children played. By some, though, they who thought it to be the excrement of the gods, it was given a measure of veneration, and they were loath to part with it. Such killjoys it became a joy to kill, indeed a virtue, since it conserved the supply of buttons and bone. Names now appeared on the charts, those of bays and capes, of towns and streams and passes between the erstwhile pristine isles, and men now knew of the Rio Grande del Norte and the Oronoque, of Cartagena and Nombre de Dios and Cozumel, and they sailed their ships from afar to fill them full with trove.

Always there was killing, and often were the killers killed in turn, and even the victors not seldom fell victim to the winds, the reefs, and rotted hulls. And then it was that the ooze became littered with old-world trash, with such contaminants as buckles and scissors and packets of needles, with beads and things of pewter and brass, and still more went dithering down to soil the abyssal plain, rigging and sail and sundials, olive wood and vials of perfume (these to smother shipboard stench); and mention must be made of cutlasses, piss-pots, and clyster-pumps (for freeing the bowel), and there were staves from casks of wine, and there were cannon lying anywhichway in the slime, culverins and sakers and falconets, and these residues too debased the new-world waters, the blood and brains of the People from Heaven—and, not to be forgotten, the bone buttons and the bits of colored glass.

Along the outer banks of Carolina, a herd of wild ponies ranged, grazing on the grasses that grew there, and on the leaves too of the live oak and the yaupon tree. Brought in the ships of Raleigh's band, they throve where the English sickened and died, and thereafter they roamed the dunes at will, their feed being sea oats and kale and such plants as they found in the marshes of the Sound. Being animals—Barbs, a Moorish breed—they dwelt not on names, neither those of flora and places, nor on the wrecks embedded in the beach. In the absence of man, they were serene save when disturbed by lightning flash, by the splash of an osprey, by the sudden flight of startled gulls—and then they'd explode across the sandhills and up or down the strand. Now and again, they'd run for running's sake alone, racing their own shadows through fringes of foam, and when blown, they'd stand staring out over the surf, over the Cold Wall, over the Stream and the sea beyond, and it may be that they sensed from afar another shore, the one where their kind had begun—Barbary.

It was lonely there, and all the more so for the turbulent air, bringing the shredded cries of plover and jackdaws and clapper rail, thin voices further thinned by the wind. It was nothing to the ponies that the *Flambeau* had gone aground near where they stood, that the *Blaisdell* lay in eighty fathoms, that only a short way off the *Monitor* rested on its turret with sixteen members of her crew. To the Berber ponies, it was nothing that six hundred ships had foundered in those waters, and it was less than nothing to the Stream, forever flowing past at a mean speed of three knots an hour.

THE MISSISSIPPI

In time, the continent would drain away through its own outfall, fill the Gulf with man and all his noble works, the rubber tires and Trojans, the peel and rind, the spittle and stool, the medley of leavings little and big; and these things too would turn and tumble down the open drain of America, feathers and flowers, trees and toys and weed; and these, loaded dice, pieces of the True Cross, chewing gum and signs that read KEEP OFF; and there'd be more in the going stream, scalps, scraps of paper that might've been treaties, maps, love-letters; and there'd be Klansman sheets, some still stained with blood; and there'd be clouds that seemed fallen from the sky—all that, together with silt and sand from the Yellowstone, from the Canadian and the Sangamon, and in time, in time, in time . . .

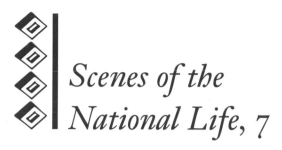

Scenes of the National Life, 7

An Island Fourteen Miles Long

It lay between two rivers—one of them merely a tidal channel and the other a broad waterway of much majesty—and most aptly did they that dwelt in that place call it Manah-atin, a name that in their tongue meant *island of the hills*. In truth, it was all hill and dale, save where a marsh or a pond had formed in a swale. There a multitude of birds could be found among the reeds—woodcock and snipe and rail—and now and then a fox would come to drink, unalarmed by an image that seemed to be doing the same. For the greater part, the island was well wooded, and the earth could scarcely be seen for its smother of birch and beech, of larch and locust and elm. So dense were these in places, so pressed for room, that they overhung the riverbanks, their skirts atrail in the stream. Here and there, a small strand had been cast up by the current, and mounds of clam-shell attested to the abundance taken from the sand. As for the waters, in the spawning season, they were stiff with shad, and always cod were to be caught, and bluefish, and the sea trout called squeteague. And, yes, mention must be made of food that came from the heavens—clouds of geese, and pigeons in such numbers that they latened the hour, sped the sun down.

That island, then, was it not Kingdom Come that the *Half Moon* fell with, had she not sailed to the end of the world, where Eden was said to be?

The Age of Information

Stored in the flexures of an electronic brain is all manner of intelligence concerning Tom, Dick, and Harry. Press this key and then that, thus sending the proper impulses through an inorganic Aqueduct of Silvius, and at once a plastic memory will flash its evergreen retrieve upon a screen—and Harry will be itemized for you, or Tom or Dick, from his first wail to his last gasp. His collar-size will be disclosed, his favorite flower, and the color of his eyes; you'll learn of his scars and birthmarks, his political views, and his turn of mind; you'll be told of the women he knows, the schools he attended, the sums he owes and to whom: through the new foramina of Monro and Majendi, you'll find Tom or Dick or Harry before you and fully exposed. But lore is no more wisdom than copulation is love, and though possessed of all that data, you still can't say why Tom would sooner hit his wife than scold his dog, and so would Dick and Harry.

The Games That People Play

Avoid those, said your father, where something is done with a ball, where it's struck, thrown, kicked, chased, or bounced off a wall—because for all the back-and-fill, for all the collisions and reciprocation, nothing will change but your age.

0 to 60 in 6 Seconds

Too slow! the people said, wherefore faster transport was provided, a very arrow from a bow, and still the people cried it was too slow. Now they were given the power to show their heels to sound, and when even that wasn't fast enough, a jigamaree was made that could outspeed light, and pleased at last, the people drove off into the past.

By the Time I Get to Phoenix, etc.

A cynic called them the love-songs of the proletariat. Sung in inane lyrics, tales are told of love on the wane, which, if spoken, would earn the yearning speakers jeering. Set to music, though, they evoke moans and tears, and clothes are torn, and young girls swoon, *and when I get to Albuquerque . . .*

We Deliver to Your Door

You don't have to go to the House of God these days: His apostles Bob and Billy will bring Him to yours. Sit around with your shoes off, smoke if you like, and swig from a can of beer. No matter: if you're at sea-level, and it's dry outside and freezing, He'll arrive at the rate of 1,087 feet per second, He'll zoom in on the zero air. Gone the day when His magic worked only under a groined vault, when you were held in spell by soaring pillars and stained pure by stained glass. You're pure where and as you are, sprawling in sock-feet, flatulent and fuming, for the voices you hear are all of them His, though the mouths are Bob's and Billy's. They're saving you the pain of shaving, of going to Him in all weathers, of hurrying home to your beer. Belching and bearded, you can receive Him unbuttoned and in comfort, and if Billy bores you, you can give Bob a try, or switch till you find a game.

Wings for the Lower Orders

He wrote for tapsters, clapswords, strumpets, and knaves. *The beached margent of the sea* was spoken to apothecaries, and *a malignant and a turbaned Turk* to pimps. For midwives in the galleries and for chapmen stinking and tumultuous in the pit, he wrote *Here I can sit alone, unseen of any,* where one less lyrical would've said *seen by none.* The place was rigid with picklocks and cutpurses, with tooth-pullers and scriveners, with creatures as common as curses, but, fresh from their base and particular tricks, they were served such verses as *Age cannot wither her, / Nor custom stale her infinite variety.* Seraphic phrases flew the Bankside air, and to stagnant ears came language so noble that it fledged the flightless, and they soared on the wings of music.

He wrote high for the low and raised them, raised whoresons and tear-sheets, raised footpads and picaroons and eaters of broken meats! Latter-day bards write for the high and lower them. They're silken and bejeweled, and their starched and studded shirts are clean; they smell of hard-milled soaps and rare perfumes; but not for them the beached margents and the turbaned Turk. Their fare is flickers of wit and froth, and, unsustained, they sink.

207

The Lamp beside the Golden Door

... a country where the unprotected always find a friend, where a kind hand is always outstretched ...
—Martí, *Impreciones de America*

He was a revolutionary, and lately released from a jail called Spain, he'd come to the States (Mother of Exiles!), where, dazed by vastness, he could see only the friendly face and the benevolent hand. How prodigal this place, he thought, how open the view! But all too soon the dazzle dimmed, and he knew he'd been bemused. The huddled masses, the refuse of the teeming shore—no marble halls awaited them, no friend, no friendly hand. In store was merely more of what they'd left behind in Zacatecas, Belfast, and Bucharest. The homeless, the tempest-tost, once inside the Golden Door, they entered another bondage.

In a sense, of course, they were free. They were free to sell a day's worth of life for two dollars; free to fall from heights, to die in a pour of concrete, or be mangled by a machine; free to be blown up, gassed, poisoned, blinded, or crazed by a routine. And if they thought the prospect vile, they were free to organize, free to strike, free to get shot by company dicks.

The lamp beside the Golden Door was out.

The Hudson River

Its source, a small pond in the Adirondacks, was a collect for snowmelt and rain from the roundabout hills. It was a pool of sky, a stillness marred now and then by the plunge of a kingfisher, by the wind, by a drinking deer. Only stirred leaves could be heard (by whom?) and the laughter of a loon. The outflow of the pond was merely a low constant, an undertone that amounted to no sound at all. Still, from that spillover, a great river grew and ran three hundred miles to the sea.

Clear and blue and wonderful to the taste, said the sailor for whom the stream is named, a lovely flow coursing what he called a good land to fall with and a pleasant land to see. Its banks were wooded with birch and elm and locust in such profusion that their limbs overhung the banks, as though they were fishing for the perch and herrings that passed in shoals. Wild grapes and berries abounded, as did the partridges and pigeons that fed on such fruits, and to that abundance, this—the forest was hard with game. Clear and blue were the waters and sweet as a swig of sky, as on some long-ago day for a faraway deer . . .

> *You said, "That summer with Pep West in the Adirondacks—it was like a last look at the past, as if the water-colors of Winslow Homer had come to life, and I could see what he saw—fallen trees, a flight of birds, white water in the Saguenay. . . . Our cabin was only a few miles from the upper Hudson, and sometimes we'd drive to Thurman and fish for smallmouth bass in the reeds under the bridge. It was quiet in that place; it was quiet in that age . . ."*

A river sweet where it rose and salt where it met with the sea, wonderful to the taste once but wonderful no more. Long since had the trees gone that dabbled in the stream. No longer do schools of shad impede the flow, and the abounding fruits are not now to be found, nor the conies, the quail, and the bear. Instead, multitudes dwell amid pots and pans and squander their lives on schemes and folly and implacable machines . . .

> *"Twain's river was the Mississippi," she said. "Yours is the Hudson."*
> *"It isn't a river any more; it's an outfall. I swam in it when it was clear and blue, as Hudson said, and wonderful to the taste. But it's laced now with the spew of millions; it's a stew of rind and stool and rubber fingerlings, of syringes and self-inflated rats. How could that happen in Paradise?"*
> *"Johnny," she said, "it always happens in Paradise."*

Other Books by John Sanford

The Water Wheel (1933)

The Old Man's Place (1935)

Seventy Times Seven (1939)

The People from Heaven (1943, 1995)

A Man without Shoes (1951)

The Land That Touches Mine (1953)

Every Island Fled Away (1964)

The $300 Man (1967)

A More Goodly Country (1975)

Adirondack Stories (1976)

View from This Wilderness (1977)

To Feed Their Hopes (1980; *republished as* A Book
  of American Women, 1995)

The Winters of That Country (1984)

A Correspondence, *with William Carlos Williams* (1984)

The Color of the Air (1985)

The Waters of Darkness (1986)

A Very Good Land to Fall With (1987)

A Walk in the Fire (1989)

The Season, It Was Winter (1991)

Maggie: A Love Story (1993)

The View from Mt. Morris (1994)

We Have a Little Sister (1995)

John Sanford was born in the Harlem section
of New York in 1904. He attended the public
schools of that city, Lafayette College, and
Fordham University, at the last of which he
earned a degree in law. He was admitted to the
bar in 1929, and at about that time, influenced
by his friend Nathanael West, he began to
write. Among his twentysome books are eight
novels, an autobiography, and a quintet of
commentaries on American history. For more
than half a century he was married to the
screenwriter Marguerite Roberts, the "Maggie"
who appears here and there in these pages.